M 29018

D1458213

A Different Drummer

A Different Drummer

Clive Egleton

HODDER AND STOUGHTON
LONDON SYDNEY AUCKLAND TORONTO

British Library Cataloguing in Publication Data

Egleton, Clive
  A different drummer.
  I. Title
  823'.914[F]   PR6055.G55

  ISBN 0-340-38136-1

This book is for Kay and John

If a man does not keep pace with his
    companions
Perhaps it is because he hears a different
    drummer.

                    Henry David Thoreau

CHAPTER I

A towering fir tree in Trafalgar Square; illuminations in Regent Street; tinsel, mistletoe and snow scenes in shop windows; a hundred Santa Clauses. It was supposed to be the festive season of peace on earth and goodwill towards men; but the authorities weren't setting much store by that expression of pious hope. The Provisional IRA might have declared a truce, but there were other terrorist groups, like Gaddafi's hit teams, who were not averse to using the streets of London as a private battleground at this or any other time of the year. No one was taking any chances; Christmas Eve was always a busy shopping day and the police were out in force in Knightsbridge, Oxford Street and Regent Street long before the department stores were due to open. The uniformed officers were the visible deterrent; as the morning wore on, they would be joined by plainclothes men of the Anti-Terrorist Squad and Special Branch, on the look-out for known international terrorists if they tried to mingle with the crowds.

Other preventative measures had already been taken. Litter bins within a mile radius of Selfridges had been quietly removed overnight, a surprising number of parking meters were now out of commission and as a further precaution, the early morning traffic bulletins on BBC and local radio stations were advising Christmas shoppers to use public transport. It was, however, a case of business as usual and while the populace were being reminded of the need to be vigilant, the potential threat was deliberately being handled in a very low-key manner.

A more robust approach was being taken in Whitehall itself. Warning notices in all government offices had been upped to State Amber for the past seven days and internal memos assessing the possibility of a terrorist attack had been circulated to staffs. By Christmas Eve, however, the number of servicemen and civil servants on duty in the various departments of the Ministry of Defence had already shrunk to less than half of the normal establishment; by mid-afternoon, only the Intelligence and Operations branches would still be functioning and even they would be down to minimum manning levels.

*　*　*

Boden was convinced that not even the Greater London Council in one of its wilder moments would be harebrained enough to slap a preservation order on Quebec House. A five-storey miscegenation of Gothic and neo-Georgian architecture ostentatiously executed in red brick and Portland stone, it looked like something out of Disneyland. Built in the early twenties as a luxury block of flats overlooking the Embankment Gardens and the Thames, Quebec House had been requisitioned during World War Two to provide additional office accommodation for the Ministry of Information and had subsequently been retained by the government on a ninety-nine-year lease. As of now, it was occupied by Defence Sales, Overseas Aid and the Joint Intelligence Bureau. Of these three departments, the JIB was of special interest to Nick Boden.

Ever since daybreak that morning, he had been keeping Quebec House under observation from the vantage point of a small room on the fourth floor of the Legal and General Building at the corner of Watergate Walk and Buckingham Street. He had witnessed the arrival and departure of the office cleaners and had been particularly gratified to see that amongst the Ministry of Defence police officers who'd relieved the night shift, two had been carrying jet bags. They had checked in at seven forty, some twenty minutes before the messengers, the post room staff and clerical assistants had started to arrive. As he continued the vigil, a dark blue Ford Transit came down Buckingham Street and turned left into the cul-de-sac to park outside the front entrance of Quebec House; then the door behind him opened and Dukes walked into the room, an earthenware mug in each hand.

"Coffee's up, Nick. Anything happening out there?"

"Not a lot, Harry."

"Well, it is Christmas Eve," Dukes said philosophically, "the whole country's coming to a grinding halt for the next ten days."

"The mail has just arrived." Boden raised the Zeiss binoculars and trained them on the transit van. "Four bags," he added, "none of them exactly overfull."

"That'll please them. Too much paperwork could ruin a good office party."

Boden nodded. Overseas Aid had held theirs on Monday, Defence Sales yesterday and now it was the turn of the Joint Intelligence Bureau. He watched the Ford Transit make a U-turn in the cul-de-sac, turn right into Buckingham Street and disappear from view towards the Strand. Checking his wristwatch, he made a note of the time on a scratchpad.

His handwriting was neat and upright – a reflection of the man himself. Boden was a shade under five foot eight, but few people were aware of his lack of inches because he carried himself erect, his back ramrod-straight, like a guardsman fresh from the drill square. When he wanted to turn it on, his image was that of a youthful Public Relations man with an ever-ready smile and a hail-fellow-well-met nature. Beneath the carefully applied veneer however, there was steel and occasionally it showed in the slate-coloured ever-watchful eyes.

"Your coffee isn't getting any warmer," Dukes pointed out.

"You'd better spell me then." Boden laid the scratchpad aside, placed his binoculars on the windowledge and vacated the upright chair. "Keep your eyes open for anyone who's carrying an overnight bag. I want to know if the pattern is being repeated."

A year ago, Defence Sales and Overseas Aid had virtually put up the shutters from Christmas until January the second; only the Joint Intelligence Bureau had stayed in business, manning the shop with a skeleton staff.

"We're looking for just three people – right, Nick?"

"Yes, three – one clerk, one watchkeeper and a Deputy Director."

"Should be a pushover."

"Nothing is ever a pushover, Harry," Boden said quietly. "On a caper like this, one must always allow for the unexpected."

"Like a car bomb?"

"The IRA has declared a truce and it's holding."

"So far, Nick. So far."

Dukes was a born pessimist: if the sky above was an azure blue, he would scan the horizon looking for the storm clouds. Yet his jaundiced outlook on life seemed wholly in keeping with his long hangdog face and dark brown eyes which drooped at the corners like those of a St Bernard. Tall and seemingly underweight for his height, he had been a good soldier, one of the best and hardest Paras Boden had ever served with.

"There are some pretty wild men in the IRA, Nick."

"No one's denying that."

"Some of them might even be tempted to go their own way."

One bomb and the whole of the Metropolitan Police Force would be buzzing around like angry bees. One bomb and they would have to back away from Quebec House and postpone the exercise until Easter or maybe even this time next year. Dukes pushed the disturbing thought to the back of his mind and concentrated on the job in hand. Time was moving on and the office workers were beginning to arrive. They were fewer in number than yesterday but that was only to be expected. Civil Servants, like most other workers, weren't above tacking a day of their annual leave on to the Christmas break to make an even longer holiday out of the festive season. Amongst the sparse crowd, one man stood out from the rest.

"Here comes the first member of the gallant stay-behind party," he said.

"Where?" Boden asked, leaning over his shoulder.

"The fair-haired guy in the knee-length topcoat, the one carrying a small suitcase. Horn-rimmed spectacles and a gammy right leg; I don't think he'll give us much trouble."

"He certainly looks harmless enough," Boden said, and laughed softly.

*   ★   ★

Hollands limped into Quebec House, showed his Ministry of Defence pass to the Special Constable on duty in the foyer and then wheeled right towards the lifts beyond the glass booth which was usually manned by two receptionists. Today, there was only one on duty, a young Jamaican girl who was busy adding a few more Christmas cards to the collection pinned on the noticeboard behind her desk. Wishing her a happy Christmas, Hollands walked on and entered the nearest lift.

There were eight other people in the elevator, none of whom Hollands recognised. Occasionally, he would see a familiar face, but like the vast majority, he hardly knew a soul outside his own department. The way he saw it, three separate communities living under one roof was not a good thing, especially when there was very little continuity amongst the security guards. It made the whole building vulnerable and anyone who possessed an MOD pass could enter the premises and wander about at will. Fortunately, the Joint Intelligence Bureau was a much harder nut to crack.

The JIB was on the fifth floor of Quebec House. When Hollands stepped out of the lift, he walked straight into a three-sided, twelve-by-ten cage with steel bars set eighteen inches apart from floor to ceiling. To gain admittance, departmental officers had to insert a pass into a keyboard, tap out their personal staff number and wait for the computer to trip the lock, then withdraw the plastic card from the keyboard and pass through a turnstile. Visitors who'd collected a temporary pass from the receptionist in the foyer had to be met at the gate by the official they were going to see before the security guard would allow them to enter the restricted area. There was one final safeguard; unlike his colleagues on duty in the foyer, the security guard on the fifth floor was armed with a .38 Smith and Wesson revolver which was kept inside the top drawer of his table. This morning, according to the Dymo name tag above the left breast pocket of his uniform, a Mr G. Whitmore was looking after them.

Hollands carried out the standard procedure and withdrew his pass when the lock tripped. Then, hugging his suitcase to his chest, he squeezed through the turnstile.

"Welcome to the club, sir."

"What?"

Whitmore pointed to the suitcase Hollands was carrying, then to a jet bag lying on the floor by his table. "The Christmas Club – somebody drew my name out of the hat too."

"Actually, I volunteered," Hollands told him. "So did the other two."

"I should have known." Whitmore raised his eyes heavenwards. "When I was assigned to Quebec House, they warned me that everyone in the JIB was nuts."

"Well, now you can tell them they were right."

Hollands turned left and moved on down the corridor. Quebec House enclosed a small quadrangle which had once served as a private car park, but nowadays the wrought-iron gates which opened into Buckingham Street were permanently chained and padlocked. This however was the most obvious change that had been made over the years for, although the fabric of the building remained much the same, the interior had been gutted and altered to such an extent that the original architects would no longer have recognised it.

The office which he shared with the other two Service representatives was on the east side of the building overlooking the enclosed courtyard and two doors up from the men's room. A lofty cubbyhole with a lousy view, the only impressive thing about it was the plaque outside the door which showed the office was occupied by Lieutenant Commander R. S. Ingersole RN, Major A. J. Hollands, Intelligence Corps and Squadron Leader J. M. Greene, AFC, RAF. In a moment of artistic inspiration, the draughtsman had executed their names in a flowing Gothic script which would not have looked out of place in an art gallery.

Squadron Leader Greene had already started his Christmas break, utilising part of the annual leave entitlement to make an already extended holiday even longer.

Ingersole intended doing the same and only happened to be in the office because he had tacked the extra days on to the end of the break so that he could spend the New Year on the ski slopes in Kitzbühel. Anxious to clear his desk before he departed, Ingersole had come in early and was busy transferring files from the in-tray to the pending.

"Morning, Ralph."

"Morning, Dutch," Ingersole said without looking up from the files in front of him.

Hollands removed his topcoat and hung it up, then opened the combination safe. His first name was Anthony but no one apart from his mother, his ex-wife and her new husband ever called him that. To his colleagues and friends, he was either Tony or Dutch. Of the two, he answered more readily to Dutch – the nickname which had been bestowed on him while an officer-cadet at Sandhurst.

"Oh, by the way, Dutch, your lady friend asked if you'd kindly drop by as soon as you came in."

"My who?" Hollands asked, his voice cold.

"Why, Lindsey Whyte, of course, our charming American exchange officer."

Lieutenant Colonel Lindsey Whyte: tall, athletic, dark brown hair and eyes, single, mid thirties; a Masters degree in Electronics from Chicago University and a graduate of the US Command and Staff College.

"For the last time, Ralph, she's not my lady friend as you so quaintly put it."

"That's not what I've heard."

"Then you've heard wrong," Hollands said.

Three dates over a period of eight months hardly constituted a romance but with a dearth of office gossip, he supposed it was something for them to rib him about.

"The duty roster over Christmas hasn't passed unnoticed, Dutch." Ingersole grinned. "I mean, people are bound to put two and two together when they see yours and Lindsey's names on the list."

"Do you know what she wants to see me about?" Hollands said, cutting him short.

"Something to do with United General Electrics."

"I thought that contract was all buttoned up?"

"Apparently not."

Against formidable opposition from the West Germans and the Japanese, United General Electrics had recently been awarded a contract to build a new, fully automated power station in Kuwait. The competition had been fierce, but the British firm had enjoyed the support of a powerful backer. Concerned about the level of unemployment on Tyneside, the government had underwritten the company's bid to the tune of fourteen million, thereby ensuring that United General Electrics submitted the lowest tender. The offer of financial aid, however, was not without strings; in return for their investment, the government expected a quid pro quo from the company. To be specific, they were required to provide a vacancy on their payroll for an Intelligence agent masquerading as a computer programmer.

"I wouldn't keep Lindsey waiting too long if I were you," Ingersole warned. "Her ladyship sounded pretty wound-up to me."

"Well, thanks a lot," Hollands said, grimacing. "That's a good start to the festive season."

The Joint Intelligence Bureau derived its name from the fact that it was staffed by the civil service and the armed forces. It was organised into four sections – Collation, Assessment, Targeting and Acquisition – each of which was usually headed by either the equivalent of a full colonel or an assistant principal whose offices were on the south side of the building overlooking the Thames and Embankment Gardens. Targeting and Acquisition were the most demanding posts and were therefore acknowledged to be the stepping stones to bigger things. Lindsey Whyte was in charge of Acquisition; confirmation, if anybody needed it, that she was going places.

She had joined the JIB from the US School of Intelligence where she had been an instructor. Despite her professional and academic qualifications and the fact that she had been in post for more than two years, Hollands got the impression that she constantly felt the need to prove herself. This compulsion to be seen to be better than anyone else even extended to her leisure activities. On hearing that he

16

was a fairly good squash player, Lindsey had invited him round to the Lansdowne Club one evening where she had totally demolished him, winning all three games to love.

But there was nothing 'butch' about her appearance. She was fashion conscious, though not a slave to it, had good taste and always looked elegant and well-groomed. Today she was wearing a green wool dress with a pure silk scarf filling in the V neckline. When Hollands walked into her office, she was perched on the edge of the desk studying a complicated chart on the opposing wall, her shapely legs crossed at the ankles.

"Good morning, Lindsey," Hollands said with a cheerful smile. "I understand you want to talk to me about the set-up at United General Electrics?"

"Yes."

"Something gone wrong?"

"Not exactly," she said, "but the Director and I were discussing it last night and neither of us is very happy with the present arrangement. Don't get me wrong, Dutch, the computer programmer you selected is okay. He's got all the necessary qualifications."

"I didn't choose him," Hollands said. "I merely asked the right questions and the computer did the rest. His name was number one on the print-out."

"Yeah, well, it just so happens we need another man to go in first."

"You mind telling me why, Lindsey?"

"Because work on the site has already started."

Hollands glanced at the wall chart again and realised it was some kind of work study programme. "We knew that before we made our choice," he said quietly.

"The situation has changed since then."

"In what way?"

"I can't answer that. All I want from you is an experienced agent who's familiar with the ins and outs of the building trade and could pass himself off as a site foreman."

"I'd do a whole lot better if you told me what else you expect of this man. The need-to-know principle is all very well but sometimes it can be carried a bit too far."

"Perhaps."

17

Lindsey walked over to the window and stood there gazing down on the Thames and the Embankment Gardens as if seeking guidance. The river was deserted, its waters mud-coloured under a grey sky. In the park below, a solitary tramp was picking over one of the trash cans looking for scraps of food the seagulls had missed. After a lengthy silence, she finally lost interest in the view and turned to face him, her manner suddenly brisk and purposeful again.

"There are too many Iranian construction workers already on the site for our liking, Dutch. HM Ambassador in Kuwait thinks a lot of them have been sent there by Khomeini with the idea of spreading his revolutionary ideals to the rest of the labour force."

"The Treasury won't like that," Hollands said drily, "especially if fourteen million quid goes down the drain."

"Well, now you know why I want a good undercover man. He doesn't have to be a professional Intelligence agent but he should know his way around." Lindsey ticked off the requirements on her fingers. "One, he should be fluent in colloquial Arabic and not one of your high-falutin' university graduates who'd stand out like a sore thumb. Two, he should have more than just a smattering of Persian. Three, he's got to be immediately available. Four, he must already be positively vetted because we haven't got time to clear him."

"Right."

"One last point, Dutch. You can eliminate anyone who isn't snowy white."

Hollands doubted if such a paragon existed and knew it for certain when he returned to his office and used the micro-computer on his desk to tap into the soldiers' data bank. When the details appeared on the visual display unit, there was only one contender, a staff sergeant in the Royal Engineers who had been a member of the British Army Training Team in Iran and had also been seconded to the Trucial Oman Scouts. Up to colloquial standard in Arabic and Persian, he was currently serving at Headquarters 1st British Corps in Germany where he was employed as an Intelligence NCO in the Engineers branch, an appointment which required him to be positively vetted. The only fly in the ointment was the fact that his name was Stefan Cazalet which suggested his father had been born in Poland.

"Shit."

"Dear me." Ingersole looked up, a pained expression on his face. "I gather you're not having a fun time," he said.

"Damn right. I've just pulled a soldier who looks ace except there's a good chance he won't be eligible to receive signal intelligence."

"Bad luck."

"You can say that again."

"Well, don't get too worked up about it. The office party starts at a quarter to twelve and I may need a helping hand to get things organised."

"Thanks a million, Ralph. You're really making my day."

Hollands lifted the phone and called his contact at the Directorate of Security to ask if he could see the file on Stefan Cazalet only to learn that the vetting unit had already closed down. Christmas, it seemed, had started even earlier this year.

* * *

The sergeant walked out of the Underground station at Fulham Broadway and turned left in the direction of Stamford Bridge Stadium. The drill hall he was making for lay a quarter of a mile beyond the football ground on the fringe of a drab shopping precinct. A single-storey wooden building tucked behind iron railings, it resembled a mission hall for down-and-outs. The sign above the main entrance told anyone who was interested that it was currently occupied by 'Z' Company of the 4th Battalion Royal Green Jackets (Volunteers).

Normally, the drill hall was looked after by a caretaker who lived in the adjoining terraced house, but he had left London the previous evening to spend Christmas with his in-laws in Kent. Opening the front gate, the sergeant strolled round to the rear of the building and unlocked the back door with a pass key.

In anticipation of the dance on New Year's Eve, the

interior had been decorated with holly, sprigs of mistletoe, bunting and paperchains as well as a giant-size Christmas tree festooned with baubles and tinsel which took up one complete corner. Only the two lecture rooms, stores, armoury and company office, which faced lengthways on to the indoor parade-ground-cum-gymnasium, still retained a military appearance.

The sergeant produced a second pass key, unlocked the door to the company office and walked inside. A methodical man, he emptied the pockets of his combat jacket and placed the contents on the desk before hanging it up. Then he consulted a small notebook to verify the number he was supposed to call and dialled it out. When Boden answered the phone, he said, "This is Macklin. For your information, Exercise Control is now operational."

He didn't need to say anything else.

Chapter II

Boden replaced the phone, glanced at his wristwatch and made a note on his scratchpad that Exercise Control had been established at 1017 hours. He planned to enter Quebec House at eleven thirty and there was nothing he could do now except check and double check every detail of the plan while he waited for the time to pass. The British Telecom map was creased, dog-eared and grubby from constant use, and he had lost count of the number of times he had studied it. Unfolding it on the desk, he again traced the subterranean route Dukes and the others would follow. They would have to crawl flat on their bellies for nearly a mile through a tunnel that jinked left and right and was about the diameter of a large sewage pipe. Three, perhaps three and a half hours of hard, grinding work that would tax the fittest of men; Boden just hoped they didn't run into any problems along the way.

"Our civil servants really believe in looking after themselves, don't they?" Dukes said, breaking a long silence. "A Fortnum and Mason van has just pulled up outside the main entrance."

"That'll be the hamper for the duty officers. Same thing happened last year."

"Regular creatures of habit."

"That's what we're banking on," Boden said.

"Yeah. What time did you say this office party of theirs was supposed to start?"

"Around twelve noon. They usually invite up to thirty guests from other government departments dotted around London; the Foreign and Commonwealth Office, Headquarters SAS, and Century House."

If they hadn't done so, Boden reckoned he was going to be in trouble. Up till now, very few visitors had dropped into Quebec House on business and it was likely things would become even more slack as the morning wore on. He needed the party guests to deceive the security guards into thinking he'd arrived and departed with them.

"You fancy another coffee, Nick?"

"No." Boden shook his head. "But don't let me stop you having one."

"Will you spell me at the window then?"

"In a minute."

Boden folded the map away, opened a small holdall and placed the contents on the desk, item by item. A glass cutter, masking tape, a Beretta 6.5 mm automatic no bigger than the palm of his hand, eighty feet of nylon fishing tackle expertly coiled and tucked inside a plastic bag that would slip into his jacket pocket without creating too much of a telltale bulge, a micro-chip audio surveillance device with an operating range in excess of a mile and a two-way radio disguised as a box of Swan Vesta matches. He checked the radio to make sure the transmitter was sending a carrier wave, and then he changed places with Dukes.

"I don't know if I'm imagining it," Dukes said with a shudder, "but this office seems to be getting colder by the minute."

"The janitor set the thermostat at fifty yesterday evening," Boden told him. "There's no point heating an empty building when Legal and General have given their people an extra day's holiday."

"No wonder this country is going broke."

"This is Christmas. No one's rushing out to buy an insurance policy – I guess that's Legal and General's excuse."

"Everyone seems to have a reason for doing nothing except us."

Boden made no comment, knowing that sometimes it was prudent to let Dukes have the last word. He re-focussed the binoculars to match his own vision, then leaned back in the chair and lit a cigarette.

The two men from Fortnum and Mason who'd delivered a hamper to Quebec House returned to their vehicle, made a three-point turn and drove off. Turning right into Buckingham Street at the T-junction, they went on up the

Strand. With the cul-de-sac now deserted, Boden raised the binoculars and scanned the offices on the fifth floor. In some ways it was a fruitless exercise since the nylon curtains effectively screened the interior; on the other hand, the heavier drapes told him which rooms on the south side of the building were occupied by the Director and his assistant principals.

Behind him, in the outer office, he could hear a disc jockey babbling away on the radio and guessed that Dukes was anxious to catch the eleven o'clock newscast. Presently, the cheerful voice gave way to a choir and the opening lines of a carol reached him, clear as a bell. 'God rest you merry, Gentlemen,' they sang, 'Let nothing you dismay . . .'

"Amen to that," Boden murmured and wondered if any of the people on the fifth floor of Quebec House were listening to the same programme.

★ ★ ★

Hollands eyed the telephone, debating whether to make a private call to Richmond in Yorkshire. No one would be any the wiser if he did: Ingersole had left the office to supervise the preparations for the office party and he could bypass the switchboard and obtain an outside line by dialling 9. But because the taxpayer was footing the bill, out-going private calls were discouraged except in the case of an emergency. Then too, Caroline knew his office number and had promised to ring him before midday to let him know whether his Christmas presents for the children had arrived safely. Unfortunately, his ex-wife was inclined to be forgetful and he didn't want a repeat performance of last year's débâcle when he'd been stationed in Belize. He'd written twice to remind Caroline that he would be phoning on the morning of the twenty-fifth to wish the children a happy Christmas only to learn from the housekeeper that Caroline and the children, together with new husband Roger Leach, had just left the house and were on their way to High Cross where they were lunching with Roger's parents.

Caroline Leach, formerly Caroline Hollands, only child

23

of Mr and Mrs Arnold Westmorland and mother of his two children, Richard aged nine and Judith aged eight. Caroline, the spoiled, selfish, wilful yet utterly captivating young woman who'd put him through the mangle and turned his whole world upside down. Hollands recalled just how many times she had failed to keep her word since they had split up, and lifted the receiver. Obtaining an outside line he dialled the area code number for Richmond, Yorks, followed by the subscriber's number. The phone rang for what seemed an eternity before a familiar small voice answered it.

"Hello, Judith," Hollands said, "how's my favourite girl?"

"Daddy?"

"How many admirers have you got?"

"Oh, lots and lots," Judith solemnly assured him.

"I bet you have."

Hollands closed his eyes, pictured his daughter standing in the oak-panelled hall of her stepfather's house. She had inherited Caroline's good looks – glossy black hair, aquamarine eyes, straight nose and rounded cheeks tapering to a firm jaw. Judith had started copying her mother at a very early age and her head was probably tilted on one side. Like as not, there would be a half smile on her lips which Caroline had always used whenever she hadn't wanted him to know what she was thinking.

"Pa says I'll be the belle of the ball when I grow up."

Pa! Hollands couldn't explain why it made him angry whenever his daughter referred to Leach as Pa, but it did. He knew it was illogical; an eight-year-old could hardly go around calling her stepfather Roger, but all the same, he couldn't help feeling it was part of some long-term plot by Caroline to make the children think of him as their natural father.

"So how are you getting on with your riding lessons, Judith?" he asked cheerfully.

"I'm learning to jump. Mummy says I can enter the local gymkhana next year." She paused, then went on breathlessly, "I'm hoping Father Christmas will bring me a pony of my own. Do you think he will, Daddy?"

"That rather depends on a number of things. Have you been a good girl?"

"Pa says I have."

"Then I expect he will."

Leach was destined to become one of the biggest land-owners in North Yorkshire and he could afford to buy Judith a whole string of ponies. When his parents died, his present thousand-acre estate would more than quadruple. It suddenly occurred to Hollands that his Christmas present to Judith was going to seem mean in comparison. What did a little girl want with a doll when she was having riding lessons? And he couldn't help wondering if the Space Invaders game for his son was destined to go down like a lead balloon, too.

"Where's Richard?" he asked, pursuing the train of thought.

"He's gone into Richmond with Pa."

"And Mummy?"

"She's here."

"Would you do me a favour, darling?" he said. "Would you tell her that Daddy's on the phone and would like to speak to her?"

"Yes, all right," Judith said, then added, "Don't go away, Daddy."

He heard his daughter put the phone down and listened to the clip-clop of her low-heeled shoes fading into the distance. The returning footsteps were heavier, more purposeful, and he sensed that Caroline was annoyed even before she picked up the receiver. Her cryptic "Yes?" confirmed the supposition. When he mentioned the children's Christmas presents, the atmosphere dropped well below zero.

"I thought we'd agreed that I would call you at midday?" Caroline said icily.

"That was the arrangement but I thought you might be busy then."

"I'm busy now, Anthony. I'm expecting the first of our house guests to arrive at any moment and we're having a drinks party for upwards of fifty people this evening."

"I'll be brief and let you get on with it then."

"I'd be grateful if you would," Caroline told him.

"About their presents – have they arrived yet?"

"Of course they haven't. I'd have phoned otherwise. When did you post them?"

"A week ago."

"It's typical of you to leave everything to the last minute, Anthony. You know very well this is the busiest time of the year for the Post Office."

"I sent them parcel post, express delivery," Hollands said angrily. The bloody things were probably still lying in the sorting office at Mount Pleasant. Express delivery, what a laugh that was; Richard and Judith were going to think the world of him tomorrow. "When's the last delivery?" he asked.

"Any time between now and twelve noon."

"Well, I'll just have to keep my fingers crossed and hope for the best."

"Like Mr Micawber," she said.

"I don't suppose you would do me a big favour, would you?" Hollands bit his lip. "I mean, if the worst comes to the worst . . ."

"You'd like me to save your bacon," Caroline said, beating him to it.

"I'm thinking of Richard and Judith."

"You sound horribly self-righteous, but of course you always have been."

It was an old and much-used accusation which Caroline had levelled at him every time he'd had to explain why it was the army expected him to place its interests above hers. The army wasn't a nine to five, Monday to Friday job; if the need arose, you were at their beck and call twenty-four hours a day, seven days a week. Other wives were able to accept this as a regrettable fact of life, but not Caroline. She had kicked, ranted and raved, taking it out on him as though it were entirely his fault whenever the system frustrated her plans. Eventually, it had led to the break-up of their marriage and memories of the bitter scenes which had preceded their divorce were still capable of arousing his anger.

"Look," Hollands snapped, "if you don't want to do it,

just say so and I'll make it up to them when they come down to London to stay with me."

"How much were you thinking of spending on the children?" The question was accompanied by a long drawn-out sigh of pure martyrdom.

"About thirty pounds each."

"All right, Anthony, I'll think of something."

"I don't know how to thank you."

"Don't even try," Caroline said and hung up on him.

Hollands replaced the phone with a wry smile. Two incompatible people, different backgrounds, different interests, different temperaments; Arnold Westmorland had tried to point this out to him when he'd asked his permission to marry Caroline, but he'd refused to listen. He'd been a gunner in those days and had been posted straight from the Young Officers course at the Royal School of Artillery to a field regiment stationed at Catterick, just in time for the Waterloo Ball. Caroline and her parents had been the guests of his battery commander and he'd been more or less detailed to look after her. It could have been the horror story to end all horror stories but Caroline wasn't the frump he'd imagined her to be. Within a month they were sleeping together, before the year was out they were married. Six weeks later, the regiment had been sent out to Northern Ireland; the first of many such operational tours that had eventually destroyed their marriage.

"We've got an emergency, Dutch."

Hollands looked round to find Ingersole standing in the doorway, a worried expression on his face as though he'd just come across a letter bomb in the mail.

"How big?"

"It couldn't be worse." Ingersole shook his head. "Half the bloody crockery supplied by the Property Service Agency for this party must have come straight off the shelf. You've never seen such a filthy collection of cups and saucers and plates in your life."

"Oh, is that all?"

"Isn't it enough?" Ingersole said irritably. "Well, don't just sit there; time is running on and we're short of a washer-up."

* * *

Boden glanced at his wristwatch and decided it was time he made a move. The staffs of Defence Sales and Overseas Aid had already begun to thin out and any minute now, those representatives from other government departments who'd been invited to the JIB party would start arriving. Moving over to the desk, he picked up the 6.5 mm Beretta automatic and tucked it into the custom-made chamois-leather hip holster. Then he checked his jacket pockets to make sure he hadn't forgotten anything and put on a green, knee-length raincoat.

"How do I look?" he asked Dukes.

"Fine."

"No telltale bulge on the left hip?"

"Not that I can see."

"Good." Boden jerked a thumb towards the outer office. "As soon as I've gone, you're to vacuum the whole place. I don't want anyone to know we were ever here. Okay?"

"Don't worry," Dukes told him. "By the time I've finished, the people who work here will be able to eat off the floor."

Boden nodded, turned away and went into the outer office. Pausing at the door, he listened intently for sounds of movement in the corridor; then satisfied that no one was about, he opened the door and stepped outside. Although Legal and General had given their employees the day off, he couldn't afford to take any chances. Just when and how often the Securicor people checked the empty premises was an unknown factor, as was the janitor. Avoiding the lift, he walked towards the emergency exit at the far end of the corridor and pushed the stairwell door open. When he reached the deserted foyer downstairs, he turned left towards the rear entrance and with the aid of a skeleton key, let himself out into the alleyway directly behind the Legal and General building. From the alleyway, he then strolled into Buckingham Street and on round the corner to Quebec House.

There was only one uniformed security guard policing

28

the ground floor, and he was standing outside the control room to the right of the swing doors. Reaching inside his jacket, Boden produced a small, cheap-looking wallet and flipped it open to reveal a Ministry of Defence pass. It looked no different to any of the others the security guard had seen that morning, and he spared it no more than a cursory glance. He also knew that anyone wanting to enter the hyper-sensitive area of the fifth floor would have to insert the pass into the keyboard and tap out his or her personal staff number before the computer would release the turnstile. And that was Boden's problem; the Exercise Director could get him into the building but he hadn't been able to provide him with a personal staff number.

Undeterred, Boden walked on past the reception desk to the lifts and pressed both call buttons. The indicator lights showed that one had just left the second floor on the way up while the other was stationary at the fourth. Behind him, he could hear a low murmur of voices, then the clack of heels drawing nearer. Glancing over his shoulder, he saw three men in sober lounge suits and a matronly-looking woman with iron-grey hair. When the lift arrived, he stood to one side and allowed them to enter first. Politeness and good manners had nothing to do with it; he was merely concerned to know where they were going before deciding which button to press. A hunch that they had been invited to the JIB party was confirmed when the woman jabbed the button for the fifth floor.

Parting company with them at the third, Boden set off at a brisk pace in an anti-clockwise direction. Despite the fact that he'd never been inside Quebec House before, his purposeful stride gave the impression he knew exactly where he was going.

As with the other floors, the men's room was in the east wing. Finding it deserted, he made for the nearest cubicle and locked the door behind him. After checking to make sure the pockets were empty, he removed his green raincoat and hung it on the hook provided, then flushed the toilet and left. The raincoat made him conspicuous; without it, he would be taken for one of the small army of civil servants who worked in Defence Sales and Overseas Aid.

Boden retraced his steps and went down to the first floor where he came face to face with a whole bevy of clerks waiting for the lift. Intent on getting home, no one took the slightest notice of him.

The office he was looking for faced out on to the Embankment Gardens and was situated directly above the control room occupied by the security guards on the ground floor. According to the Exercise Director, the room number was either twenty-six or twenty-eight. Because of this uncertainty, Boden had intended to recce the area before carrying out the next phase of the operation, but the premature thinning out of the staff of Overseas Aid had now presented him with an unexpected opportunity to combine the two.

There was only one snag. Once the staff had left, the Branch Security Officer of the day had to check each office to ensure that everything had been locked away, and there was no telling how soon he would start on the south wing. Resisting the urge to pick up speed, Boden walked on to Room 28, then doubled back to 26.

Room 26 was the larger of the two offices and he was satisfied that the dividing wall overlapped the control room on the ground floor. Go or no go? He glanced left and right, then went inside. The task could be accomplished in a couple of minutes and nobody ever got anywhere without taking a few risks along the way.

One glance at the central-heating plant was enough to convince him it was as old as the building itself and twice as decrepit. It was also apparent that over the years extra radiators had been added willy-nilly so that the whole system was a plumber's nightmare. Around every water pipe that had been driven through to the floor below, there was a gap of at least one eighth of an inch between it and the floorboards.

The micro-chip surveillance transmitter supplied by the director was roughly the size of a 2p coin. About the same thickness, it incorporated a miniature battery with a twenty-four-hour lifespan and an extending wire microphone wound around the circumference. Boden felt the rim, got a fingernail under the release catch and pulled out the mike to its fullest extent. Then, crouching down, he eased the semi-rigid mike through the gap in the floor-boards and clamped the magnetised transmitter behind the steel pipe where it couldn't be seen.

Boden left the room and started back the way he had come. Before turning the corner into the east wing, he stopped to listen for sounds of movement that would indicate the Branch Security Officer was making his rounds. Hearing none, he continued on towards the lifts and went up to the fourth floor. From there on, he expected to be playing a game of hide-and-seek with the security guards and the BSO of Defence Sales until everybody, with the exception of the JIB duty staff, had left Quebec House.

As he'd found on the previous occasion, the men's room provided a temporary refuge. Locking himself in a vacant cubicle, he took out the two-way radio, selected channel 1 and held the receiver to his right ear. The minutes passed, then from inside the control room on the ground floor, he heard a voice say, "We'll give it another hour, Bert. Then you can check the building from Defence Sales to the basement."

Smiling to himself, Boden switched to channel 2. "This is Sunray," he said. "I'm on the inside and so far everything's looking good."

Chapter III

Dukes switched off his two-way radio, picked up the phone and dialled 736 0028. The Fulham number rang out briefly, then Macklin answered the call and said, "Exercise Control."

Dukes said, "Sunray's on the inside and everything's jake. How are things your end?"

"Quiet," Macklin told him. "Quiet as the grave."

"Good, let's hope it stays that way. You've got a boring wait ahead of you but five, maybe six hours from now you'll need to have your wits about you."

"When have you ever known me to goof off?"

"There's always a first time."

Dukes put the phone down, collected his travel bag and left the office. Like Boden, he avoided the lifts and went down the internal fire escape; like Boden, he also had a pass key to the back door which opened into the alleyway behind the Legal and General building. Turning left outside, he made his way via Villiers Street to Charing Cross station.

The lead story of every newscast that morning had been the great exodus from the capital. The police and AA had reported heavy traffic on all major routes out of London; Heathrow and Gatwick were handling extra flights to the Continent and British Rail were claiming that more people than last year were travelling by train. There was, however, little evidence of the holiday bustle at Charing Cross. With fewer than a hundred passengers waiting for trains to Dover, Ramsgate and Hastings, the concourse looked about as busy as it would be on a Sunday morning.

Dukes strolled through the main hall to the ticket office, bought a single to Charlton and returned to the concourse. Although the IRA had declared a truce, no one was taking any chances; half a dozen police constables positioned at vantage points around the terminal were on the look-out for anyone behaving suspiciously and every litter bin had been removed from the hall. Checking the departure board, Dukes saw that his train left from platform 1 and made his way towards the gate. The travel bag he was carrying contained two sleeping bags, a portable radio, an electric kettle, the leftovers from breakfast and Boden's shaving tackle. Although fairly light, the canvas holdall looked bulky and he was uncomfortably aware that the young policewoman standing by the gate was observing him closely as he strolled along the platform and boarded the train.

The rolling stock was typical of a suburban line – obsolete, dirty and long overdue for the junkyard. Slowly, as though reluctant to leave, the train pulled out of the terminus and clanked across Hungerford Bridge. Six stops and nineteen minutes later it arrived at Charlton.

Leaving the station, Dukes headed north, crossed the Woolwich Road and made his way to the Speedwell Garage in Anchor Lane. Situated next door to an abandoned fire station in a dockland area scheduled for redevelopment, the building looked as though it would fall down of its own accord long before the demolition contractors moved in. None of the pumps on the forecourt were in working order and a healthy crop of weeds had taken root in the fractured concrete. Given its dilapidated appearance, Dukes thought the owner must have been pleasantly surprised when Boden wanted to rent it. Crossing the forecourt, he entered the workshop by the side door facing the abandoned fire station.

Of the three men who were waiting for him inside, Roach was the only one he'd known for any length of time. They had served together in the same Para Battalion in the mid seventies and had kept in touch ever since. Small, wiry and extremely fit, he was an experienced potholer and was a member of the Pennine Cave Rescue Team. Apart from his valuable skills, Dukes liked and respected him because he was modest and unassuming, which was more than could be said for Josef Kardar.

Kardar had been born in Croydon of Hungarian parents who'd fled their native homeland in 1956 at the time of the

Uprising. He was twenty-four, had light brown wispy hair and a moon-shaped face that was entirely in keeping with his flabby condition. A man who lived and breathed computers, he considered himself something of an intellectual. Given his innate air of superiority, there was bound to be friction between them, but the thing that really got under Dukes' skin was the knowledge that the whole success or failure of the operation would ultimately depend on him. He just wished that Boden had found someone else for the job.

"Anything wrong, Harry?" Roach asked, moving forward to greet him.

"Not that I know of." Dukes forced a smile. "As a matter of fact, things are going better than I expected. How about you?"

"See for yourself."

Roach turned away, walked over to the shrouded vehicle which was positioned above the inspection pit and beckoned the third man, Franklin, to join him. With his help, he then removed the dust cover to reveal a Dodge van identical to the fleet operated by British Telecom.

"I reckon Franklin has done a pretty good job, don't you?"

Dukes placed his holdall on the ground and walked round the vehicle, inspecting it closely. The body had been resprayed, then sanded to remove the gloss so that the yellow paintwork looked weathered and matched the age of the truck. For added realism, Franklin had obviously used a wire brush to produce a number of scratchmarks around both door handles.

"Not bad," Dukes murmured, "not bad at all. You want to show me the Vehicle Registration Document?"

"Sure." Franklin climbed into the cab, opened the glove compartment in the dashboard and gave him the computer print-out supposedly issued by the licensing department at Swansea. "You won't find anything wrong with it," he said.

"I don't take anything on trust," Dukes told him. "There's nothing personal about it, you understand, just one of my little quirks."

34

It was also a fact that he hardly knew Franklin. An ex-Royal Corps of Transport driver who'd left the army when his six-year engagement was up, he had been recruited by Roach, and this was only the second time they'd met.

"You're the boss of this detail," Franklin said affably.

"That I am."

Dukes compared the document with the licence number and tax disc, then raised the hood and checked that the engine and chassis numbers tallied.

"Satisfied?" Franklin asked him.

"You'd know soon enough if I wasn't." Dukes turned his back and faced Roach. "Where do I find my working clothes?"

"In the office, Harry."

"And the rest of the gear?"

"It's already on board the truck."

"Good." Dukes rubbed his jaw. "You'd better give the street the once-over. If there's no one about, get the truck out on to the road and lock up the workshop. I'll leave by the side exit and join you as soon as I've changed. Okay?"

"No problem."

Dukes collected the holdall, walked into the lean-to office behind the inspection pit and stripped off his clothes, exchanging them for a pair of blue overalls. Then he went through the pockets of his suit and transferred his personal belongings to the overalls. Leaving the office, he joined the others who were waiting for him outside with the truck.

"Do you know the way?" he asked Franklin as he climbed into the cab.

"Like the back of my hand."

"Then what are we waiting for?"

Franklin started the engine, shifted into gear and drove up to the Woolwich Road. Turning left, he made for the Blackwall Tunnel under the river.

★   ★   ★

Boden walked past the lifts and used the adjoining staircase to reach the intermediate landing below. Once there, he positioned himself behind the lift shaft, his back pressed against the inner wall. It was the hiding place he'd used when the Branch Security Officer of Defence Sales had made his rounds before going off duty, and he saw no reason why the same tactics shouldn't be equally successful the second time around.

A faint whirring sound told Boden that one of the lifts was on the move and he listened intently, trying to decide whether it was going up or down. A minute or so ago, the sensor had picked up a conversation in the control room on the ground floor which had informed him that one of the security guards was about to check out the building. On the other hand, it could be some of the guests leaving the JIB office party.

The whirring noise grew louder, then ceased abruptly. A few moments later, he heard the lift doors open, followed by the sound of a man's footsteps on the landing above. The measured tread and the creak of leather suggested that he was wearing boots, the tuneless whistle implied he was not particularly alert.

Boden allowed the security guard a head start, then went after him. He moved slowly, testing each wooden step to see if it creaked before putting his full weight on it. Three quarters of the way up the flight, he adopted a semi-prone position and raised his head just high enough to peer over the top step. The security guard had started the check in the east wing and was steadily drawing away from him. As he neared the next office on the left side of the corridor, Boden ducked below the top step and timed him with his wristwatch.

It took the guard barely a minute to check that all the windows, filing cabinets and desks in the room had been properly secured and that the wastebins did not contain any classified material. If he kept that up, Boden calculated it would take him roughly eight minutes to reach the end of the corridor. He waited, eyes on the second and minute hands. When the time was up, he slowly raised his head again and caught a brief glimpse of the guard before he turned the corner and disappeared into the south wing.

Satisfied that it was now safe for him to follow on, Boden got to his feet and climbed the last few remaining steps to the fourth-floor landing.

The guard was moving in a clockwise direction which would eventually bring him back to his original starting point by the lifts. If he was feeling idle, he would ride down to the third but if he was going to do the job properly, he would use the staircases to make sure nobody was loitering between floors. Although the MOD constable had given every indication of being slapdash, Boden chose to play it safe: by moving forward to occupy one of the offices that had already been cleared, he avoided the danger of having to retreat.

Boden walked on past the men's room and entered the next office along on the right-hand side of the corridor which overlooked the inner courtyard. It was exactly fifteen minutes past one and he had at least five hours to kill before it would be safe to make the next move. He wished he'd thought to bring a paperback to help pass the time.

★   ★   ★

The JIB's Christmas party was being held in the conference room situated in the west wing just round the corner from Lindsey Whyte's office. A large room, it was possible for about thirty people to sit round the conference table in comfort. When the table was pushed against the outside wall, twice that number could move about with some degree of freedom. By the time all the guests had arrived, eighty-five were jammed into the room and Hollands found himself trapped in a corner with Stan Edwards.

Edwards was a short roly-poly man who suffered from a wheezy chest and smoked like a chimney. A civilian clerical officer in the Collation section, he was easily the longest-serving member of the Bureau and had attended every office party since 1951. Hollands also knew that he was a widower with two grown-up children and had volunteered for duty over Christmas.

"I hope you're a dab hand in the kitchen, Stan," he said, making small talk.

"I can look after myself, had to for the past ten years ever since Edith died. How about you, Major?"

"I'm pretty good with a frying pan. Any idea what's in the hamper from Fortnum and Mason?"

"Not a clue."

"You weren't on duty last year then?"

"No." Edwards looked round for an ashtray, found an empty saucer amongst the debris on a side table and stubbed his cigarette out in that. "I spent last Christmas with my son and his wife in Birmingham. They emigrated to Australia in February after he'd been made redundant. They want me to go and live with them in Melbourne when I pack this job in."

"When's that?"

"Eighth of May next year. I'll be sixty-five then. No more travelling up to town on the Central Line – shan't know I'm born."

"Where are you living now, Stan?"

"Northolt," Edwards said, wheezing for breath. "Got a nice little semi in Moat Farm Road. Linda – that's my daughter – she wants me to sell up and join her and Dick in California. I suppose I could always make myself useful in little ways but I don't know too much about the catering business."

It transpired that Dick had been a cook in the USAF stationed at Lakenheath whom Linda had met when working in an hotel on the outskirts of Cambridge. When his hitch was up, they'd settled in San Diego where they'd opened a diner.

"The climate's all right," Edwards went on, "none of your raw, wet, windy days we get over here, but upping sticks and moving to a strange country at my time of life isn't as easy as Linda thinks it is. Besides, there's the British Legion."

"Oh yes." Hollands did his best to seem interested. "Didn't someone tell me that you're a branch secretary?"

"That's right; we've got over two hundred active members." Edwards frowned at his empty glass. "I could go another beer," he said.

"I'll get you one."

38

Hollands edged his way towards the bar in the window. It was a typical office party, the men and women congregating separately and subdivided again according to the pecking order. There were a couple of notable exceptions; Ingersole was doing a great line with the girls from the typing pool and Lyndsey Whyte was surrounded by a group of male admirers. When he returned from the bar with a Carlsberg and a glass of white wine, Edwards had lit another cigarette and was helping himself to a sausage roll.

"You want to try one of these," he said, "they're not at all bad."

"Thanks, but I'm not hungry."

"Take a tip from an old infantryman, Major. Always fill your stomach while the going's good because you never know when your next meal's coming." He wiped a crumb from his lip, then said, "Still, I don't suppose that maxim applies to your lot."

"Oh, I don't know," said Hollands. "I used to be a gunner."

"Really? What made you transfer to the Intelligence Corps?"

"I'd worked with them in Northern Ireland and liked the look of them."

In reality, other factors had prompted the transfer. While on his third tour in Northern Ireland, Hollands had been ordered to investigate a suspect car outside the Europa Hotel in Belfast. As soon as the patrol he was leading had cleared the immediate area, he'd moved forward with the bomb disposal expert to take a closer look at the vehicle when it had suddenly been ripped apart by twenty-five pounds of plastic explosive. The blast had killed the bomb disposal expert and swept Hollands off his feet, hurling him through the plate-glass window of a jeweller's shop. Shards of glass had entered his eyes, nearly blinding him, and both his legs had been broken. Although the surgeons at the Royal Victoria had done their best to put him back together again, his sight had been permanently impaired and the Achilles tendon in his right leg had never healed properly. As a result of these injuries, he had been medically downgraded to the point where he was no longer fit enough to remain in a 'teeth-arm' unit. That meant he either transferred to some other less physically demanding branch of the service or took a medical discharge. Since the Intelligence Corps were willing and able to find a niche for him he'd opted to stay in the army. At the time, he'd also believed that his future career would be less turbulent and would therefore give his marriage a second chance. Subsequent events had proved him wrong on both counts.

"I see our friends from the Foreign and Commonwealth are beginning to make a move."

Hollands glanced round and saw the Director shepherding three of the more senior guests towards the door.

"They only come to put in an appearance," Edwards continued.

"I wonder how long before the others follow their example?"

"It's the hardened drinkers you want to worry about, Major. A few of the more determined ones hung on until after three o'clock last year."

"First-hand knowledge, Stan?"

"Somebody had to see them off the premises," Edwards said unabashed.

★   ★   ★

They were making better time than Dukes had anticipated, but most of the traffic had been flowing out of London in the opposite direction to them. From the Blackwall Tunnel, Franklin had skirted the East India Docks and followed Commercial Road as far as the junction with the A11 where he'd turned left. Cornhill, and on past the Bank of England into Victoria Street, then right into Cannon Street. St Paul's Cathedral, Ludgate Hill and Fleet Street; Franklin hadn't been exaggerating when he'd claimed he knew the route like the back of his hand.

Dukes glanced left and right: there was very little sign of life in Fleet Street. He could see the law courts up ahead when Franklin turned left into the narrow entrance of Crown Office Row.

Crown Office Row was the heartland of the legal profession. All the terraced houses facing the small enclosed park in the centre of the square had been converted into offices and were occupied by various chambers, each consisting of some fifteen to twenty barristers-at-law. With the law courts now in recess, the area was deserted, every office locked and barred. Franklin drove round the square and stopped on the west side opposite the park gates, some eight feet beyond a manhole cover.

Both men got out and moved round to the back of the vehicle. While Dukes lifted the manhole cover with a special key, Franklin opened the offside rear door, removed a canvas folding screen and erected it to form a hollow square around the tunnel entrance. Dukes then climbed down into the manhole and crawled forward on his stomach, using a small flashlight to probe the darkness ahead of him. Kardar left the van and followed him into the hole, leaving Roach, who was carrying a holdall containing a variety of special tools, eighty feet of nylon rope and a lightweight grapnel, to bring up the rear. As soon as Roach had disappeared into the narrow tunnel, Franklin replaced the metal cover, dismantled the canvas screen and stowed it away in the truck, then closed the rear door, got into the cab and drove off.

Crown Court Row was still the same oasis of peace and quiet it had been since the previous evening. No one had seen the vehicle arrive, nor had anyone witnessed its subsequent departure.

Chapter IV

Eight minutes past two: Boden did a quick calculation in his head and figured the guard would soon complete his security inspection of the building. Reaching for the two-way radio on the desk, he checked to make sure it was on channel 1, then switching it on, he turned the volume down low and held the receiver close to his ear. Somewhere downstairs in the control room, he could hear Gilbert O'Sullivan singing 'I'm not dreaming of a white Christmas', then the water gurgled in the central heating and drowned the rest of the refrain. The belly-rumbling noise was a long time in dying; when finally it did stop, Boden found himself listening to a phone-in. The caller was truculent and aggressive; he'd been unemployed since leaving school in July and was busy telling everybody just how lousy the festive season was going to be for him. The woman conducting the phone-in was all heart and sounded equally indignant. She was just getting into her stride when the sergeant in charge of the control room exercised his prerogative and switched off the transistor.

The ensuing silence was short-lived and ended with the sound of footsteps. Listening to the measured tread, Boden recognised the familiar creak of leather and knew who the man was before he even opened his mouth.

"Fancy a raincoat for Christmas, Sergeant Cantwell?"

"I wouldn't mind that one," Cantwell said, "it looks brand new. Where did you find it, Bert?"

"In the men's room on the third floor. Some berk left it in a cubicle."

"Any name tag in the collar?"

"No. There's nothing in the pockets to identify the owner either."

"Better stick it in the lost property cupboard until someone comes forward to claim it."

"Right."

"And while you're at it, put the kettle on," Cantwell told him. "I could do with a cup of coffee."

Subject closed, Boden thought, and was proved right. From then on, football and Liverpool's chances of bringing off the League and Cup double became the main topic of conversation in the control room.

*　　*　　*

Franklin glanced into the wing mirror, spotted a police car two vehicles back and immediately eased his foot on the accelerator. After leaving Crown Court Row, he'd doubled back to Ludgate Circus, crossed Blackfriars Bridge and was now heading out of town on the Old Kent Road, on his way to Wrotham. He checked the wing mirror again, saw the police car was signalling a left turn and heaved a sigh of relief.

Everything was still going like clockwork. In a little over half an hour from now, he would be deep in the Kent countryside and within easy striking distance of the woods on the escarpment above Wrotham where he was to ditch the truck before making his way on foot to the secluded cottage a mile from the village which Roach had pointed out to him a fortnight ago. A weekend retreat belonging to a wealthy businessman who was on their side and had agreed to let them use it was what Roach had told him, and he'd been content to leave it at that. You weren't inclined to ask too many questions when you were involved in a caper like this one where the stakes were high and the people around you had made it very clear that a man who showed signs of becoming nosy could well find himself in serious trouble. It was sufficient for him to know that the operation had been planned with a meticulous eye to detail.

Nothing had been left to chance and Franklin had been told to the precise minute how long it would take him to reach the cottage on foot. As of now, the place was unoccupied, but there was a Ford Escort in the stables, the fridge had been stocked with food and he had a key to the back door. All he had to do was make himself comfortable until the man he knew only as Sunray telephoned to warn him that the operation was about to enter the final phase. Then, and only then, would he be told how, when and where he was to pick up the team. Taking one hand off the steering wheel, Franklin reached for the packet of cigarettes he'd placed on the adjoining seat and put one to his lips. The accident occurred seconds later when, fumbling with his lighter, he momentarily took his eyes off the road.

A horn blasted a warning. Startled, Franklin looked up and saw that an elderly black woman wheeling a shopping basket had stepped off the pavement straight into the path of an oncoming juggernaut. At the same time, his mind registered the fact that the Volvo truck driver was swerving to the right in an effort to avoid her. Reacting instinctively, he steered towards the nearside kerb and stamped on the brakes. Even so, he was still doing close on thirty when the juggernaut ploughed into him.

There was a rasping cacophony of tortured metal as the Dodge was struck broadside on. The offside wing and the door crumpled as though made of cardboard and he heard his right arm snap above and below the elbow. The impact flipped the Dodge over on to its back, the seat belt parted company with the door pillar and his head struck the roof. The vertical body struts buckled inwards, jamming both doors, and the windscreen disintegrated with a loud report that sounded like a pistol shot. Coolant spewed out of the radiator, mingled with fuel escaping from the ruptured petrol tank and spilled over into the gutter. As though crushed between the jaws of a huge vice, the floor and roof of the cab were compressed until the gap between them was less than three feet.

The police officers in the patrol car which Franklin had spotted earlier on were the first to arrive at the scene of the accident. A few minutes later, they were joined by an ambulance crew from King's College Hospital in Bessemer Road and a fire engine from the nearby station house. After the potential fire hazard had been neutralised with foam, it then took the firemen another hour to cut their way into the cab and release the unconscious Franklin. With his skull looking as though it had been flattened with a smoothing iron, they were more than a little surprised to discover that he was still alive.

*　　*　　*

By two fifteen, the office party in the conference room had thinned out enough for Hollands to make a tactical withdrawal. All the VIP guests had departed and the Director, together with his four departmental heads, was no longer in evidence. Only Edwards and a few of his cronies were still propping up the bar, but Ralph Ingersole had had his beady eyes on them for some time and had already cut off the supply of booze. Hollands also had the feeling that if he didn't make himself scarce, Ingersole would call upon his services to help with the clearing up.

Returning to his office, he made another trunk call to Richmond. This time it was Leach who answered the phone.

Hollands said, "Hello, Roger. How's the world treating you?"

"Pretty good, all things considered." His voice sounded like that of a much older man, one who was overly fond of the good things in life and had become indolent and altogether too pleased with himself in the process of enjoying them. "How about you, Anthony?"

"I have my moments."

"I'm glad to hear it. You know what they say, all work and no play . . ."

Leach was full of platitudes and well on the way to becoming one of life's crashing bores. In time, no doubt, even Caroline would find him a bit wearing. But, of course, there were the obvious compensations; whatever she wanted, Roger provided.

"Is Caroline there?" Hollands asked.

"Afraid not, she went into town to do some last minute shopping. She's in a bit of a flat spin about this drinks party we're giving this evening. Anything I can do?"

"Caroline didn't say anything about my presents for the children, did she?"

"Not that I recall." Leach paused, then said, "I see there

45

are a couple of large parcels by the hall table. They must have arrived while I was out."

"Are they from me?"

"Hang on, I'll have a look."

There was a loud clatter as Leach put the phone down; moments later, he started muttering to himself. Listening to him rummaging about, Hollands marvelled that anyone could make such a big production out of such a simple task.

"Don't recognise the printing . . ." Leach sighed as he picked up the phone again. "You live in Clapham, don't you, Anthony?"

"Yes."

"Must be from you then. We don't know anyone else in that part of the world."

"Thank God for that. Have yourself a happy Christmas."

"And you, Anthony."

Replacing the receiver, Hollands walked over to the security cabinet and unlocked it. His in-tray was empty, so was the out and most of the stuff in the pending was for information only. The print-out on Staff Sergeant Cazalet, the combat engineer whom he'd earmarked for the Kuwait assignment, didn't offer much scope either. Although Cazalet's record of service looked impressive, the picture was incomplete without the security file and there was no way he could lay his hands on that until after the Christmas break.

For want of something better to do to help pass the time, Hollands sat down at his desk and began to read the latest Intelligence summary of the political and military situation in the Horn of Africa. The report consisted of twenty-four pages and he had barely started it when Lindsey Whyte interrupted him.

"Busy, Dutch?"

Hollands looked up and saw that Lindsey had changed out of the green wool dress and was now wearing navy-blue slacks with a matching reefer jacket over a white roll-neck sweater. A pair of gloves was tucked into the outside pocket of her shoulder bag.

"Not particularly." He indicated the file on his desk. "I

was just bringing myself up to date, but it's nothing that can't wait."

"Good. The Director has just been having a word with me. He thinks the duty officer's phone should be manned now that most of the staff have left. I wonder if you'd mind holding the fort?"

"Yes, of course."

"Thanks." Lindsey pulled on her gloves. "I'm going out for an hour or so. I forgot to bring a book and I'll be bored out of my mind unless I have something to read."

"I know the feeling."

"Is there anything I can get for you while I'm at the book store?"

Hollands shook his head. "Thanks all the same, but I came prepared."

"I guess you're better organised than I am," she said, waving a hand in goodbye.

Hollands doubted that very much. Returning the file to the cabinet, he pulled the shutter down, spun the combination and reversed the hanging card on the locking bar from red to green to show that it had been properly secured. That done, he left the office and made his way to the duty officer's room opposite the central registry in the north wing.

The room set aside for the duty officer had been furnished in accordance with the minimum barrack scale. This meant the Property Service Agency had provided a tallboy, a divan bed, a writing desk, a small nine-by-nine woven carpet and two chairs, one of which was an upright ladder-back. There was also a Chubb safe behind the door which had been fitted with a combination dial instead of the usual lock and key. As an added precaution, the safe had been bricked in so that it was now virtually immovable. The portable monochrome fourteen-inch TV set, together with the microwave oven and the two-ring electric cooker in the adjoining storeroom-cum-kitchen, were not standard issue. They had been purchased with a grant from the Directorate's contingency fund in order to make life slightly more agreeable over a weekend when the minimum manning cover during silent hours was increased by the addition of a resident clerk. While not exactly plush, these

47

facilities were adequate enough under normal circumstances; they were however considerably overstretched at Christmas and other bank holidays when standing orders required that one of the four department heads should also be on duty. On such occasions, it was customary for the duty officer to sleep elsewhere and there was every indication that Lindsey Whyte had already anticipated this.

Hollands closed the door behind him, switched on the TV set and settled into the armchair. Moments later he found himself watching the umpteenth repeat of *The Longest Day*. It was, he thought, a singularly inappropriate movie for Christmas Eve but before the night was over, he would have cause to revise his opinion.

★   ★   ★

The air was stale and oppressively warm, rather like the atmosphere inside a greenhouse. Their rate of progress was agonisingly slow because the amount of headroom varied so that at times Dukes was crawling flat on his belly, his protective helmet frequently scraping the roof. It was a dark, claustrophobic and tomb-like world which the beam from his small flashlight did little to dispel, and even though he had known what to expect, there were moments when his mind was paralysed with fear.

The map he'd studied and committed to memory was not a hundred percent accurate. Despite the large scale, it did not reflect every twist and turn and if he didn't take care, there was a very real danger that he would become totally disorientated. Dukes stopped crawling, rubbed the sweat from his eyelids and stole another glance at his wristwatch. Eleven minutes past three: more than an hour had passed since they'd entered the tunnel in Crown Court Row and there was still no sign of the first junction point.

"What's the matter now?" Kardar asked him, his voice breathless but sarcastic enough to get under his skin.

"Nothing." Dukes sucked in his cheeks, trying unsuccessfully to work a little saliva into his mouth. "I just thought we deserved a short break, that's all."

They deserved a break all right. According to the map, the junction point where they were supposed to turn left was exactly nine hundred and twenty-five feet from the manhole in Crown Court Row. If he hadn't missed the junction point, it meant they had covered less than three hundred yards in over an hour. To have expended so much energy in achieving so little? It didn't seem possible. Christ alone knew how much time they would lose if he had overshot and had to back up, but it sure as hell was going to make a dog's breakfast of the schedule that Boden was working to.

Dukes closed his eyes; he should have allowed Roach to take the lead. Roach was an experienced potholer and had explored damn near every cave in the Pennines. He was a human mole, blessed with an uncanny sense of direction which made him at home in the dark below ground.

"I can't go on." Kardar again, and beginning to wheeze like an asthmatic.

"What do you mean, you can't go on?"

"I can't breathe properly in this atmosphere and my chest is killing me."

"I have news for you," Dukes said grimly. "If your chest doesn't kill you, I just may."

"Hey, come on, take it easy," Roach said quietly. "Josef is not as fit as you and I, but he's a specialist and we've got to make allowances. Without him, this whole operation will crumble."

"You think I don't know that?"

"Well, okay," Roach said, "so it's up to us to help him in any way we can."

"You're a regular boy scout," Dukes told him and started inching forward again.

The junction point was a psychological hurdle; when, a couple of minutes later, they reached it, their morale soared.

"We've cracked it," Dukes said triumphantly. "You hear that? We've cracked the bastard."

They were, in fact, a long way from doing that but at least they were now moving downhill towards the river and in places it was even possible for them to crawl on all fours.

★　★　★

Robert Mitchum and the United States 1st Infantry Division were still pinned down on Omaha Beach when Lindsey Whyte returned from her last-minute shopping expedition. Observing a slight frown as she glanced at the TV set, Hollands got up and switched it off.

"You needn't have done that, Dutch," she told him. "It doesn't bother me."

"Nor me," he said. "As a matter of fact, I've seen that film so many times that I'm thinking of putting in for the France and Germany Star."

"You and me both." Lindsey removed her shoulder bag and sat down on the bed. "Talking of battles, how's the office party going?"

"It finally broke up around three o'clock. Ralph poked his head round the door about half an hour ago to say that everything was shipshape again."

"So who did all the work? The girls from the typing pool?"

Hollands nodded. Whenever the Chiefs gave a party for the Indians, it was always the same, the Indians ended up doing most of the chores.

"Well, now that everyone's gone home, you might as well do the security check," she said.

"Right." Hollands got up and moved towards the door. "Will you stay by the phone while I'm making the rounds?" he asked.

"I thought Edwards might do that."

"I believe he's having a snooze in the central registry."

"You mean he's had too much to drink and is sleeping it off." Lindsey shook her head. "Whenever there's a job in the offing, you can bet your bottom dollar he's some place else. If there was an award for the goldbricker of the year, he'd win it hands down. I doubt if anyone will miss him when he retires in May."

"Oh, I don't know," Hollands said drily. "Who's going to organise the sweepstake on the Derby and the Grand National when he's gone?"

"Ralph told me you'd volunteered to do it."

"He would say that."

Hollands left the duty officer's room, sought out Constable Whitmore who was manning the cage opposite the lifts and told him they might as well carry out the security check together. By mutual agreement, they started with the offices in the east wing and continued in a clockwise direction so that, some fifteen minutes later, they arrived back at their original starting point. Collecting his overnight bag, Whitmore then removed the .38 Smith and Wesson revolver from the desk drawer and took the lift down to the ground floor where he subsequently reported to the sergeant in charge of the control room.

The time was nineteen minutes past four. Although not the shortest day of the year, it was already pitch dark outside and would remain so until the moon rose at 2145 hours. The department stores in Oxford Street and Regent Street were still open but the crowds were rapidly dwindling. In Trafalgar Square, a few drunken revellers had gathered round the giant Christmas tree to form an impromptu but raucous choir for the Salvation Army band who were playing on the steps of St Martin-in-the-Fields. To the south, Whitehall, Parliament Square, the Embankment and Northumberland Avenue were ghost areas. Even the tramps who normally bedded down under the arches of Hungerford Bridge had disappeared, whisked off to a Congregational Hall in Victoria where they would be fed and sheltered over the Christmas holiday by a small band of dedicated social workers who'd volunteered for the job.

But not everybody was celebrating. Below ground, the assault team led by Dukes had reached the third junction point and were now roughly two hundred and fifty yards from their final objective. There were also those who were simply killing time, like Boden, who was occupying a fourth-floor office in the east wing of Quebec House, and Macklin over in Fulham who had his feet up on the desk belonging to the officer commanding 'Z' Company, 4th Battalion the Royal Green Jackets. Finally, there was the detective constable who was waiting in the corridor outside the intensive care unit of King's College Hospital. He was there to get a statement from John Matthew Franklin, the driver of a vehicle belonging to British Telecom.

There were two reasons why the traffic accident which had occurred earlier that afternoon in the Old Kent Road was not what it had seemed at first sight. Firstly, British Telecom were adamant that John Matthew Franklin was not one of their employees, and secondly, they did not own a Dodge pick-up with the licence number TLA 298Y. In the detective constable's opinion, these two indisputable facts raised a number of interesting questions which he hoped the man in the intensive care unit would be able to answer. Franklin, however, was unable to oblige him. At ten minutes past six that evening he died without regaining consciousness.

Chapter V

At exactly six fifteen, Boden left the office where he'd been lying up and entered the men's room next door. Moving past the urinals to the sashcord window which overlooked the inner courtyard, he unlatched the lower half just high enough to give himself a better view than the frosted glass afforded. He scanned each of the visible wings in turn, working from the ground floor up. As soon as he was satisfied that none of the offices were occupied, he raised the window to its fullest extent. Then, leaning out, he checked the rooms in the east wing beneath him before twisting round to look up at the fifth floor. There was no sign of activity, merely a faint glare from the odd fluorescent light that had been left on in the corridor.

Boden climbed up on to the sill, turned sideways to face the wall and, ducking his head, planted a foot on the windowledge outside. Then he reached up with his right hand, got a fingertip hold on one of the horizontal beadings which subdivided the pane of glass in the upper half of the window and eased himself out on to the ledge. Slowly turning round again until he was facing inwards, he raised one foot and pushed down on the frame to close the lower half of the window.

The drainpipe was to his left, roughly four feet beyond the ledge. Inching towards it, Boden saw that the ring bolt which anchored the pipe to the wall was not on the same level and realised that spanning the gap was going to be much more hazardous than he'd anticipated. He had to get it right first time or he would end up in the courtyard sixty feet below with his head split open like an over-ripe watermelon. Total concentration, total co-ordination. Boden took a deep breath, grabbed hold of the drainpipe with his left hand and wedged his foot on the ring bolt. Then, maintaining the momentum, he launched himself across the abyss, got a second hand and foothold on the pipe and hung there like a monkey on a stick.

As soon as he'd regained his breath, Boden straddled the pipe, planted the rubber soles of his shoes against the wall and leaned out, his back a drawn bow. Then he literally walked up the wall, left arm, right leg alternating with right arm, left leg. He was roughly at the halfway point when he noticed there was a U-bend in the pipe, while directly above it, a thinner pipe hived off the main waste outlet and went on up to the guttering.

Boden didn't hesitate. The slimmer pipe was easier to hold and it was physically impossible to climb diagonally. Furthermore, it didn't matter a damn which ledge he perched on in the end so long as he made it to the fifth floor. Suddenly his head was on a level with the windowledge; another upward heave and it was his hip, then finally the stone projection was below him and without thinking about it, he side-stepped across the gap.

He found himself looking into a small, narrow office. Somewhere in the corridor, one of the overhead fluorescent lights was still burning and he could just make out the furniture, a security cabinet to the left of the door and a swivel chair and steel executive desk which had been positioned diagonally across the near corner of the room. Boden dipped into his jacket pocket, took out the glass cutter and unsheathed the blade. Pressing down on it, he cut the glass in the upper half of the sashcord window parallel with the bottom frame and six inches above it. Then he tucked the knife into his top pocket and fished out the reel of adhesive masking tape.

Biting on the tag, he unwound the tape and pressed it over the incision he'd made in the window. Then he went to work with the glass cutter again and fashioned a slot which was about the size and shape of an ordinary letter-box. When he'd finished, the masking tape acted as a hinge and he was able to push the glass inwards, slip his hand through the opening and undo the catch.

The rest should have been easy. Two metal handles resembling a pair of stirrups were attached to the underside of one upper frame and by inserting a foot into each one in turn, Boden figured he would be able to exert sufficient downward force to open the window. But, for some reason, it refused to budge. Either the wood had warped or else the window hadn't been opened since being re-painted.

Using the knife again, he scoured both sides, then attacked the top, digging the blade between the brick surround and the wooden frame. At the same time, he pushed down on each stirrup in turn, frequently taking his other foot off the windowledge in order to bring his full weight to bear. It was an agonisingly slow business and always at the back of his mind was the worry that some-body would spot him out on the ledge. Suddenly, the window gave an inch or so on the left and he changed his stance to deal with the other end.

Rain, frost, snow and ice had worn away the window-ledge over the years, polishing its surface so that in some places it was as slippery as a skid-pan. Although aware of the treacherous surface, Boden had grown careless in his anxiety to finish the job and an accident was almost inevi-table. As he side-stepped along the ledge, he trod on some moss and lost his footing. In sheer desperation, he clawed at the window so that the knife slipped from his grasp, sailed through the air and landed with a clatter in the inner courtyard. Then his fingernails encountered the strip of beading and arrested his fall long enough for him to grab hold of the nearest stirrup with his right hand.

For some moments he hung there in space, his body swinging from side to side, the tension on arm and shoulder muscles unbearable. The motion finally stopped and Boden placed the palm of his left hand on the ledge and levered himself up until he was able to kneel on the stone projec-tion. Then, very slowly, he hauled himself upright.

Boden closed his eyes. A steam hammer was pounding away inside his chest and he felt sick, as though someone had kicked him in the groin. 'You're okay,' he told himself, 'the panic's over and you're safe.' Gradually the nausea passed and his limbs stopped trembling, and as he struggled to recover his composure, he discovered that his dead weight had partially opened the window and that there was a gap of some nine inches.

Placing his hands either side of the centre point, Boden pushed downwards. The gap became twelve inches, then eighteen; at a shade over two feet it was wide enough for him to squeeze through head first. Supporting himself with one hand on the interior windowledge, he turned sideways and was able to get one leg at a time through the opening. Then he stepped down on to the floor and, satisfied that no one had heard a thing, closed the window.

He glanced round the room, saw there was a noticeboard on the wall behind the desk and took a closer look at it. There was just sufficient light for him to see that amongst the notices was a copy of the duty officers' roster. It was the one vital piece of information he lacked and although it meant chancing his arm, Boden had never been one to look a gift horse in the mouth. Unpinning the sheet of paper, he took it out into the passageway and held it up to the light. As soon as he'd committed the names to memory, he returned to the office, picked up the phone and dialled 736 0028. When Macklin answered, Boden told him to grab a notebook and pencil, then said, "Take this down. The following officers are on duty from the twenty-fourth of December to inclusive the twenty-seventh; Lieutenant Colonel L. Whyte, Major A. Hollands and Mr S. Edwards."

* * *

Hollands opened three tins of fruit and emptied the peaches, pineapple and mandarin oranges into a bowl. To round it off, he added a few maraschino cherries from a glass bottle.

"There you are," he said, "instant fruit salad."

"We'll make a chef out of you yet, Dutch." Lindsey Whyte removed the lid from the saucepan which was simmering on the two-ring electric cooker and jabbed a fork into the potatoes. "Hard as bullets," she muttered. "They won't be ready for at least another ten minutes."

Hollands opened a packet of frozen peas, poured them into a saucepan of water and added a pinch of salt. "What do we do about this chicken pie? According to the instructions on the carton, it should be heated in an oven for fifteen minutes at three hundred and fifty degrees, but there's no mention of how long it takes in a microwave."

"Two, possibly three minutes should do it," Lindsey told him. "Where's Stanley got to?"

"I believe he's laying a table in the registry."

"Do you suppose he'd mind if we sampled the wine?"

"Don't worry about Stan, he'll catch up on us." Hollands uncorked a bottle of Sancerre, filled three glasses, and raised one to Lindsey. "Here's to you," he said.

"And a merry Christmas to you, Dutch."

"Yeah." His face clouded. "I guess it's a fun time for children – at least I hope it is."

"So when are you going to see yours?"

"I'm collecting Judith and Richard on New Year's Day. They're staying with me for a few days."

"And you wish it could be longer."

"I'm frightened of losing them." Hollands chewed on his bottom lip, staring into the glass of wine. "Oh, I've been granted reasonable access – every other weekend and half the school holidays – but it's not always practicable. Before I came here, I spent nine months in Belize when I didn't get to see them at all."

"It must be very unsettling for the children, Dutch."

"I mean to go on seeing them," Hollands said obstinately. "It was Caroline who wanted the divorce, not me. I'm just the one who's supposed to have made her unhappy."

"And did you?" Lindsey frowned. "On second thoughts, don't tell me – it's none of my business."

"We started out all right," he said, ignoring her request, "then everything seemed to go sour. I don't know where I went wrong, I really don't."

"You and I are pretty much alike, Dutch. We've both gone down the same road. I've been married too."

"I didn't know that."

"It's not something I usually talk about."

Hollands waited, expecting her to tell him more, but it seemed Lindsey didn't intend to break her golden rule, after all. The complete liberated woman, he thought, doing her own thing and very sure of herself. The past was dead and buried and she wasn't about to resurrect it. Then a wry smile materialised to soften her face, an indication that the hard-as-nails posture was only skin deep.

"Maybe neither of us were to blame, Dutch, but we failed, you and I, and the knowledge still hurts, doesn't it?"

There was only one answer to that. Ducking the question, Hollands said, "You want to try those potatoes again?"

★   ★   ★

Dukes crawled out of the tunnel into the vertical shaft below the manhole cover and slowly straightened up. Every muscle ached, his kneecaps and the palms of both hands were grazed and under the blue overalls his shirt clung damply to his back.

"Are we there?" Kardar's plaintive voice wheezed at him from inside the tunnel, then died in a paroxysm of coughing as he struggled to regain his breath.

"I think so."

Dukes licked his lips but there was no spittle there and his mouth was as dry as dust. Are we there? Kardar's question had sown an ugly seed of doubt and he went over the route again in his mind, mentally comparing it with the map Boden had shown him. Three turns: left, left, then right. Even a half-wit wouldn't have found it difficult to follow those simple directions. One thing was certain; in a few minutes from now he'd know just how good a navigator he'd been. Bending almost double, he called down the tunnel to Roach and asked him to open the holdall and get out the special key.

The manhole cover was held in position by four metal flanges which rotated anti-clockwise to engage with the recesses in the steel ring which had been set into the concrete some three inches below the rim. To unlock it from below ground, it had been necessary to design a special key consisting of a cylindrical bar and a spanner with two prongs at one end which fitted snugly either side of the metal flanges. Once the prongs had been engaged, leverage was obtained by passing the cylindrical bar through the near round hole in the shaft.

Taking a firm double-handed grip on the bar, Dukes attempted to turn the key in a clockwise direction. At first,

58

the flange refused to budge, then suddenly he felt it give and exerting all his strength, he was able to rotate it through ninety degrees. Repeating the process until all four had been unlocked, he then lifted the manhole cover just high enough off the ground for him to place it to one side without making a noise.

The moment he raised his head above the lip and looked about him, Dukes knew there had been nothing wrong with his navigation. The side exit into Buckingham Street was directly to his front, the wrought-iron gates padlocked and chained the way they had been ever since the IRA had first started their bombing campaign in London. Unbuttoning the top pocket of his overalls, he took out the transistorised walkie-talkie and held the mike close to his mouth.

"This is Sunray Minor," he said in a low voice. "How do you read me?"

"I have you in sight," Boden told him softly. "Let me know when you are ready."

Dukes acknowledged the message, instructed the other two to follow him and climbed out of the hole. When Kardar emerged a few moments later, it was plainly evident he was physically exhausted. Despite the fact that he'd been able to take it easy for the past five minutes or so, he was still wheezing and, as he tottered towards the dark shadows in the south-east corner of the quadrangle, Dukes wondered how long it would be before his legs buckled under him.

"We've got a problem," he murmured to Roach. "Our computer whizz-kid is never going to make it. The way Kardar is now, he couldn't climb a foot, let alone seventy to eighty."

"Then we'll just have to haul him up, Harry."

"Yeah, like a bloody sack of coal."

Dukes picked up the access plate and carefully replaced it, lowering one end at a time on to the steel rim inside the manhole shaft. That done, he called Boden on the radio and told him they were ready. Up on the fifth floor, a light flicked on and off in a room to the left of the waste outlet, and shortly afterwards he heard a faint scraping noise of wood against wood, a sign that Boden was opening the window. Signalling Roach to bring the holdall with him, he moved forward to the drainpipe and side-stepped five paces to position himself directly below the office on the fifth floor.

The nylon fishing line was virtually invisible against the dark background and he didn't spot it until it was almost at eye level. Once he'd got hold of it, Roach passed him the rope end and he tied the fishing line on to it below the grapnel and buried the lead hook into the strands. Then he removed his protective helmet, placed it in the holdall and told Roach to make sure he collected Kardar's. Knowing it was essential to keep the line away from the building in case the grapnel scraped against the wall, Dukes moved out into the quadrangle, uncoiling the rope as he did so. After taking up the slack, he then gave the line a couple of quick tugs.

Eighty feet above, Boden began to haul in the rope by winding the nylon fishing line on to a plastic ruler he'd found in the bottom drawer of the desk. As soon as the grapnel came within reach, he leaned out, grabbed hold of it and anchored the prongs under the projecting edge of the windowsill. Then he called Dukes on the radio and told him to come on up.

Dukes took a double-handed grip on the rope high above his head and lifted himself off the ground. Drawing both knees up to stomach level, he crossed his legs at the ankle to nip the rope between his feet. Stretch, jack-knife, clamp; his co-ordination was so perfect that he made the long climb seem effortless. When his head was just below the window, Boden seized his collar and dragged him into the room.

"Thanks, Nick." Dukes inspected the graze and burn marks on his palms and gave them a cursory lick. "I'm afraid we've got a problem," he said, still breathing heavily.

"Kardar?"

"Yeah. Roach is going to tie him on to the rope and we'll have to winch the slob up. There's no way he's going to make it on his own."

"Relax, Harry," Boden said quietly. "Kardar may be a little overweight but he's not in the Guinness Book of Records. Between the two of us, we'll have him up here in no time."

Boden couldn't have been more wrong. Kardar was in no physical shape to do anything and was merely a hundred and sixty-four pounds of dead weight at the end of a very long rope. As though members of a team engaged in a tug of war, Boden and Dukes took up the strain, leaned back and side-stepped towards the corridor. When they reached it, Dukes performed the job of anchor man while Boden returned to the window and took a fresh grip. As soon as he had anchored the rope, Dukes let go of his end and moved forward to join him.

It was a process they were to repeat over and over again until finally, some twelve minutes later, Kardar's head and shoulders were level with the window and they were able to pull him into the room. After that, the rest was easy, Dukes merely lowering the rope to Roach who shinned up it like a monkey, the holdall containing the rest of their gear slung across his back, bandolier fashion.

The time was seven thirty-five and they were within easy striking distance of the unsuspecting trio who were on duty in the north wing. Only Kardar seemed less than elated. He was sitting hunched up behind the solitary desk, his face waxen.

"How do you feel now, Josef?" Boden asked softly.

"Terrible. My chest is killing me, and that's not all . . ." Kardar looked up and swallowed hard. "I think I'm going to be sick."

"It'll pass," Boden told him. "A couple of aspirins washed down with a hot cup of tea will soon put you right. Meantime, you'd better rest here."

"Maybe I should stay with him," Roach suggested. "After all, it doesn't matter when I isolate this floor, as long as the JIB duty staff are confined to one room."

"I want it done now, starting with the telephones in the south wing. Do I make myself clear?"

"Very."

"Good." Signalling Dukes to follow him, Boden left the office and made his way to the central registry. From that moment on, he became Captain James Redmond, 22nd SAS Regiment.

Chapter VI

Edwards was in reminiscent mood and was telling them how he'd spent the Christmas of '42 when the intruders appeared. The door had been left ajar so that they could hear the telephone in the duty officer's room across the passageway, and Lindsey was facing the corridor with Hollands on her left at one end of the table and Edwards to her right at the other. The clerical officer had been talking non-stop for close on twenty minutes and his latest anecdote was even more boring than those he'd previously recounted. But the glazed expression suddenly vanished from Lindsey's face and Hollands wondered why she should now seem both surprised and puzzled. Glancing to his left, he saw that they had been joined by two men, the taller of whom was dressed like a maintenance engineer. His companion could have been a clerk of works except that Hollands had yet to meet one who wore a suit that must have cost at least a couple of hundred pounds while he was busy getting his hands dirty.

"My name's Redmond," the smaller, fair-haired man said before anyone had a chance to ask him. "Captain James Redmond."

He had an engaging smile; he also had a military identity card which he rapidly produced for their inspection.

"Do you mind explaining how you got up here without an escort?" Hollands asked.

"Are you Colonel Whyte, sir?"

"No, I am," Lindsey told him.

"Oh, I'm sorry, Ma'am. The Directing Staff omitted to tell me that the JIB had an American exchange officer."

"What Directing Staff?"

"The umpires who are controlling exercise Silent Night. I think it might be a good thing if you spoke to SAS Headquarters and got them to put you in the picture."

Hollands left the table and walked over to the nearest desk to pick up a phone, but Redmond got there first and started dialling. Then, halfway through the code, he calmly handed the telephone over to him. "The Duke of York's barracks," he said. "You want 0028 for Exercise Headquarters."

"Thanks."

"You're welcome, Major."

Hollands dialled out the extension and waited. The number rang just four times before someone lifted the receiver and identified himself as the chief umpire at Exercise Control.

Hollands said, "This is the duty officer, JIB. I have a Captain Redmond here who claims he's participating in an exercise called Silent Night."

"That's correct."

"I see. What's the aim of this exercise? And, more importantly, who's sponsoring it?"

The chief umpire chose to answer the questions in reverse order. The exercise, he said, had been organised and sponsored by the Director of Army Training at the request of the Cabinet Office, the basic concept subsequently being approved by the Prime Minister. The purpose of Silent Night was to assess the reaction of the security forces to a hostile situation.

"What sort of hostile situation?" Hollands asked.

"A surprise attack on a government building."

"Yes? Well, I hope you know what you're doing. The JIB is a highly sensitive department."

"That's exactly why it was selected and the fact that Captain Redmond has apparently penetrated Quebec House without being challenged is more than a little disturbing. It only goes to show how right the PM is to be concerned about the general lack of security awareness in Whitehall."

Sarcastic, condescending, supercilious; the anonymous voice was a blend of all three and was more abrasive than a sheet of sandpaper. "I'd like to know just who I'm dealing with," Hollands snapped. "For all I know, you and Redmond could be a couple of smart-arsed reporters."

"My name is Macklin and this is not a newspaper stunt. No pressmen would be in a position to know that Lieutenant Colonel Whyte, Major Hollands and Mr Edwards are on duty from the twenty-fourth to the twenty-seventh of December. Do you get the drift?"

"More or less."

"Good. Are there any other questions?"

"Only one," said Hollands. "What are the ground rules for Silent Night?"

"There are none. This is a free play exercise," Macklin said brusquely, and hung up.

The disarming smile was still there on Redmond's mouth, only now it seemed a little smug as though he knew exactly what the chief umpire had said to him.

"Well, what's the score?" Lindsey asked.

"It's an exercise all right." Hollands slowly replaced the receiver. "But there's no pink."

"Pink?" Her eyebrows drew together in puzzlement.

"The detailed scenario for an exercise which indicates the way it is to develop. It's printed on pink paper and issued to all the umpires. Silent Night is different because there are no guidelines and no one knows how it is going to end or when."

"That's not quite correct," Redmond said cheerfully. "This exercise will end either when I have accomplished my mission or you have succeeded in raising the alarm and the security forces are seen to be reacting to the situation."

"So what is your mission?" Lindsey asked.

"Now, you don't really expect me to tell you that, do you, Colonel?"

"There's a lot of sensitive information in this department," Hollands said curtly. "Do you have the necessary clearance to see any of it?"

The military identity card merely told him that Redmond was an officer. It did not indicate whether he had been positively vetted, nor did it show any of the caveats that would give him access to codeword material and signal intercepts.

"Run a check on me, if you like."

"You bet I will." Hollands pointed towards the corridor.

"There's a VDU in my office. It'll only take a couple of minutes to get a verification."

"Why not? Harry can keep an eye on Colonel Whyte and Mr Edwards while we're away." He turned to Lindsey, the friendly agreeable smile again on his lips. "Don't let Harry's appearance fool you, Ma'am; he may look a weakling but he's really as hard as nails."

"A real tough guy, huh?"

"Well, I wouldn't pick up the phone and try to raise the alarm if I were you. It could be a painful experience."

"I'll bear that in mind."

"Good." He nodded sagely, then turned to Hollands. "Let's go," he said. "The sooner we get started, the sooner this exercise will be over."

Redmond made it sound as though he personally found the whole business a tremendous bore and that if they all pulled together, they could bring Silent Night to a satisfactory conclusion in the shortest possible time. But Hollands noticed there was no togetherness as they made their way to his office in the east wing. For all his bonhomie, the younger man kept well clear of him and when they entered the room, the first thing he did was to move the phone on the desk.

"It's best to avoid any unpleasantness, Major Hollands. If I left the phone within reach, you might be tempted to use it, and I wouldn't like that."

"I thought you were keen to get this thing over and done with?"

"Oh, I am. But there's a right way and a wrong way to go about it. You and I would find ourselves on adverse reports if Macklin suspected we'd deliberately sabotaged his precious exercise."

"Is Macklin an army officer?"

"No, but he's the equivalent of a brigadier."

Macklin hadn't acted like one when Hollands had snapped at him. The man who claimed to be the chief umpire had been sarcastic and condescending, and wouldn't a senior civil servant have made it very clear just who he was dealing with? Leaning across the desk, Hollands switched on the VDU, then sat down.

"I'll need your ID card," he said.

"Yes, of course."

Redmond placed the card face up on the desk in front of him. As Hollands tapped out his P number, rank, name and initials, he moved round behind him and stood there, peering over his shoulder at the visual display unit. Presently, his personal record sheet began to appear line by line, box by box, in a sickening ambience of yellow letters against a green background. Halfway down the sheet, the box relating to security clearance showed that Redmond had been positively vetted. Depressing the key appropriate to retain the information on call, Hollands then asked the computer for his record of service to date. Moments later it appeared on the screen.

Commissioned into the Coldstream Guards in 1972 at the age of nineteen, Redmond had spent the first four years of his service with the 2nd Battalion in the UK, Germany and Northern Ireland. After an eighteen-month tour in Dhofar with the Sultan of Muscat and Oman's forces, he had then transferred to the Parachute Regiment, serving with the 3rd Battalion in Cyprus. Subsequently, he had been accepted by the SAS and from 1979 onwards had been stationed at Hereford.

"Well, now you know the story of my life, Major."

"It would seem so." Hollands instructed the computer to give him a print-out and leaned back in his chair. "I wish I could say the same for Harry and the rest of your team."

"No way."

"What do you mean, no way?"

"Just that. It would be a gross breach of security if I disclosed their names and service numbers, and you know it."

"The JIB holds a lot of sensitive material," Hollands said.

"So you keep telling me, but I'm afraid you'll just have to take my word for it that they have all the requisite clearances." He waited until the teleprinter had stopped chattering, then plucked the print-out from the machine. Folding the tear sheet in four, he tucked it into his jacket pocket. "It wouldn't be very prudent to leave that document lying around."

"Give yourself ten out of ten for security awareness," Hollands said drily.

"You have an engaging sense of humour, Major Hollands."

The ready smile came back again but it didn't extend to the slate-coloured eyes. They were predatory, unblinking, watchful and dangerous. Hollands was conscious of them boring into his back as they returned to the central registry and had the feeling that Redmond was just longing for an excuse to take him apart.

There was a similar air of menace in the registry even though Lindsey and Edwards were doing their best to pretend otherwise. The clerical officer was leaning back in his chair, hands clasped together over his corpulent stomach, his eyes downcast at the half-empty glass of Sancerre in front of him as if, mellowed by the wine, he was about to drop off at any moment. Lindsey had gone one better; she had her nose buried in a paperback, seemingly indifferent to the brooding presence of the tall, thin character in workman's overalls. When they walked back into the room, she looked up slowly, her face a picture of studied boredom. Her expression didn't change when Hollands told her that Redmond was in the SAS and had been cleared for Top Secret.

"I suppose that's something," she said. "What happens now?"

"I noticed the duty officer's room is locked and that tells me the safe must be open, Colonel."

"So?"

"So I'd like the key to the door."

"What makes you think I've got it?" Lindsey demanded.

"Well, Mr Edwards certainly won't have it. That leaves you and Major Hollands." He shrugged. "But if you're determined to be difficult, Colonel, I guess we'll just have to search you."

"Give him the key," Hollands said tersely. "None of the documents in the safe are graded higher than Confidential."

He could tell the suggestion didn't meet with Lindsey's

approval but if they were going to raise the alarm, they would have to catch the intruders off guard and right now they were far too alert. He caught her eye and tried to make her understand that she would gain nothing by provoking them at this stage. For a while it looked as though he'd failed to get the message across then suddenly Lindsey opened her shoulder bag, took out the key and tossed it on to the table.

"Thank you." Redmond scooped it up and walked round the table to get at the keyboard between the two filing cabinets near the window. "What do you keep in the storeroom?" he asked, pointing to the fourth key from the left in the top row.

"Stationery," Edwards said, suddenly coming to life.

"That seems as good a place as any." Redmond unhooked the key, checked the room number on the metal disk, and turned to Lindsey. "I hope you and Major Hollands won't find it too cramped in there, Colonel."

"Are you proposing to lock us up?"

"Only while I'm questioning Mr Edwards."

"This is getting ridiculous."

"Most exercises are," Redmond said, cutting her short. "And this one will become even more farcical if we have to use force."

Hollands edged a little closer to the younger man. The odds were just about in their favour and if he started to mix it, either Lindsey or Edwards would have a chance to grab the phone and raise the control room on the ground floor. Then a voice behind him warned Redmond to watch his back and glancing round, he saw that they now had to contend with a third intruder.

"You couldn't have arrived at a more opportune moment," Redmond told the newcomer. "That is Major Hollands, the lady is Lieutenant Colonel Whyte. Harry and I were just about to move them into alternative accommodation. Right, Major?"

"It's your party," Hollands said.

"Good. Then perhaps you'd like to lead the way?"

The storeroom was next door but one on the same side of the corridor. Little bigger than a walk-in cupboard, it

measured nine feet by six and could just about accommo-
date the meccano-type racks on which the bureau's supply
of stationery was kept. There was a window above the
door but it didn't open, and the only source of ventilation
was a small grille at ceiling height on the dividing wall
between the storeroom and the office used by the typing
pool. The floor was uncarpeted and none too clean but
there was nowhere else for them to sit.

"I don't know about you," Lindsey said when they were
alone, "but I think this whole thing stinks."

"So does Redmond."

"I'm not exactly wild about him either."

"He can't be more than five eight," Hollands said. "Yet,
according to the print-out, he was originally commissioned
into the Coldstream Guards. It's not usual for the Household Division to accept an officer that small."

"Are you saying he's an impostor, Dutch?"

"In my book, he's a very plausible con man."

Lindsey frowned. "Come to think of it," she said slowly,
"I noticed he did a double-take when he discovered who I
was."

"Yes." For Hollands, the initial seed of doubt had been
sown as a result of Redmond's reaction. He'd thought it
highly unlikely that the Directing Staff would have omitted
to include a detailed character briefing when they told him
just who was on duty. "You can be sure of one thing," he
went on, "this operation has been well planned and even
better executed. Somehow these intruders managed to
reach the inner courtyard without being seen and roped
their way up here. So far, the security guards don't know
they're inside the building but if he's to stay in business,
Redmond has got to isolate this floor. If he hasn't already
done it, you can bet the third man is busy sabotaging every
phone except the duty officer's."

"There are other phones, Dutch, and we've each got an
ace up our sleeves."

Hollands nodded. They were thinking along the same
lines: the MOD pass was their ace card. If he could make
it to the gate and feed his personal staff number into the
computer, Redmond and the others would be unable to

follow him once he'd passed through the cage. There was, however, one major snag.

"Redmond's been well briefed," Hollands said, broaching the subject. "When he questions us, the MOD pass will be the first thing he asks for."

"Then one of us will have to pretend they left it at home."

"That's exactly what I had in mind. I'll tell him that I didn't have to obtain a temporary pass from the reception desk because Ralph Ingersole came down to the lobby and vouched for me. If you think about it, there's no way Redmond can prove I'm lying. Oh, he'll make me strip off but I won't have the card on me."

"Because I'll be carrying it," Lindsey said.

"Yes. When he asks you for your pass, hand it over under protest. Mine, you keep next to your skin until he's finished interrogating you, then you'd better hide it some place else. If Redmond doesn't buy my story, he may subject you to a body search."

"What do you think of our chances, Dutch?"

"Pretty good, provided he leaves me to last." Hollands reached inside his jacket and took out his MOD pass. "My staff number is 5495. You'd better memorise that in case he decides to keep us apart after we've been interrogated."

*   *   *

At noon the maximum temperature recorded on the Air Ministry roof had been six degrees centigrade, forty-three Fahrenheit. Some four hours later, the cold front which had been building up near Sule Skerry had begun to move south, its onward march heralded by snow flurries over the high ground in north-east Scotland. By nineteen hundred hours, the temperature in central London was down to minus four degrees centigrade, twenty-five Fahrenheit, and still falling. Although it wouldn't be a white Christmas, a heavy frost on the morrow would create the illusion of one.

The atmosphere seemed even chillier in the TA centre on the Fulham Road. As part of a year-long economy drive to reduce costs, the caretaker had switched off the gas-fired central heating before leaving to stay with his in-laws in Kent. Since no one had thought to provide him with a key to the boiler room, Macklin had therefore spent a large part of the day performing various physical exercises in order to keep himself reasonably warm. The tension he'd been under for the past ten hours had also sapped his energy to the point where he had found it increasingly difficult to stay awake.

Although Dukes had warned him that he would need to have his wits about him once the operation got under way, that high spot had long since passed. Having convinced the duty officer of the JIB that Silent Night was an official exercise, Macklin had felt he could afford to unwind and take things easy. Hunched up in the chair, both hands thrust deep into his pockets, he was indulging in a quiet snooze when the telephone rang and set his pulse racing.

Lifting the receiver, he nervously cleared his throat and said, "Exercise Control."

"Relax," Dukes told him. "It's only me."

"Thank God for that. How's it going?"

"Everything's fine. Sunray says you did a great job on Hollands. As a matter of fact, he reckons we don't need you any more."

"You mean I can leave this god-awful dump?"

"Just as soon as you like."

"Great. Have a happy Christmas."

"Up you," Dukes said and hung up.

Macklin put the phone down, took out a handkerchief and carefully wiped the receiver and cradle. Cigarettes, notebook, pen, lighter and a crumpled sheet of tinfoil that had contained his sandwiches: he checked his pockets to make sure he hadn't forgotten anything. Then he left the drill hall, locking the office and back doors behind him. For some minutes he waited in the shadow of the building, alert and tense, like a deer scenting danger, but apart from the occasional vehicle in the Fulham Road he neither saw nor heard anything untoward. Crossing the yard, he opened the gate and stepped out into the street.

There were no pedestrians in the immediate vicinity and the road was completely free of traffic. Confident that no one had seen him leave the premises, Macklin turned right and headed towards the Underground station in Fulham Broadway. He was less than fifty yards from the entrance when the Ford Escort cut across on to the wrong side of the road and pulled up alongside him.

There were two men in the vehicle and he knew them for what they were – a couple of hard-nosed police officers on plainclothes duty. They had that aura about them which suggested they would welcome a spot of aggro to enliven what was, for them, a very dull evening.

The driver wound the window down, looked Macklin over, then said, "Working overtime, Sergeant?"

"I haven't been to a fancy dress party," he said and almost instantly regretted the air of bravado.

"Very comical. You want to tell us where you're going?"

"You want to tell me why I should?" Macklin said, then switched on a contrite smile the moment the driver showed him his warrant card. "Forget I asked," he added.

"That's all right, Sergeant. You weren't to know we're police officers."

"No, that's a fact."

"But now that you do, how about satisfying our curiosity?"

"Sure." Macklin nodded eagerly. "I'm on my way home. Our commanding officer is a regular, like me, only keener. He's very hot on security; that's why he insisted his permanent staff should check out all the drill halls twice a day over the Christmas break. We drew lots for it and I lost."

"Tough luck. You got an identity card on you?"

"Yes." Macklin unbuttoned his hip pocket. "You want to see it?"

"That's what I had in mind, Sergeant."

"Right. I guess you can't be too careful these days." Shit, shit, shit: relaxed on the outside, nervous as a kitten within, Macklin stooped down and passed the plastic card through the open window. "37945600," he said, reeling off his army number.

"I can read, Sergeant."

The driver reached above his head, switched on the

courtesy light in the roof and studied the photograph in the top right-hand corner. As if wanting a second opinion, he showed the identity card to his companion before returning it to Macklin. Then he wished him a merry Christmas, started the engine and pulled away from the kerb, the offside indicator winking as he steered across the road.

Macklin walked on, turned into the Underground station and bought a ticket to Hammersmith from one of the vending machines in the hallway. He tried to persuade himself that it could have been worse, that at least the police officers hadn't asked him for his home address. But it was a small consolation and he drew little comfort from it. They knew his real identity and could trace him through his serial number any time they wanted.

CHAPTER VII

The Nuits St Georges was one of four bottles of wine Mr Fortnum and Mr Mason had seen fit to include in their bumper Christmas hamper. Coming on top of the two glasses of Sancerre he'd already consumed, it had a twofold effect on Edwards, heightening his colour and loosening his tongue to the point where he'd become positively loquacious. Although nothing he'd said about the various personalities in the JIB had so far been of the slightest value, Boden was content to string him along. A skilled interrogator, he was an exponent of the softly, softly approach.

"How long did you say you'd been a civil servant, Stan?" he asked casually.

"Thirty-seven years next May."

"And the rest."

"What do you mean?"

"You're an old soldier, right?" Boden stared at the small emblem in the lapel of Edwards' sports jacket. "I mean, that is a British Legion badge you're wearing, isn't it?"

"You know it is."

"Well, there you are then, you were obviously a clerk. When your time was up, you simply turned in your uniform and carried on doing the same job."

"I was an infantryman," Edwards said indignantly, "not a bloody pen-pusher."

"Really? What regiment?"

"The Royal Berkshires – 1st Battalion. I joined up in 1937 at the age of nineteen, seven years with the colours, five on the reserve."

"And spent the whole of the last war guarding the Orkney Islands." Boden looked beyond him and winked at Dukes who was standing at ease in the doorway, hands loosely clasped behind his back. "It must have been tough up there in the frozen north, hundreds of miles from civilisation and only the sheep for company. I reckon you earned your Defence Medal the hard way, Stan."

"Bollocks, you don't know what you're talking about." Edwards downed the rest of his wine and pushed the glass across the table, inviting Boden to re-fill it. "Listen," he continued, "we were in 6 Brigade, 2nd Infantry Division, from the third of September 1939 to the thirty-first of August 1945 and saw the bloody lot."

The phoney war in the Maginot Line near Metz, and the blitzkrieg. The Royal Berkshires had been in the thick of it during that long and bitter rearguard action from Tom Beck to the beaches of Dunkirk via the River Escaut, the Bois de Wannerheim south-west of Lille, and the La Bassée Canal.

"We were up against the SS Totenkopf Division; the bully boys from Danzig. I don't know what sort of reputation they earned for themselves in Poland, but we gave them a right hammering." Edwards smiled at the memory of those days and emptied his glass again, then wiped his mouth on a liver-spotted wrist. "We heard later that they took it out on the Royal Norfolks – shot a hundred of them down in cold blood after they'd surrendered."

"I bet you paid them back with interest on D Day, Stan," Boden said, leading him on.

"2 Div was sent to India in April '42. When the landing on the Normandy beaches took place, we were advancing towards Imphal."

But before that, there had been Kohima and the bloody fight to relieve the minuscule garrison. The Royal Berkshires had taken over Summerhouse Hill above the Deputy Commissioner's bungalow, where for the next twelve days and nights they had slugged it out with Major General Sato's 31st Infantry Division. Below them, they could see the 2nd Durham Light Infantry and the 1st Royal Welch Fusiliers dug in at one end of the tennis courts with the Japanese facing them across the nets, except that the nets had vanished and the once lush grass courts had become a moonscape of shell craters.

"You make it sound like it was only yesterday," Boden told him.

"Sometimes it seems that way."

"My father used to say much the same. He was a cavalry-man and spent his war in the Western Desert, serving under every commander from Wavell to Montgomery."

"Oh, yes?" Edwards was having difficulty with certain words now and the 'yes' acquired an 'h'.

"He must have been about your age when he died, Stan, but his mind was still very clear at the end. Or at least I thought so until I discovered that most of his vivid recollections had been culled from a stack of old regimental journals that he kept in his study."

"What are you getting at?"

"Well, maybe you've read a lot of books on the subject too," Boden said gently. "After all, Stan, thirty-eight years is a long, long time."

"Some things you don't forget."

"Like your old army number?"

"Yes."

"So what was it?"

"861750," Edwards said promptly.

"861750?" Boden looked doubtful. "That doesn't sound right to me. Shouldn't there be eight figures?"

"It's an old pre-war regimental number."

"I don't know, Stan. I think you're confusing it with the combination to your security cabinet."

"Rubbish – that's 45 22 0 . . ." Edwards bit his lip and stared at him pop-eyed. "You almost caught me out," he mumbled.

"You've got to admit it was a nice try," Boden said cheerfully.

It was better than that. The last figure was obviously somewhere between 1 and 9 and the cabinets were fitted with a standard Manifoil lock. To open it, Boden knew the dial had to be moved in alternate directions starting with five complete revolutions clockwise to the first key number. Thereafter, the number of revolutions decreased progressively to the point where the dial only had to be moved a quarter turn from zero to disengage the locking bar. By repeating this sequence a maximum nine times, he would discover the final digit which Edwards had held

76

back, a task that was unlikely to take him more than ten minutes. And when he'd succeeded in opening the security cabinet, he would find a brown envelope inside containing the combinations of two other related safes, a requirement that was laid down in standing orders.

"I've dropped a clanger, haven't I?" Edwards said morosely.

"Don't worry about it, Stan," Boden told him. "I shan't put it in my report. If anyone comes out of this exercise with egg on their faces, it'll be Lieutenant Colonel Whyte and Major Hollands."

"Does that mean you aren't going to open my cabinet?"

"No. I'll wait until after I've questioned the other two. Then you can put the blame on them."

Opening the cabinets was merely to be a diversion to hoodwink the opposition. The real damage would be done by Kardar once he and Roach had picked the lock to the computer centre and neutralised the infra-red intruder system.

"I wouldn't like to lose my pension."

"You won't, Stan, believe me." Boden pushed the bottle of Nuits St Georges towards him. "Here," he said, "you may as well finish the rest. Perhaps it'll help cheer you up – not that you've anything to worry about."

"I only wish that was true," Edwards said gruffly.

★   ★   ★

The computer centre was located in the north wing on the same side of the corridor as the duty officer's room. It was protected by a heavy wooden door backed with a half-inch steel plate and secured with a Yale lock, the key to which was kept in the control room during silent hours. A warning notice on the door stated that the premises were guarded by an infra-red intruder system.

The lock was hardly a serious deterrent to a man like Roach. He had operated with the special reconnaissance group in Northern Ireland and, as part of his training, Special Branch had given him a thorough grounding in the art of breaking and entering. One of the more useful implements he'd acquired was a strong, flexible probe about the thickness of a playing card which could be inserted in the narrow gap between the door and the jamb to spring the lock.

The infra-red intruder system was much more difficult to neutralise. The sensors were mounted on the dividing walls, some eighteen inches beyond the threshold, and projected a solid but invisible fence across the width of the room from floor to ceiling. The alarm was controlled by a switch outside the infra-red fence which was concealed behind a metal panel in the wall to the left of the door. As an additional safeguard, it was fitted with a Manifoil lock. Only three people knew the combination; the senior executive officer in charge of the computer centre, his deputy, and the branch security officer. Furthermore, a probe that could manipulate and disengage the vertical locking bars had yet to be invented.

The one foolproof method of dealing with the intruder system was to isolate the sensors from their energising source. To be sure of locating all the wires, Roach decided to attack the wall directly above the metal panel. His tools were a hammer and chisel and he used them with a delicate but incisive touch. It was a long, slow business and he could have done without Kardar breathing down his neck, constantly asking him how much longer he was going to be.

"This isn't the kind of job you can rush," Roach explained patiently for the umpteenth time.

"You're making a hell of a mess," Kardar said plaintively. "Look at all the plaster on the floor."

"That's inevitable."

"But they'll know we've been here."

"Christ almighty," Roach exploded. "Hollands and the other two have already seen us."

"But you don't understand. I mean here, in the computer centre."

"You're supposed to be the expert, Josef. You'll just have to make it look as though we tried to get into the system and failed."

Roach lined up the chisel, gave it a judicious blow with the hammer and dug out another chip of plaster. A minute piece of flex caught his eye and moistening a fingertip, he rubbed away the dust and discovered that he'd exposed one of the leads.

"Well," he grunted, "it looks as though we're almost there."

Taking care not to chisel through the flex, Roach enlarged the hole until all the leads had been uncovered. Then he went through his holdall and found a contact breaker.

"Okay," he said, his voice heavy with sarcasm, "before we go any farther, is there anything you need? Another glass of water? More aspirins? A leak?"

"No."

"You'd better be very sure, Josef, because once the power is interrupted, you've got just ten seconds to reach the computer terminal, and there's no coming back until I return."

"I'm ready when you are," Kardar told him.

Although he still looked pale and drawn, his eyes were now suddenly bright with expectation.

"All right, get set."

Roach spliced the contact breaker into the leads and switched off the current. Like an habitual gambler who couldn't wait to try his luck on a line of one-armed bandits, Kardar made it to the console in record time.

★   ★   ★

Four hours after Franklin had died, the only progress made by Scotland Yard had been entirely of the negative kind. What had started out as a routine investigation of a fatal traffic accident had rapidly become a major operation involving the Anti-Terrorist Squad, Special Branch, the Serious Crimes Squad, the forensic scientists of 'C' Department, and the uniformed branch of just about every police district in the Metropolitan area.

The fact that the mystery vehicle had obviously been camouflaged for a specific purpose had led the police to assume that some major British Telecom installation had been targeted by the IRA. Consequently, every exchange, repeating station and depot had been searched, as had the homes of known IRA sympathisers amongst the Irish community in Kilburn. But, apart from a number of seditious pamphlets which Special Branch had seized, the operation had been largely abortive.

It was the forensic scientists who'd provided the only worthwhile leads. After analysing paint scrapings taken from the Dodge, they had been able to identify the manufacturer, the batch number of the product and how long it had been on the shelf before being sold to a customer. They had also persuaded the vehicle licensing centre at Swansea to feed the engine and chassis numbers into their computer. The programme had started running at 1630 hours; by 2115 the police knew that the Dodge was owned by Leslie William Tyler of Willowdene, Burleigh Crescent, West Harrow. Unfortunately, Tyler had previously reported that his vehicle had been stolen from outside his house some time during the night of 16 December.

★ ★ ★

Hollands listened to the footsteps in the corridor and knew it was the tall thin man before he opened the door. It seemed that ladies not only came first with Redmond, they also received preferential treatment. Edwards had been questioned for over an hour, but now, less than fifteen minutes after Lindsey had been summoned to appear before him, Harry was back again.

"You needn't have hurried on my account," Hollands told him.

"We didn't."

"That was meant to be a joke."

"Then it wasn't very funny, was it?"

Hollands got to his feet and moved towards the door, Harry retreating until they reached the corridor when he was then careful to stay a pace or two in rear. When they walked into the duty officer's room, he saw that Redmond had re-arranged the furniture, moving the table away from the wall so that he faced the entrance. The ostentatious display of a large number of Secret and Top Secret files was clearly meant to shake him. So also were the two MOD passes which had been placed in a prominent position on the table where he was bound to see them.

80

"I hope you're going to be equally co-operative, Major Hollands," Redmond said pleasantly.

"Concerning what?"

"I'd like your MOD pass."

"Ah, well, that's a little difficult." Hollands smiled apologetically. "I'm afraid I left it at home along with my season ticket. I keep them in the same plastic wallet."

"So where's your temporary pass?"

"I didn't have to ask for one. I rang Ingersole from the reception desk and he collected me from the lobby."

"How very convenient."

Hollands shrugged. "You can always ring him at home if you don't believe me. He lives in Godalming; his phone number is in the duty officer's folder."

"And if I did call him, you know very well that would give the game away."

"It's up to you, isn't it?"

"Indeed it is. Now, suppose you empty your pockets and persuade me you're not being obstructive."

Hollands reached inside his jacket and placed a leather wallet on the table, then produced a key ring and a handful of loose change before turning the linings of his pockets inside out.

"Are you satisfied now?" he asked.

"You're too eager, Major." Redmond counted the banknotes in the wallet and examined the rest of the contents. "Cheque card, American Express, Military ID." He looked up. "I don't see a return ticket."

"I bought a single to Waterloo."

"Somehow I thought you'd say that." Redmond paused, then said, "Okay, Harry, search him."

Hollands found himself shoved up against the wall, body at forty-five degrees from an upright position, legs and arms spread wide apart. Hard, talon-like fingers began to frisk him from head to toe, probing every crevice. A perfectionist, Harry then undid the leather waist belt, unzipped his fly and yanked his trousers and under-shorts down around his ankles. His jacket was raised and draped over his head, so was the blue check shirt he was wearing. Finally, Harry reluctantly conceded he was clean.

Redmond snapped his fingers. "Colonel Whyte has got his pass," he said. "Hollands gambled we'd leave him to last and gave it to her."

"I'd go along with that," Harry said.

"She took us in, hook, line and sinker. The fuss she made, the tug of war over her handbag and her pathetic request that at least I should give her a receipt for the pass because it was an accountable document. She put on an act to hoodwink us into thinking she was worried about finding herself on an adverse report."

"So what are you going to do? Search her?"

"Not unless I have to. Get Roach in here, I want to have a word with him."

Roach: was it a real name or an alias? The hard edge to his voice told Hollands that Redmond had made an error and was beginning to lose his cool. Roach, Roach, Roach; he committed the name to memory, convinced it was genuine. Moments later, the hitherto anonymous intruder walked into the room. Without any preamble, Redmond asked him what he made of the American girl.

"An attractive woman." Roach laughed. "She doesn't like us, that's for sure. Cut me dead when I tried to talk to her."

"What else?"

"Well, nothing really. She just turned her back on me and began reading a paperback."

"She hasn't asked to use the ladies' room?"

"Not since I've been watching her."

"She will, sooner or later. The lady is carrying Hollands' MOD pass. That means she'll either try to use it herself or set it up for him."

"So how are we going to play it?"

"Very cool. We'll just keep them apart – Whyte, Hollands and Edwards."

"Now?" Roach asked.

"We can afford to wait a bit longer. Meantime, tell Harry I want him to search the storeroom. He'll know what to look for."

Hollands listened to the retreating footsteps, and mentally crossed his fingers. The plastic wallet containing his season ticket wasn't in the storeroom. Shortly after Lindsey had been removed, he'd pushed it through the extractor fan into the office allocated to the typing pool. At the time, it had seemed a good hiding place and he still thought the wallet would be safe there provided Harry didn't use his initiative. Then a twinge of cramp in his calf muscles gave him something else to think about.

"Hey, Redmond," he said. "How much longer do you expect me to hold this position?"

"Beginning to feel the strain?"

"A little."

"Then you're obviously out of condition."

The minutes dragged by, time sliding towards eternity. The humiliation of having to stand there half-naked made it easy for Hollands to hate. The onset of cramp in his right leg concentrated his mind wonderfully on the problem of just how he was going to destroy Redmond, Roach, Harry, the faceless Macklin, and the unknown intruder whom he could hear in the computer centre. He was still grappling with the conundrum when Harry returned and slapped Hollands' plastic wallet on to the table.

"Clapham Junction to Waterloo," Richmond mused, then said, "Where did you find it, Harry?"

"On the floor in the typing pool. Looks as though our friend here thought he could put one over on us."

"Yes. We shall have to do something about that."

The attack happened fast; so fast that Hollands didn't have a chance to defend himself. Hit by a savage left and right to the kidneys, he moaned in agony and sank down on to his knees. Then as if anxious to make amends, Harry slipped both arms around his chest and helped him to his feet. The haze in front of his eyes cleared momentarily and he thought Redmond too seemed concerned for him, but that was before the younger man punched him under the heart and butted him in the face.

Chapter VIII

The sky was pitch black except for a thin yellowish streak on the horizon. Puzzled by the phenomenon, Hollands wasn't sure whether it was the final ambience of the moon or the first glimmer of daybreak until it slowly dawned on him that he was lying on the floor of the storeroom, and then the rest fell into place. The door had obviously shrunk over the years and the crack of light he could see at eye level was coming from one of the fluorescent tubes in the corridor.

He wondered how long he had been unconscious and tried to glance at his wristwatch, only to find that his hands had been lashed together behind his back. He couldn't straighten his legs out either; they were drawn into an inverted 'v' by the cord around both ankles which had then been tethered to his wrists. He could taste congealed blood and there was a lot more of it encrusted on his chin and in both nostrils; closing one eye, Hollands squinted at his nose and saw that it had swollen to almost twice its normal size. The nagging ache from his kidneys was another reminder that he wasn't exactly in the best of health.

Scattered around him on the floor were packets of A4 typing paper, carbons, and government issue ballpoint pens that Harry had swept off the shelves when he'd been searching for the elusive MOD pass. Only it wasn't so elusive any more; the bastard had found his plastic wallet in the typists' office and Redmond had put two and two together. Even if Lindsey still had the pass, there wasn't a damned thing she could do with it; forewarned was forearmed and from now on they would be watching her every move.

And in the meantime, the intruder who'd broken into the computer room was free to take MIDAS apart. MIDAS, the all-knowing Multilateral Intelligence Data

Access System: if they could get into that, they could tap the National Identification Bureau at Scotland Yard, the SIS discs at Century House and the Security Service. That was an incentive to strike back, but there was another which was entirely personal and far more compelling. He had been duped, humiliated and beaten up and, on that level, it was simply a question of restoring his injured pride and self-respect. Crawling was impossible but lying there on his left side, he could at least wriggle like a worm, using his shoulder and kneecap to give himself the necessary momentum. Slowly but surely, Hollands inched his way towards the nearest rack. A mere two feet away, it took him the best part of fifteen agonising minutes to reach it.

The shelves were above him, half-inch wooden slats which were held in place by a metal frame that resembled a giant-size Meccano set. Gritting his teeth, he turned over on to his right side and backed up to one of the vertical struts. The inside edge was sharp, and although not as keen as a honed knife, he thought it would eventually cut through the cord binding his wrists. Just what he could do after that was far from clear; he was on his own, pitted against insuperable odds, and without a pass there was no way he could get to a telephone. Then suddenly an idea occurred to him which was so simple yet so effective that he couldn't understand why he hadn't thought of it before. Like a man inspired, he began to saw away at the cord.

★   ★   ★

Lindsey turned the page, scanned a few more lines, then gnawed her bottom lip. She pressed her knees together and started fidgeting again, squirming this way and that to give the impression she was becoming more and more agitated. Finally, she placed the paperback face down on the table and glared at Harry.

"It's no good," she snapped. "I'm getting desperate."

"Aren't we all."

"I mean, I've got to go to the john."

"The what?"

"I want to use the ladies' room, goddamn it."

"Why didn't you say so in the first place?"

"I told you I was getting desperate, I didn't realise I had to spell it out."

The creep knew she was shamming. He also knew she had an MOD pass in her possession.

"Okay, you've made your point. Just hold your water."

"Are you going to let me use the john," she demanded, "or do I have to sit here and wet myself?"

For a moment or so it seemed Harry was prepared to let her do just that, then with an audible sigh, he opened the door and motioned her to go ahead. As she drew level with him, he side-stepped to shield the door with his body so that she couldn't slam it in his face. A savage back heel into his shins, then run like hell; the idea was still crystallising when he grabbed the fleshy part of her arm above the elbow.

"Let go of me," Lindsey said furiously. "I don't like being pawed."

"The ladies' room happens to be in the west wing," Harry told her.

"I know that."

"You were making for the lifts."

Lindsey knew he hadn't thought anything of the kind. The name of the game was psychological intimidation and the creep was simply trying to convince her that he had her number.

"You're being paranoic," she said curtly. "Keep it up and you'll be a candidate for the funny farm."

It had about as much effect as water on a duck's back. Still gripping her arm, he walked her down the corridor and on around the corner into the ladies' room.

"You can just back off," she told Harry. "Men aren't allowed in here."

"I've got news for you, they are now. That window behind you overlooks the inner courtyard and we wouldn't like it if you went out on the ledge."

"Neither would I," Lindsey said acidly.

Harry grinned at her wide enough to show that his teeth had been capped. "So why don't you be a good little girl and lock yourself in one of the cubicles?"

Lindsey glared at him, then stormed into the nearest

cubicle and slammed the door. Making as much noise as possible, she pushed the bolt home and raised the toilet lid.

"Temper, temper," Harry told her and sniggered.

It was exactly the kind of reaction she had been working for. Unzipping her navy-blue slacks, Lindsey reached inside her panty hose and fished out the MOD pass that Dutch had given her. After a suitable pause, she flushed the lavatory. Then she transferred the pass to her shoulder bag, unlatched the door and left the cubicle.

"Mind if I wash my hands?" she asked Harry.

"Be my guest."

"Thanks."

Lindsey moved past him to the washbasins and placed her shoulder bag on the shelf directly below the wall mirror. As she started to run the hot tap, Harry grabbed it and went through the contents.

"Nice try," he said, and waved the pass in her face. "Too bad it didn't work."

"Oh, go boil your head."

Her lips met in a thin straight line, giving expression to a sourness she didn't feel. It didn't hurt to let the creep enjoy his moment of triumph; he had taken the bait and would choke on it before the night was over. Next time she asked to use the ladies' room, he would be a damn sight less vigilant.

Harry had found the missing pass, therefore she was trapped on the fifth floor. A sound hypothesis, except that in the event of a fire, there was an emergency exit in the Xerox office next door to the conference room in the south-west corner of the building. A Heath Robinson contraption, its sole purpose was to relieve the congestion which would inevitably occur at the turnstile should the staff be ordered to leave the building. Consisting of a hinged trap door and a lightweight ladder that had to be lowered into the room below, the emergency exit had not been used since the last practice fire drill back in July. On that occasion it had taken the girls in the Xerox office just one minute to get the ladder into position and Lindsey knew she couldn't afford to take that long. Once she had given Harry the slip, it was vital she got to a telephone on the fourth floor before Redmond and the others caught up with her. There was only one way to do that; as soon as the trap door had been sprung, she would have to lower herself to the fullest extent her arms would allow and then let go. Lindsey just hoped she wouldn't end up with a broken ankle when she hit the floor twelve feet below.

*　　*　　*

The credits for the hour-long comedy show rolled off the screen and were followed by a commercial break. Curious to know what was coming on next, Whitmore picked up his newspaper and opened it at the TV page. BBC 1 was definitely out; he didn't like chat shows and after that there was only the midnight mass from Wells Cathedral. There was a travelogue on BBC 2, a documentary on ITV, and an old French movie with subtitles had just started on Channel 4. Big deal, he thought, then glanced sideways at Cantwell who was sleeping peacefully in his armchair, and gave him a nudge. It was some moments before the sergeant reluctantly opened his eyes.

"Was I snoring?" he asked and yawned.

"Only now and again."

"Sorry about that. Anything on the box?"

"Not a thing," Whitmore said. "That's why I thought I'd do the rounds."

"Right." Cantwell yawned again, stretched both arms above his head. "There'll be a cup of tea waiting for you when you get back."

"Thanks."

Whitmore got to his feet, dumped the newspaper on the seat of his armchair, and started towards the door. Halfway there, he happened to glance at the infra-red monitor next to the public address system, and stopped dead.

"Hey, Sarge," he called, "come and have a look at this magic box. The bloody thing's gone haywire."

"Be with you in a minute.

Cantwell switched on the electric kettle, then ambled across the room to join Whitmore by the monitor. He looked at the digital display, saw that instead of the usual

88

double zero in the frame, the numerical counter had moved up to fourteen.

"Fourteen intruders in the computer centre?"

"That's what the machine is telling us," Whitmore said.

"Then it's on the blink. The alarm never went off; I'd have heard it if it had."

Whitmore was inclined to doubt it. The way Cantwell had been snoring, it would have taken an atom bomb to wake him. In any case one of the snags with the infra-red intruder system was that it had been designed for use on active service and the alarm it emitted was just loud enough to alert a sentry. In the circumstances, he thought it unlikely that either of them would have heard its low-pitched buzz above the noise from the TV.

"What's the phone number of the JIB duty officer?" Cantwell asked.

"0526. You want to ask for Major Hollands."

★   ★   ★

Boden was on his way to the computer centre to see how Kardar was making out when he heard the telephone. For a split second, its discordant jangle unnerved him and he froze, uncertain what to do. Then a gut feeling that every second the call went unanswered would put them at risk made him turn around and run back to the office. Stay cool, act naturally, he told himself.

Lifting the receiver, he said, "Duty officer."

"Major Hollands?"

"Yes." Boden frowned, cleared his throat. "Who's that?"

"Sergeant Cantwell, sir. I'm in charge of the control room downstairs."

Boden nodded instinctively. He could place the voice now, had heard it before on channel 1 of his two-way radio. He wondered if Hollands and the sergeant were acquainted.

"I've been looking at the infra-red monitor," Cantwell went on, "and it seems to be acting up. According to the digital display, fourteen people have entered the computer centre."

"How many?" Boden said and forced a laugh.

"Fourteen, sir. Mind you, neither Constable Whitmore nor I heard the alarm."

"I'm not surprised; there's no one in the computer centre. I reckon the intruder system must have developed a fault."

"We think so too," Cantwell told him. "But the machine's never gone on the blink before, and it is serviced once a month."

"That doesn't mean it can't go wrong in between times." Boden closed his eyes, had a sudden flash of inspiration. "Come to think of it, there was a momentary loss of power up here about twenty minutes ago. The lights dipped, then surged; that could have been enough to throw the infra-red. The sensors would have reacted to the interruption in much the same way as if the fence had been broken. In other words, the digital counter would have been triggered into action."

"You know about these things, do you, sir?" Cantwell asked, seeking reassurance.

"I wouldn't claim to be an expert, but I've had some experience of operating a similar model under active service conditions. Naturally, I'll mention the defect in my report." Boden opened the duty officer's folder and checked the roster. "And I'll also warn Mr Ainsley when he relieves me on the twenty-seventh. I suggest you do the same with your relief; then we can both draw it to the attention of the administrative officer once things are back to normal after the Christmas break."

"That should take care of the problem." Cantwell sounded positively relieved that the decision had been made for him. "Thank you for your advice, sir," he said. "I'm sorry to have troubled you."

"Not a bit, you were only doing your job, Sergeant."

Boden wished Cantwell a happy Christmas and put the phone down. Despite the satisfaction of knowing he'd fooled the sergeant, the fact remained that a potentially dangerous situation could have been avoided had he continued to monitor the control room. It was a task he should have delegated to Roach as soon as they'd taken over the JIB, but it simply hadn't occurred to him while so much else was going on. Angry with himself for having been so remiss, Boden took out the two-way radio and switched it on just in time to catch the tail end of a conversation between Cantwell and Whitmore.

A security check? Boden caught his breath, wondered if it was purely a routine affair or whether he'd said something that had aroused Cantwell's suspicion. Maybe the sergeant knew Hollands well enough to realise that he had been talking to a stranger. Boden pushed the thought aside and went back to the duty officer's folder again. Finding the appropriate enclosure, he saw that Hollands was required to check every office on the floor at least once during his tour of duty but nowhere in the instructions did it say that the night security guard would visit the JIB. It was, of course, entirely possible that the routine check only applied to Defence Sales and Overseas Aid which were not manned during silent hours, but a lot would depend on just how observant Whitmore was. If he noticed that the lower half of the sashcord window in the men's room on the fourth floor had not been properly secured, they could well find themselves in serious trouble. Hesitating no longer, Boden picked up the two-way radio and left the office.

Hollands was trussed up like a chicken in the storeroom, Whyte was under guard in the central registry, and Edwards had been shifted into the adjoining office. The clerical officer had been docile right from the start and with all that wine inside him, he didn't need a minder. Any lingering doubt on that score was dispelled when Boden poked his head round the door and saw Edwards fast asleep on a camp bed. Crooking his index finger, he beckoned Roach to join him in the corridor.

"We've got a slight problem," Boden told him when they were alone. "There's a chance we may have to entertain an unwelcome visitor."

"That's terrific news," Roach said, his voice flat.

"It's not the end of the world. We can handle the situation as long as you do what I tell you." Boden gave him the two-way radio, then said, "I want you to monitor the control room. There are two security guards on duty – a Sergeant Cantwell and a patrolman called Whitmore who is about to check out the building. Let me know the minute he's finished. The same applies if you hear anything that suggests Cantwell is going to make a 999 call."

"Right."

"One last point. Should the phone ring in my absence, pretend you're Edwards and ask whoever is calling to hang on while you fetch Major Hollands. You'll find me at the other end of this passageway watching the lifts."

Boden turned away and moved on down the corridor to position himself just beyond the end room where he could observe the cage from a safe distance. If Whitmore took it into his head to visit the fifth floor, he would have to grab him. But it wouldn't end there; much as Boden disliked the possible change of plan, he realised they would be forced to take over the control room. It would be easy enough to accomplish; he had Edwards' pass and with a little judicious pressure, the clerical officer could be persuaded to disclose his personal staff number. Smiling to himself, Boden reached inside his jacket for the Beretta 6.5 mm automatic and jacked a round into the breech.

*   *   *

The cord was tougher than Hollands had expected and was about as pliable as baling wire. Yet just when it seemed he was getting nowhere, the strands suddenly parted and his wrists were free. But the cord had bitten deep, reducing the flow of blood so that he had lost all sense of touch. His fingers were swollen fat as pork sausages and proved twice as useless when it came to untying his ankles. Angry and frustrated, he massaged them into life and went back to work, plucking at the granny knot until he finally managed to undo it.

Like an old man crippled with arthritis, Hollands slowly got to his feet and straightened up. His kidneys ached so much he could hardly bear to move. 'You're tougher than you think,' he told himself and started walking backwards and forwards, pacing the length of the tiny storeroom. The pain didn't vanish but it gradually became more tolerable and, after a while, he began to look around for a weapon which he could use to defend himself when the time came.

*   *   *

Boden heard footsteps, glanced to his left and saw Roach coming towards him. His jubilant smile said it all and Boden put the Beretta on safe and holstered the automatic with a profound sense of relief.

"We've got it made," Roach said, punching a clenched fist into the air. "The security check's over; friend Whitmore has just told Cantwell that everything is okay."

"Good," Boden said evenly. They had been lucky, damned lucky but it wouldn't do to let the others know that.

"What do you want me to do now?" Roach asked. "Keep Edwards company?"

"No." Boden shook his head. "No, he doesn't need a minder, but you might look in on him every so often. Meantime, hold the fort while I have a word with Kardar."

"Right."

"We're almost finished here."

"Really?" Roach stared at him in astonishment. "That's funny," he murmured, "Dukes told me it would take all night to get the information we need."

"Harry's a good man, but sometimes he doesn't know what he's talking about."

'Give me four hours with the computer,' Kardar had boasted, 'and MIDAS will never be the same again.' All he'd asked for were the right codewords to get into the system.

But it seemed, nevertheless, that he was behind schedule. When Boden walked into the computer centre, Kardar was still busy keying in yet another question.

"For Christ's sake," Boden hissed, "how much longer are you going to be?"

Kardar jumped, then swivelled round to face him. "Don't come any nearer." His voice rose to a petrified squeak. "Another step and you'll break the infra-red fence."

"I asked you a simple question, I want a simple answer."

"The erasures have been done but the list of names is incomplete."

"How many have you got so far?"

"Half a dozen." Kardar licked his lips. "I've only just started on that part of the programme. Your friends aren't going to like it if we pull the plug now."

Boden glanced over his shoulder to make sure they were alone. "Screw them," he said fiercely. "You've got thirty minutes to gum up the works, then we're getting out of here."

"All right, it's your decision."

Leaving him to get on with the task, Boden returned to the duty officer's room and told Roach to get his gear together.

"Kardar's cracked it?"

Boden nodded. "Sooner than any of us expected."

"Well, it's not too soon for me," Roach said. "I've been on tenterhooks ever since we busted into this place."

Boden waited until he'd left the room, then lifted the receiver and dialled the number of the safe house in Wrotham. The number rang out loud and clear but Franklin didn't answer the phone. Boden hung up and tried again but there was still no reply. Reluctant to put the phone down, he sat there staring into space, trying to figure out what had gone wrong.

He cursed himself for not having checked the Wrotham number earlier, but it simply hadn't occurred to him. Had Franklin been apprehended? Boden discounted the possibility almost in the same instant it came into his head. If he'd been arrested, the police would have been knocking on the door of Quebec House by now. Maybe he'd met with an accident, or had simply lost his nerve and chickened out? The permutations were limitless and they too were wholly irrelevant. What mattered was the fact that Franklin was missing and they would be left high and dry unless he acted quickly.

Tyler: he could ring Leslie Tyler in West Harrow and get him to stand in for Franklin. Tyler had supplied the Dodge van and was a member of the National Front, except that nigger-bashing was more in his line, and when you came right down to it, he didn't have too much stomach for that unless the odds were heavily stacked in his favour. No, this was a problem for the Exercise Director; Silent

Night had been his idea and he would be waiting by the phone, anxious to know how it had gone.

Boden broke the connection to Wrotham, obtained an outside line again and called the Exercise Director. Their conversation was brief, acrimonious and largely one-sided but, in the end, he got what he wanted.

★   ★   ★

Hollands gripped the wooden slat in his right hand and whacked it into the palm of his left. As a truncheon, it was less than ideal, but it wasn't necessary to club a man over the head to immobilise him; there were other, more certain ways of doing that. He looked at the door, thought he might as well get started, and gave it a solid kick. Shouting at the top of his voice, he went on kicking it until Roach came running.

The key turned in the lock, the door was flung open, and Roach charged into the room. Hollands met him, his left arm raised and crooked at the elbow to guard his face and chest, right hand loose at his side holding the wooden slat parallel with the floor. Timing it to perfection, he aimed low and drove the stave into Roach, jabbing him in the groin. Roach screamed and grabbed his testicles, then sank down on to his knees and rolled over.

Hollands stepped over his prostrate body and ran out into the corridor. Redmond had left the duty officer's room and was bearing down on him, the tall thin man a few paces to the rear. Wheeling right, Hollands sprinted towards the Xerox office in the south-west corner of the building. Every stride tore him apart, the knife thrusts coming at millisecond intervals; yet he seemed to be moving in slow motion. Even with a five yard head start, he had a long way to go and they were gaining on him all the time.

He ran on, eyes fixed on the distant fire alarm, willing it to come nearer. At any moment, he expected Redmond to reach out and grab him by the collar. But somehow he made it and drove the wooden slat through the thin protective covering of glass to hit the button on the nose. They were on him then, boots and fists flying, and the

95

darkness began to close in again. But somewhere, a long way off, he thought he could hear a bell ringing.

*   *   *   ·

The fire alarm in the control room rang loud enough to wake the dead and its effect on Cantwell and Whitmore was electric. Both men swore, leapt to their feet and simultaneously made for the gap between their respective armchairs where inevitably they met head to head. Cantwell, who was two stone heavier and had a thicker skull, came off best and though dazed, managed to reach the telephone a few strides ahead of his colleague. But the element of farce still had some way to run. In his haste, Cantwell succeeded in knocking the telephone on to the floor and then, having stooped down to retrieve it, he completely forgot the desk was in the way and bumped his head for the second time as he straightened up. While rubbing the tender spot with one hand, he somehow managed to dial 999 with the other.

A cool, female voice said, "Emergency – which service do you require?"

"Fire," Cantwell said, then added, "better send an ambulance too."

"And the police," Whitmore yelled at him. "The bloody monitor's clicked up to fifteen."

"It's faulty," Cantwell said ponderously.

"Not any more it isn't. For Christ's sake, get the police."

"We are the police."

"Don't be a fucking idiot, I mean the real police. We've got an intruder in the computer centre."

"Don't you dare speak to me like that," Cantwell said angrily, "I'm in charge here."

"And a right bloody disaster you're making of it."

Almost speechless with rage, Cantwell longed to give him a piece of his mind but the Fire Service was on the line and the incident officer was becoming a mite impatient. Taking a deep breath, he gave his name and the location of Quebec House. While he was busy doing that, Whitmore opened the firearms locker, grabbed the .38 Smith and Wesson and a box of ammunition off the top shelf and headed towards the lifts.

Boden ran into the office next door to the men's room in the east wing and opened the lower half of the sashcord window. Roach had laid out the abseiling gear before he'd rushed into the storeroom to deal with Hollands, but nothing else was ready. Only too aware that every second counted, he hooked the grapnel under the windowledge, dropped the nylon rope into the courtyard, and then slipped his arms through the handles of the canvas holdall so that he could carry it on his back like a rucksack. By the time the others entered the room, he had already clipped himself on to the line and was about to go out of the window.

"Don't tell us you're deserting us, Nick," Dukes said icily.

Boden glared at him angrily. "You know me better than that," he said, and then looked at Roach, sizing him up. "Think you can make it on your own?" he asked.

"Just about."

"Good. I'll go first, you follow, then Kardar, then Harry. Got it?"

Boden climbed out on to the sill, planted both feet against the wall and arched his back. Then he kicked off and went down the wall in a series of bounds.

*   *   *

Lindsey was in a destructive mood. Caught on the hop when Hollands had broken out of the storeroom, it angered her that she had been slower to react to the situation than Harry. Before she could hurl her bag at him and make a dash for it, he'd nipped into the corridor and locked the door, trapping her inside the central registry. The fire alarm however had given her an idea; realising it had been triggered in order to alert the security guards, Lindsey decided she would ram the message home.

The means were ready to hand, two old-fashioned Imperial typewriters weighing all of twenty pounds apiece which the clerks had scrounged from the typing pool light years ago when they'd been replaced by more up-to-date models. Grabbing the nearest one, she hefted it as though putting the shot and hurled it at the window, shattering the glass in spectacular fashion. The second typewriter also landed in Buckingham Street and exploded on impact with a loud crump that sounded like a mortar bomb.

★   ★   ★

Boden heard both impacts as he scuttled towards the wrought-iron gates which opened into Buckingham Street. Shucking off the holdall, he opened it up, took out a pair of heavy-duty shears and cut through the padlock and chain. The gates however remained firmly closed, secured by a mortice-type lock. To deal with the problem, he exchanged the shears for a length of steel tubing which had been specially designed for the job and inserted it into the keyhole. As soon as the tube engaged the spindle, he turned the improvised key in a clockwise direction and sprang the lock. Boden then withdrew the top and bottom bolts and opened the right-hand gate a fraction.

Although the rope would still be hanging from the fifth-floor window when the police arrived, Boden hoped the partially open gate would lead them to assume that they'd made their getaway into Buckingham Street. If that didn't work, he reckoned the police wouldn't get very far without a map of the telecom system for the area and it wouldn't be easy to obtain a copy at this hour on Christmas Eve. Given an hour's breathing space, Boden was confident they could get within striking distance of the alternative safe house in Lumley Court before the police cordoned off the immediate area around Quebec House. After that, it would be up to the Exercise Director to pick them up when he thought it was safe to do so.

The off-key warble of a fire truck moving at speed along the Strand brought him up with a start and he spun round to see how the others were faring. They were all there in the courtyard, Kardar, Roach and Dukes. Without him being aware of it, Harry had taken the manhole key while he had been working on the gate and was busy unscrewing the retaining bolts.

"You ready, Nick?" he called.

Boden gave him a thumbs up, grabbed the canvas holdall

98

and loped across the courtyard to join them. There was no argument as to who should go first; he was the only one who knew the escape route and, therefore, had to lead the way. Kardar followed him into the shaft, then Roach. As the last man down, it fell to Dukes to manoeuvre the access plate into position and lock it home. By the time he'd completed the task, Boden had reached the first junction point and was crawling north towards the Strand.

★   ★   ★

Moments after he'd stepped into the lift, it occurred to Whitmore that he was being extremely foolish. Although he had been on a small arms course, he couldn't forget that the last time he'd fired a .38 revolver on the range, he'd missed a six-foot figure target with every other shot from a distance of fifteen yards. Apart from that consideration, there was the unpleasant possibility that the intruders might also be armed and far superior marksmen. Quickly re-assessing the situation, Whitmore stopped the lift at the fourth floor and used the staircase to reach the JIB.

Two things were immediately apparent; the building wasn't on fire and someone was making an unholy racket in the north wing. Inserting his pass into the lock, Whitmore tapped out his personal staff number and passed through the turnstile. Still ultra-cautious, he checked out each office in turn as he inched towards the north wing. His back to the wall, he slowly approached the central registry, saw the key was still in the lock and turning it, threw the door open and stormed into the room.

"About time," Lindsey said. "What kept you?"

Whitmore lowered the Smith and Wesson and stared at the shattered window, seemingly mesmerised by the few shards of glass that still remained in the frame.

"I was looking for the intruders," he said in a hollow voice.

"Well, you won't find them in here." Lindsey moved nearer, stretched out a hand for the Smith and Wesson. "Better let me have that," she said quietly, "before you put a hole in your foot."

Gently but firmly, she prised the revolver from his grasp,

99

then moved swiftly to the duty officer's room across the corridor and opened the window.

The moon was well up over the horizon now and bathed the deserted courtyard in an eerie light. To her left, Lindsey could see a rope dangling from an open window in the east wing, while directly opposite, one of the wrought-iron gates facing Buckingham Street was slightly ajar. Above the caterwaul of police, fire and ambulance sirens, she could just hear the bells of St Martin-in-the-Fields.

"And a merry Christmas, one and all," she muttered angrily.

Chapter IX

The house at Osborne had been built by Thomas Cubitt
in 1845 on the lines of an ornate Italian villa because the
view across the Solent had reminded the Prince Consort
of the Bay of Naples. Set in grounds that had once extended
to a thousand acres, it had been Queen Victoria's favourite
residence, a secluded country retreat where she and Albert
and the children could lead a normal family life away from
the bustle of London. But with the passage of time, it had
ceased to be a haven of peace and quiet; bequeathed to the
nation by Edward VII after his mother's death, the house
and grounds had become a major tourist attraction. From
April to September, visitors to the Isle of Wight came in
their thousands to troop through the royal apartments and
to see the Swiss chalet at the top of the High Walk where
the royal children had learned to keep house, as well as the
model fortress the ten-year-old Prince Arthur of Con-
naught had made, complete with fieldworks, barracks and
wooden cannon. Only the east wing which had been turned
into an officers' convalescent home at the express wish of
Edward VII still remained inviolate.

Currently, there were just four patients – two Royal Navy
officers, a captain in Queen Alexandra's Royal Army Nurs-
ing Corps, and Hollands, who'd been there a fortnight following three months in hospital. As far as he was concerned,
there wasn't much to do and all day to do it in. Each morning
after breakfast, he adjourned to the anteroom to read the
newspapers, then took a stroll through the grounds, returning in time for a cup of coffee at ten thirty. The bar opened
at twelve, lunch was served between one and two, and his
afternoons were spent either answering letters when there
were any, or taking another even longer walk until it was
time to change for dinner. Occasionally, to break the monot-
ony, he would hop on a bus into Newport to do some

shopping and see a movie but always it was dinner at eight, the best of five frames of snooker, and early to bed.

This morning, however, was different. As he entered the loggia from the terraced garden, the mess steward greeted him with the news that a Mr Gattis was waiting for him in the library. The name didn't ring a bell with Hollands but there was nothing odd about that; any number of strangers had called on him while he was in hospital. The only surprising thing was that after an interval of six weeks, somebody had evidently decided to re-open the inquiry on Silent Night.

Gattis was about five foot nine, had reddish-brown hair, brown eyes and a strong-looking face that seemed appropriate for a man who introduced himself with a slight Glaswegian accent. Hollands thought he must be pushing forty, but appearances were often deceptive and as Caroline had frequently observed, he'd never been much good at guessing a person's age.

"My ID," Gattis said, and showed him a plastic card with the usual passport-size snapshot. "I always think it's best to clear the decks before we start."

"Are you with the Security Service?" Hollands asked.

"Sort of." Gattis sat down, opened the black, executive briefcase beside his chair and took out a tape recorder. "You don't mind if we use this, do you? Saves a lot of writing."

"We're in for a long session, are we?"

"No, I don't think so. There are only a couple of points I want to clear up about the man you said was James Redmond."

"You've got it wrong," Hollands said. "I never vouched for him; he showed me an identity card bearing his photograph and the computer produced Redmond's record of service. It would be more accurate to say I didn't really know what to make of him. I'd no grounds for thinking Redmond wasn't an SAS officer; he was tough, knowledgeable, efficient and intelligent, the very qualities you'd expect of someone in that elite regiment. On the other hand, he was supposedly working under the direction of Macklin, the chief umpire, and as soon as I spoke to that man, I had a gut feeling there was something very wrong about him." Hollands shook his head. "He just wasn't my idea of a senior civil servant and naturally that raised a question mark against Redmond."

And always at the back of his mind there had been the unspoken thought that there was something distinctly odd about Silent Night. Even if the aim had been to gauge the effectiveness of their security measures, Hollands had never known an exercise to get off the ground without some kind of forewarning. At the very least, he would have expected the Director to drop a veiled hint that things might not be so peaceful as they seemed and that they'd better be on their toes over Christmas and the New Year. In his opinion, the senior officer had yet to be born who was prepared to risk the possibility that his own organisation would be found wanting.

"Tough, knowledgeable, efficient and intelligent." Gattis eyed him thoughtfully. "Anything else you'd care to add about Redmond? Could you place his accent for instance?"

"Home counties," Hollands said unhesitatingly. "Surrey, Middlesex, Essex, Berkshire – take your pick. He was very smooth, the hail-fellow-well-met type who reminds me of a PR man. But underneath, Redmond was as hard as nails and pretty vicious."

"And the other two – Harry and Roach?"

"I've already described them to your colleagues."

"I'm not asking you for their physical characteristics," Gattis reminded him politely.

"The trouble is I don't have much else to offer. They were very close-mouthed about themselves and didn't give much away. I think Roach came from somewhere up north and was trying to hide it. I'm also reasonably sure that Harry is a Londoner. He seemed to be on more familiar terms with Redmond than Roach."

"Would you say they were close friends?"

"They seemed to know one another rather well." Hollands frowned. "Maybe I was imagining it, but I got the impression that Redmond was a little wary of Harry and inclined to handle him with kid gloves."

"That's interesting," Gattis murmured.

"But it doesn't get you very far, does it? Personally, I'd concentrate on Roach. Apart from the fact that he must have done a bit of rock climbing in his time, I'm sure he was the only one of the three who wasn't using an alias. Dig deep enough and the chances are you'll find he is a trained electrician."

"Did you mention this to my colleagues?"

Hollands pursed his lips. "Yes," he said eventually.

"You don't seem very sure."

"If I sound hesitant," Hollands told him, "it's because you're the third interrogator who's questioned me. I know I told your Mr Lawrence and that's definite."

"A serviceman born in the north of England, has some experience of rock climbing and is a trained electrician." Gattis repeated the key identity factors to himself, then shook his head. "You'd have thought the computer could have matched those characteristics."

"You drew a blank with the army?"

"And the other two services."

"Did your people try the deadsack?" Hollands asked.

"Deadsack? What's that?"

"The last resting place for the non-effectives. When a soldier is discharged, his personal details and record of service are wiped off the data base which means the computer can't locate him. But his documents are never destroyed; they are all there at the depot in Hayes – record of service, confidential reports, medical history and dental charts. The RN and RAF do the same."

"Is that a fact?" Gattis inclined his head. "Of course, with his military background, I daresay Lawrence knows about the record office at Hayes and has already been in touch with them."

"Maybe he has," said Hollands. "Then again, maybe someone told him not to bother."

"Just what is that supposed to mean?"

"Redmond had a lot going for him – a fake military identity card which would stand up when checked against the micro-computer, the requisite codewords to get into the MIDAS system, and a highly sophisticated eavesdropper that enabled him to monitor the control room on the ground floor."

"Who told you that?" Gattis asked sharply.

"Colonel Whyte. She came to see me when I was in the Queen Elizabeth Hospital at Woolwich. Lindsey said your people went over Quebec House with a fine-tooth comb and found this magnetised bug in an office on the first floor directly above the control room."

"Colonel Whyte has been talking out of turn."

"So have a lot of other people, right across the board. You don't have to be a genius to realise Redmond couldn't have got as far as he did without the help of a number of moles in and around Whitehall. And we all know how much embarrassment they have caused the government. That's why I have this feeling that the Security Service has been told to go easy."

"Are you one of them?"

"Me? A mole?" Hollands shook his head. "If that wasn't so bloody laughable, I'd sue you for libel."

"Some of us think Redmond's timing was more than just fortunate."

"So?"

"So what prompted you to volunteer for duty over Christmas?"

"Well, like I told Lawrence, I had nothing better to do."

"Bit of a loner, are you?"

Gattis had obviously read his security file and knew that his father had died when he was sixteen. It was also on record that his mother had subsequently married a South African born stockbroker and was now living with him in Johannesburg. He hadn't seen his sister, Ruth, since 1978, either, but only because she was married to a Gurkha officer who was stationed in Hong Kong.

"You shouldn't take everything you read at face value," Hollands said calmly. "It so happens there's an unwritten rule in the JIB that the Services Liaison officers should arrange their leave so that two of them are always present. Ingersole jumped the gun way back in September and arranged to go skiing immediately after Christmas. I wanted a few days off over the New Year; volunteering for duty was simply a means of twisting the Director's arm."

"Where does Colonel Whyte fit into the chain of command?"

"She's my immediate superior officer," Hollands told him.

"Do you need her okay to go on leave?"

"Yes."

"So how do you get on with her?"

"We have a good working relationship but that's as far as it goes."

Gattis nodded. "Colonel Whyte said much the same thing. She also told us that she relies on you to put her straight."

"Only about the British Army, its customs, traditions, and way of doing things." Hollands smiled wryly, then said, "So far as everything else is conerned, the shoe is very much on the other foot."

"I think you're being a little too modest, Major. According to Colonel Whyte, you're a very switched-on operator. That's why she didn't query your assertion that Silent Night had been sponsored by the Directorate of Army Training."

"What exactly are you implying?"

"I'm not implying anything," Gattis said coldly. "I'm merely quoting from the statement made by Colonel Whyte. She told Lawrence that you telephoned the Headquarters of the Special Air Service Group and spoke to the chief umpire on extension 0028. Correct?"

"Yes."

"And after you'd had a word with Macklin, you informed her that Silent Night was a free play exercise. You actually said, 'It's an exercise all right, but there's no pink', and then you went on to explain precisely what it meant."

"What if I did?"

"There is no such extension as 0028 at the Duke of York's barracks in Chelsea and the SAS do not have anyone by the name of Macklin on their strength. The same goes for the Security Service."

"I didn't make it up," Hollands said angrily.

"Quite a number of people are beginning to think you did. Some of them go even farther; they say you were on Redmond's team then changed sides when things started to go wrong."

"They've got to be out of their tiny minds."

Gattis smiled in a way that suggested he almost felt sorry for him. By the time he'd finished outlining their case, Hollands was beginning to feel the same way.

It seemed the events that night were open to a number of wildly differing interpretations. So okay, he was the man who'd had the bright idea of withholding an MOD pass, but the plan had misfired because he had subsequently blown the gaff to Redmond. The way Lawrence and the others saw it, his aim had been twofold: firstly, to pre-empt any suspicion that he might be involved and secondly, to make damn sure Lindsey couldn't throw a monkey wrench into the works.

"You've overlooked something," Hollands said. "If I was so pally with those people, why did they beat me up?"

"That's easily explained. To get into the MIDAS system, Redmond had to know the appropriate codewords. Someone had told him that you would provide them and he refused to believe that you weren't in the know. He thought you were holding out for more."

"More what?"

"Cash, of course," said Gattis. "You're pretty strapped for it right now, aren't you?"

Standard operating procedure, Hollands thought. Without a motive, they didn't have a case and so they'd scratched round until they'd found one. They had talked to Caroline and she had told them how he'd refused Roger's offer to help him with the children's school fees. Then there was the flat he was buying in Clapham. The mortgage repayments ran to £282 a month and he'd had to go to a finance company to raise the additional capital he'd needed for the deposit or lose it to another buyer. Throw in the premiums on four life insurance policies and they could prove that he had to watch every penny.

"That's the way it was," Gattis continued. "You sold some information to a middleman and hinted there was more to come. When Redmond pushed you into a corner, you had to protect yourself. Changing sides seemed the perfect solution."

"You know something?" Hollands grated. "That's the biggest load of crap I've ever listened to in my life."

"I'd be inclined to agree with you but for that phone call you made."

"I didn't make it."

"Colonel Whyte says you did."

"I only dialled the last four digits. Redmond suggested that one of us should talk to SAS Headquarters, then got to the phone ahead of me and started dialling. I thought he was going through on the MOD tied line . . ." Hollands could see him now, his stubby index finger picking out the numbers one by one. Low left seven o'clock on the dial when it should have been two o'clock high right. Then suddenly he could visualise the rest of the sequence. "Redmond obtained an outside line," Hollands continued, "then he dialled the area code which began with a seven. The next figure was either a four or a three, but the last was definitely six."

"So the area code was either 746 or 736, and the subscriber's number which you dialled was 0028?"

Hollands nodded. "We were standing shoulder to shoulder with our backs to Lindsey and she didn't see him hand the phone over to me. After that, he stepped to one side and she saw me holding the receiver and assumed I'd dialled the whole number."

"Yes, well I think that will do to be going on with." Gattis switched off the tape recorder and put it away inside his briefcase. "You've been very helpful, Major."

"Who to?" Hollands asked.

"Ah, now that would be telling," Gattis said and flashed him the kind of faraway smile politicians reserve for the electorate.

⋆   ⋆   ⋆

Subversive Warfare was the smallest government department in Whitehall. Referred to in the trade as DSW, its full-time staff consisted of a chief executive, a financial adviser, seven desk officers, four clerk/typists, two armourers and a personal assistant. The bastard love child of the wartime Special Operations Executive, it had been raised, nurtured and preserved in the face of considerable opposition from the Treasury and the Foreign and Commonwealth Office by its founder, Cedric Harper.

Despite the vicissitudes of his job, the years had been kind to Harper in so far as he had managed to retain a youthful appearance. At fifty-nine, his hair, neatly parted on the left side, was still predominantly brown and the only lines on his face were those around his mouth which seemed permanently on the point of breaking into a smile. He was quiet yet authoritative, but saddled with a streak of obstinacy, a man who, once he had made up his mind that he was in the right, would not be deflected by argument. In the eyes of his supporters, he was resolute, loyal, far-sighted, intelligent and decisive; on the other hand, ruthless, devious and deceitful were among the more polite adjectives bandied about by his detractors. In the mid seventies, Harper had expressed a desire to retire at fifty-five; the fact that he had subsequently changed his mind was, as far as his enemies were concerned, the biggest and most unforgivable sin he'd ever committed. The more optimistic of them now looked forward to his sixtieth birthday when, like it or not, he would be compulsorily retired; the pessimists, however, were convinced that somehow an exception would be made in his case and he would soldier on for ever.

But it was the organisation as much as the man that they loathed. Unlike the Security Service and the SIS whose activities were controlled to some extent by the Home Office and the Foreign and Commonwealth, the Department of Subversive Warfare was a completely autonomous body. Answerable only to the Cabinet Office, it frequently trespassed into areas which were considered by other intelligence agencies to be strictly their preserves. Silent Night was a classic example of this bone of contention.

Because they were all locked into the MIDAS system, the repercussions from the incident had affected the Ministry of Defence, the Home Office, the SIS, and the Security Service. Although of necessity each department had had to carry out its own 'in-house audit' to ascertain whether any of their material had been compromised, no one in Whitehall had thought it odd that the Security Service should conduct the subsequent investigation. The demarcation lines were very clear; counter-espionage was their business and they were the obvious people to handle the JIB affair. It was only after the Security Service had submitted their findings that the wires had become crossed. Wanting a second opinion, the Cabinet Office had immediately referred the report to the Department of Subversive Warfare.

The report which had eventually reached Harper was about the size of an average novel and a good deal less entertaining. Subject interviews had been reproduced verbatim and even the summary of conclusions ran to a dozen pages. Having read it from cover to cover, Harper had been convinced that there was no point in going over the same ground again. Since the Security Service had concentrated their efforts on identifying the insider, he decided the DSW would go after the man who'd passed himself off as Redmond. Sending Gattis down to the Isle of Wight had been the first step in that direction and there was just a chance that it had paid off. Somewhere between Osborne House and Ryde, Gattis had broken his journey to call the office with two very similar phone numbers. Now Harper waited impatiently while his PA endeavoured to obtain the names and addresses of the two subscribers.

As though willing it to come to life, Harper stared at the intercom on his desk. Along with the secure speech telephone, it was one of the very few items of modern equipment in his office. Data word processors, visual display units and micro-computers left him cold, but even if he had been enthusiastic about such gadgets, the Treasury would have moved heaven and earth to ensure he lacked the funds to purchase the latest models. Financial stringency was their principal weapon in a long war of attrition against the department. If they had their way, Harper would remain where he was, in a dingy turret office with a peep view of the National Gallery across Trafalgar Square. The only natural source of light in the room came from a porthole window which the pigeons roosting on the ledge outside regularly fouled.

A noise like a stiff breeze came from the squawk box, then a cool voice said, "About those phone numbers, Mr Harper. 746 would appear to be an incorrect area code but Directory Enquiries were able to find a listing for 736 0028. The subscriber is 'Z' Company, 4th Battalion the Royal Green Jackets, and their address is The Drill Hall, Fulham Road, London SW1."

"Thank you, Miss Nightingale."

"It's Mrs Swann, sir."

"Yes, of course. How forgetful of me."

Harper smiled lopsidedly. Either he had made a Freudian slip or old age really was catching up with him. Nightingale had been his PA for more years than he cared to remember but, to his complete astonishment, she had left the department some eighteen months ago to marry a widower.

"Will that be all, Mr Harper?"

"Not quite. I'd like to ring Special Branch and get hold of Detective Superintendent Marsh."

"That may not be easy, sir. He's a very elusive man."

"I don't think you'll have too much trouble," Harper said calmly. "At least, not when he hears that I'm inviting him to lunch at the Silver Grill."

CHAPTER X

William Marsh was another of the new faces Harper had
had to get used to. Unlike his predecessor, the ponderous
somewhat lugubrious detective Chief Superintendent
Wray who'd retired in 1980, Marsh was a bundle of suppressed energy. Aged forty-two and roughly five foot nine,
he had the build of a second row forward – broad shoulders,
barrel chest, heavy thighs and wide hips. Although his
suits were made to measure, they always looked as though
they were about to come apart at the seams. His thick head
of hair caused just as many problems for his barber; short,
dark and wiry, it refused to lie down and resembled a stiff
brush. Although he claimed to enjoy the good things in
life, to Harper's way of thinking his tastes were remarkably
unadventurous. Before they'd even sat down to lunch at
the Silver Grill, he had known that Marsh would start with
a prawn cocktail and would then opt for a medium rare
filet mignon with French fries and a side salad before
rounding off the meal with a slice of chocolate gâteau. And
since Harper was paying, he would also have a Corona
with his brandy.

There was, however, nothing conservative about his
curriculum vitae. Marsh had done a stint with the Anti-
Terrorist Squad and had been seconded to the Northern
Ireland Office at Stormont before he'd become Wray's
deputy. He was sharp, quick-witted and in common with
a lot of other Special Branch officers, he professed to
despise the Security Service.

"I hear our mutual antagonists are in trouble again,
Cedric."

"Which ones?" Harper asked innocently.

"The Curzon Street mob – who else? Their report on
the Silent Night affair is said to have gone down like a lead
balloon with the Cabinet Office."

"Really?"

"Oh, come on, Cedric, don't be coy with me. You know damn well that right from the off they were determined to paper over the cracks."

"You've seen the report?"

Marsh shook his head. "No, but I can make a shrewd guess. They were on the scene minutes after the first police car arrived at Quebec House and they had that computer centre quarantined before you could say knife. None of the plods were allowed within sniffing distance of it; same thing applied to the CID officers."

"I would have done the same in their place," Harper said mildly. "Very few police officers are cleared for Top Secret material and the MIDAS was still running. As it happened, most of the stuff it was churning out was pure gobbledegook, but they weren't to know that at the time."

The experts claimed that MIDAS had gone into a loop following the input of a codeword it had failed to recognise. Lawrence, who'd led the investigation, had reduced a few random sheets of print-out to A4 size and had attached them to his report as proof of this contention. The computer language hadn't meant a thing to Harper; all he knew was that every government department with access to MIDAS was satisfied that their classified material had not been compromised.

"Gobbledegook or not, they elbowed the plods out of the way and virtually dictated the initial press release." Marsh leaned forward and tapped his cigar over the ashtray. "Quote: 'At approximately twenty-three hundred hours on Friday the twenty-fourth of December, four men attempted to break into a building occupied by the Ministry of Defence. The alarm was raised immediately and the intruders made off, having failed to gain entry to a sensitive area. Police inquiries are proceeding.'" His lip curled. "Unless my memory is at fault, that was the gist of the official statement, wasn't it?"

"I don't see what you're getting so uptight about," Harper said cheerfully. "It was pretty close to the truth."

"Including the inference that the Provisional IRA was responsible?"

"It was a reasonable enough assumption in view of what was happening elsewhere in London at the time."

"You mean the furore over the suspect vehicle which allegedly belonged to British Telecom? Well, I can tell you the deceased, John Matthew Franklin, didn't have any adverse Irish connections. Oh, he'd served in Belfast and Londonderry on a couple of occasions when he was a corporal in the Royal Corps of Transport, but the Ulster Constabulary had nothing on him."

"What about his next of kin?" Harper asked.

"None, apart from a sister living in New Zealand. Mother and father are both dead and his ex-wife didn't want to know. We had the devil's own job persuading her to come down from Manchester to identify the body."

"I presume the lady was interviewed by the Anti-Terrorist Squad?"

"Of course she was, Cedric, and a fat lot of good it did them. She'd neither seen nor heard from Franklin since they split up in 1978. She claimed she'd left him because he was for ever putting the army first and neglecting her. The fact is, Franklin bought himself out and got a job as a long distance lorry driver in an effort to save the marriage." Marsh studied the glowing ember of his cigar, eyes narrowing viciously. "Well, he lost her just the same and his job too when the haulage firm he was working for went bust. He was on the dole for the last eight months of his life. The way I see it, Franklin agreed to drive that truck because he needed the money."

"In other words, he was a small-time crook?"

"That's about the size of it."

"Without any previous form?" Harper said.

"Only because he'd never been caught. The Social Security people reckon he was doing a little moonlighting on the side – driving a mini-cab and the like – but they could never prove it. Franklin didn't have a bank account and we didn't find any folding money in his room." Marsh aimed his cigar at the ashtray again and, missing it, dropped a pile of ash on to the tablecloth. "His landlady could have nicked it, but I reckon he spent every penny he earned on his collection of medals."

"Medals?"

"World War Two stuff, mostly campaign stars but he had a few decorations too – an Iron Cross Second Class and a Knight's Cross with swords and diamonds which must have set him back a few bob."

Harper nodded. Except for the German decorations, Marsh hadn't told him anything new. He wondered why Lawrence hadn't mentioned the Knight's Cross in his report, then decided the security officer had probably thought it irrelevant.

"There was no IRA involvement," Marsh said emphatically. "I know the Provos; if they'd broken into Quebec House, they would have been on to the Press Association claiming the kudos. There was no shortage of phone calls but they were all from the lunatic fringe groups."

"I think you're wrong, Bill."

Marsh stared at him, pointing like a gun dog. "Have you got a mole, Cedric?"

"A ferret would be a more apt description."

Before leaving his office, Harper had spoken to the Vice Adjutant General. As a result of their conversation, Hollands was now on his way to London, puzzled no doubt as to why he had been sent on indefinite leave by his personnel branch. He would be kept under surveillance from the moment he arrived by car at Ryde Pier Head; exactly how he would be employed by the Department of Subversive Warfare would depend on his subsequent actions.

"This ferret of yours," Marsh said quietly. "How's he shaping up?"

"It's early days yet but Gattis thinks he may be able to use him."

"Yes, well I'm told Iain was a pretty good copper before you got hold of him, Cedric – the best detective sergeant the Glasgow CID had had in a long time according to my informant."

"Then you won't be surprised to hear that the best detective sergeant has come up with a lead." Harper smiled. "It's a pretty thin one but I'm hoping you can put some flesh on it."

"I had a feeling our lunch date would end up as a Dutch treat."

"I'm not asking for much. All you've got to do is ask a few questions in the right quarter."

"And where might that be?"

"V District," Harper said promptly. "To be specific, I want to know if anyone was seen behaving suspiciously in the area of Fulham Road on Christmas Eve between seven thirty and midnight. Talk to the police officers who were on duty that night and see if they noticed anyone loitering near the TA drill hall."

"You'll be lucky."

"So it's a bit of a long shot," Harper said calmly. "But that traffic accident in the Old Kent Road did spark off a red alert. The Anti-Terrorist Squad thought the IRA were planning to attack a British Telecom installation and everyone had been warned to be on their toes."

"I don't know, Cedric; seems to me you're looking for a needle in a haystack."

Harper thought it might well come to that. If Marsh drew a blank, he would have to obtain a voice print of every officer and man on the strength of 'Z' Company and even then he might not get anywhere. The mere fact that Macklin had set himself up inside the drill hall was hardly conclusive proof that he was a member of the Royal Green Jackets.

"Do you think any good will come of it?"

"You won't be doing yourself any harm," Harper told him.

It was another way of saying that he would put in a good word for him in the right quarter and he could tell by the speculative glint in his eye that the inference had not been lost on Marsh.

★   ★   ★

Hollands left the ticket office at Waterloo station and made his way across the concourse to the W. H. Smith bookstall near the lost property office on platform 16. He'd received a totally unexpected phone call from AG 18, the personnel branch at Stanmore, shortly after Gattis had departed; less than four hours later, he'd walked into his flat in Clapham Common and unpacked his things.

The retired colonel in charge of the officers' convalescent home at Osborne House couldn't have been more helpful and had laid on a car to take him to Ryde Pier Head before Hollands had even thought of asking for one. If he hadn't known him better, Hollands would have said that, like the JIB, he'd been anxious to see the back of him. Although AG 18 had been evasive when he'd raised the point, he'd been left with the distinct impression that the JIB didn't want him back at any price. "We've got a manning problem, Dutch," the staff officer had told him airily. "Two chaps have been promoted to Lieutenant Colonel sooner than we'd anticipated and replacing them in their present appointments has created a knock-on effect. We also had to find a stand-in for you while you were in hospital and the Director feels it would be wrong to move him on just when he's settled into the job. Besides, we've got a really high grade job lined up for you – SO2 G2 Headquarters Allied Land Forces South East in Ankara. It doesn't become vacant until June, but who's complaining? A spot of gardening leave won't come amiss and, take it from me, a couple of good confidential reports in your new post and two years from now, you'll find yourself on the promotion list."

The hard sell had had more holes in it than a colander. The way Hollands saw it, the JIB had decided to get rid of him weeks ago; he'd had more than an inkling of that when Lindsey had visited him at the Queen Elizabeth Hospital. Curious to know who else had been purged, he'd rung the office from his flat only to find that every extension he dialled was unobtainable. 'Enquiries' hadn't been able to help him either; having changed their phone numbers, the JIB had also gone ex-directory, and Hollands had declined to give his name to the operator. In the long run, he'd figured it was safer to contact Ingersole direct.

Ingersole was a nine-to-five man with a strong aversion to working overtime. On a few occasions he'd been known to catch the ten to six out of Waterloo but usually it was either the five thirty-two or the five forty. Except in bad weather, he made a point of walking to the station, believing the exercise did him good. Tonight, with inter-mittent rain showers in the offing, Ingersole might well be inclined to abandon his keep-fit programme in favour of the Underground. If he did, it wouldn't matter; from W. H. Smith's bookstall, Hollands was able to observe the escalators from the Underground as well as both main entrances at the York Road end of the concourse.

Five thirty-two came and went. Roughly three minutes later, Ingersole pushed his way through the swing doors opposite the bookstall and moved purposefully towards platform 15, his umbrella still partially open. Hollands gave him a head start, then tagged on fifteen to twenty yards in rear. By the time he passed through the gate, Ingersole had gained several more yards on him. Although it was standing room only in the rearmost coach, Hollands decided to board the train while his back was still turned. A few moments later and right on schedule, the train pulled out of Waterloo.

Vauxhall Bridge, Queenstown Road, Clapham Junction, Wimbledon: the suburban stations passed in a blur as they picked up speed and headed out of London into the Surrey countryside. Night came early with a leaden sky and a sudden cloudburst of rain that stayed with them until they reached Guildford when it then began to ease off. It was however still drizzling when Hollands got off the train at Godalming and followed Ingersole through the booking hall to the car park in the station yard beyond. Catching up with him as he was about to unlock his Toyota, Hollands tapped him on the shoulder.

"Hullo, Ralph," he said cheerfully. "How's the world treating you?"

Ingersole jumped and spun round to face him, his jaw sagging. "Dutch!" Recovering his composure, he greeted Hollands with a hasty smile. "Well, this is a surprise. What are you doing in this neck of the woods?"

"There was no other way to get in touch with you. I thought we might stop off at a pub and have a drink."

"Why don't we do that? Julie won't mind if I'm a little late; we never dine before seven thirty." Ingersole got in behind the wheel, chucked his briefcase and umbrella on to the back seat, then leaned across to open the front nearside door for Hollands. "We've got a lot of catching up to do, right, Dutch?"

"You've heard I'm being moved on?"

"To bigger things by all accounts."

"Don't believe everything you hear, Ralph."

"Now you're being overly modest." Ingersole started the engine, shifted into gear and drove out of the car park. "Listen, after the show you put up, you deserve whatever promotion is coming your way. I just hope the army isn't planning to send you to Northern Ireland again. You must be numbered amongst the top ten on the IRA's hit list."

"Quebec House was one of their operations, was it?"

"Well, I don't know of anyone who thinks the KGB were behind it – unless you do?"

Hollands didn't, but he had yet to meet the Irishman who could disguise his accent a hundred per cent of the time. And he was equally certain in his own mind that the IRA man who could pass himself off as a Londoner or a Yorkshireman born and bred was an even rarer species. But he didn't bother to make the point to Ingersole; whether he believed it or not, Ralph was sticking to the official line.

"So how's everyone at the office?" Hollands asked, taking a different approach.

"Your replacement's a nice enough chap and he seems to be settling into the job. He's got a lot on his plate with this United General Electric thing – the Kuwait project has really boiled up since you left, Dutch. Poor devil doesn't know whether he's coming or going."

"Lindsey's giving him a hard time?"

"You are out of touch. Lindsey left us a month ago, around the beginning of March." Ingersole signalled he was turning left at the intersection ahead and shifted into third. "I'm surprised she didn't write to you."

"Yes, it's not like Lindsey to fold her tent and steal away in the middle of the night." But it was perfectly understandable if they'd given her the same line of shit he'd had from Gattis that morning and she'd believed that, up to a certain point, he'd been working hand in glove with Redmond. "Kind of sudden, wasn't it, Ralph?"

"Oh, I don't know. Lindsey would have been relieved in May when her two years were up; the Pentagon just moved the date forward by a few weeks. After all, we're not the only people who have manning problems. Chances are they had to fill a slot at short notice and Lindsey was caught up in the domino syndrome. Not that she minded; when all is said and done, you couldn't ask for a better posting than Rome." Ingersole signalled he was turning left again and pulled off the road into a car park. "This is it," he said. "The Hare and Hounds, my favourite watering hole."

"Looks a nice place." Hollands released the door and opened it a fraction. "How about Stan Edwards?" he asked. "Is he still with you?"

Ingersole shook his head. "He retired in February."

"Don't tell me he was caught up in the domino syndrome, too?"

"Hardly. Between you and me, he was given the elbow; full pension rights, of course, and he received the usual send-off. The Director even made a speech at his farewell party thanking him for all he'd done for the JIB, which was pretty ironic when you think he was probably an IRA sympathiser."

"Stanley – an IRA sympathiser? Aw, come on, Ralph, you've got to be joking."

"You think so?" Ingersole twisted round to face him. "Obviously you've never seen his security file, but I have, and believe me, Stanley had adverse Irish connections going way back. His late wife might have been born in London but her family came from Enniskillen in County Fermanagh and most of them are still there. A second cousin of hers is serving ten years in the Maze for the attempted murder of an RUC inspector."

"So what was Stanley doing in the JIB? Why didn't we move him on?"

"Because our writ doesn't include Northern Ireland and the vetting people were satisfied that there was virtually no contact with that branch of the family."

"But that didn't stop us sacking him."

"Damn right it didn't," Ingersole said heatedly. "Soon after they'd started their investigation, the Security Services discovered that his American son-in-law was a regular contributor to Noraid and that was enough to raise presumptions of unfitness."

They'd needed a scapegoat and Edwards had seemed tailormade for the part. His family connections lent substance to the IRA theory and the fact that he was being retired early probably hadn't bothered Stanley one little bit; his pension hadn't been affected and he'd always said how much he loathed travelling to town and back again on the Central Line.

"We're not going to sit here all night, are we, Dutch?"

"Not when the pub's open."

Hollands got out of the car, waited for Ingersole to join him, then followed him into the bar. At that hour of the evening they had the place pretty much to themselves. The hushed atmosphere rubbed off on Ingersole who became decidedly quiet and glanced repeatedly at his wristwatch as though he was thinking Julie would be worried if he was more than a few minutes late. Taking the hint, Hollands finished his whisky and soda in rapid time and said he would have to be making tracks. There was a pay phone in the bar but Ralph wouldn't hear of him ringing for a taxi and insisted on running him back to the station.

Throughout the short journey, neither man saw the black Ford Cortina which tagged on behind them soon after they left the car park. Nor were they aware that the same taxi cab had followed them to the Hare and Hounds.

*　　*　　*

Bernard Jago occasionally worked for the National Council for Civil Liberties, in which capacity he was a constant anathema to the police. A committed Marxist, he was also deeply involved with the CND, Greenpeace, the League of Anti-Blood-Sports and the political wing of the Provisional IRA, as well as those anarchist fringe movements which provided him with a useful platform in his campaign to undermine the Special Branch. An authority on the Race Relations Act, there were strong grounds for thinking he was not above manufacturing incidents to further his own ends but, as yet, the police had not come up with sufficient evidence to prove this in court.

Although most women found him physically attractive on first acquaintance, they rapidly discovered that he was self-centred, supremely egotistical and impossible to live with. He had a sharp tongue and a hectoring manner and, by any yardstick, was a thoroughly unpleasant man. Not surprisingly, his wife had walked out on him less than six weeks after they'd been married. Now aged thirty-one, he lived alone in a detached house near Hedley Court, nine miles beyond the outskirts of Leatherhead, a property he'd inherited from his parents.

There was not the slightest doubt in Dukes' mind, as he drove towards Hedley Court, that Jago deserved to die. He and his kind were helping Moscow to bring the country to its knees and, according to the print-out, Special Branch were pretty sure that one of their informers whom the IRA had blown away with a sawn-off shotgun had been fingered by him. Maybe, Dukes thought, the Jew-boy should have got what was coming to him a long time ago, but Boden had been right to insist that they should wait for the heat to cool down before they moved in on him.

Before Silent Night, the party had been all talk and no action but it had been a vastly different story after they'd broken into Quebec House. Then those same committee members who'd practically crapped themselves when the operation had been mooted had suddenly become lions, eager to go after the prey. The way Boden had told it, he'd had his work cut out to make them see that the one sure recipe for disaster was to act first and think later. If the job was to be done clinically, they'd need to choose the right time, the right place and the right men to carry it out.

Right time, right place – a dark night and a secluded house in a woodland clearing off a minor road nine miles from the nearest town. Dukes glanced at the man sitting next to him in the Fiat and wondered if he would live up to his reputation. They had only met twice before and would go their separate ways when the job was done; two strangers who'd never been formally introduced because it was safer if they remained in ignorance of each other's surname. Dukes just hoped the Geordie from Sunderland was the hardnose Boden had claimed he was. Two, possibly three minutes from now and he'd know the answer.

"Better get ready," he told the Geordie. "We're almost there."

Dukes switched off the lights, shifted the gear lever into neutral and cut the engine. Coasting round a sharp bend in the road, he put the wheel hard over to the left and turned into a gravel driveway that looped round to a white stucco house surrounded by dense, overgrown rhododendrons. Applying the brakes, he brought the car to a halt in the shadow of a tall evergreen where it couldn't be seen from the road.

"Doesn't look as though Jago is at home, Harry. One light above the porch, the rest of the house in darkness."

"He's round the back."

"How do you know?"

"Because I phoned him from the pub back down the road while you were swilling down whisky. I told him I must have dialled the wrong number."

"Smart."

"Yeah, well, you need a lot of brains for this job." Dukes reached between the front seats, unzipped the airline bag and took out a couple of Hallowe'en masks. "Put one of these on," he said. "It'll improve your looks."

"Thanks a lot."

"Don't mention it."

Dukes handed him a 12 bore sawn-off shotgun, then opened the door and got out of the car. Like a cat after a bird, he crossed the gravel drive stealthily and cut the telephone wires with a small pair of shears. The front door was solid oak and the spyhole suggested it was probably fitted with a security chain. Signalling the Geordie to follow him, he moved round to the back of the house where, to his amusement, he found Jago had opened one of the fanlight windows in the kitchen. The rest was easy; climbing on to the sill, Dukes opened the fanlight to its fullest extent, squeezed his head and shoulders through the gap and unlatched the side window.

Jago was sprawled in an armchair watching TV when they walked in on him. For several moments he gazed at them, mouth open and eyes bulging at the sight of their Hallowe'en masks and the sawn-off shotgun. Then everything clicked and he dropped the gin and tonic he'd been drinking and leapt to his feet, hands raised high in the air.

"That's what I like to see," Dukes said. "Now lie down on the floor, hands crossed behind your back."

Jago nodded dumbly, lowered his arms and did exactly as he'd been told. Crouching down, Dukes trussed him up like a chicken, drawing his ankles to the sashcord above his locked elbows so that he was forced to raise his head and shoulders. Over the years, Jago had used a glib tongue to talk his way out of many a tight corner and it seemed he believed that his court room tactics would stand him in good stead in this situation. Eager to co-operate, he offered no resistance and even gave them the combination of his wall safe before they thought to ask him for it.

It was only after they had gagged him and put a noose around his neck and tied the loose end to his ankles that he began to realise what they had in mind. The pillowcase, which Dukes found in the linen cupboard upstairs, was not a particularly effective hood but it certainly provided the final macabre touch. And the towel they subsequently wrapped around his face made it difficult for Jago to breathe so that he instinctively tossed his head from side to side in an effort to shake it off, and in so doing, drew the noose tighter and tighter around his throat.

Chapter XI

The phone rang barely two minutes after Harper arrived in the office. As he lifted the receiver, he heard his PA say, "You're through", then Detective Superintendent Marsh came on the line. There was no cheerful 'good morning' from him, just a crisply expressed hope that Harper had his pen and scratchpad handy.

"37945600 Sergeant Preece, Gary Trevor," he said slowly and emphatically. "I reckon he's the man you're after. Two plainclothes officers on patrol in the Fulham Road stopped and questioned him at approximately twenty hundred hours on the twenty-fourth of December."

"Why?"

"No special reason. It was Christmas Eve, they were probably fed up and in a mood to be bloody-minded. Anyway, it seems that Preece gave them some lip and they took his name just to be awkward."

"And that's all there was to it?" Harper persisted.

"You've got a name, rank and serial number of a soldier who was in the right place at the right time. What more do you want, Cedric?"

"Nothing. You've opened a door and I'm very grateful. I hope I can do the same for you some day, Bill."

"Maybe you can. What do you know about the National Socialist Liberation Army?"

In a world-wide economic depression, international terrorism was one of the few growth industries. Hardly a week passed without another embryo organisation being added to the card index and, at the last count, the department had over a hundred on their list. Harper took pride in the fact that, even if he couldn't name them all off the top of his head, there was not a single one he couldn't recall, given a little prompting. The National Socialist Liberation Army was, however, an exception. Telling

Marsh to hold on, he buzzed Mrs Swann on the intercom and asked her to check the index. Although the check proved wholly negative, he was gratified to learn that at least his memory hadn't been at fault.

"It would seem the NSLA hasn't come to our notice," he said.

"It has now," Marsh told him. "At three o'clock this morning a man claiming to be their official spokesman telephoned Radio London and informed the news desk that the political agitator, Bernard Jago, had just been tried and executed for high treason. The night editor thought he was a nutcase; so did the Yard until he called every newspaper in Fleet Street and gave them Jago's home address and ex-directory telephone number. Then we began to take him seriously."

Hedley Court, where Jago lived, was outside the Metropolitan Police area, so the incident room had passed the message on to the Surrey Constabulary at Guildford and had tactfully suggested they might care to look into it. They in turn had contacted the police station in Leatherhead and some two hours after the NSLA spokesman had called Radio London, a patrol car had eventually arrived at the house.

"The police constable found the house in darkness and no one answered the door when he rang the bell. Round the back it was a different story; the lights were on in the drawing room and one of the kitchen windows was wide open. There were also a couple of footprints on the sill, and that clinched it." Marsh took a deep breath, then said, "The constable found Jago lying on the floor trussed up like a chicken, gagged and hooded with a pillowcase. As a final touch, the killers had wrapped a towel around his face."

"And he'd suffocated?"

"You don't smother traitors," Marsh said grimly. "In their book, you hang them by the neck until they are dead. Only they couldn't do that because there were no beams they could use for a gallows, so they had to improvise."

Marsh sounded matter-of-fact and somehow his flat voice made it seem all the worse. Harper was not the squeamish type – in Sicily, as a young infantry officer of not much over nineteen, he'd seen one of his soldiers literally decapitated by an 88 mm super velocity shell that had failed to explode – but the way Jago had died sickened him. There had been nothing quick about it; convinced he was going to suffocate, Jago had panicked and in attempting to shake off the hood, had slowly strangled himself.

"Jago may have given us a hard time, Cedric, but I want the men who killed him before they go after the next victim on that list."

"What list?"

"They opened Jago's wall safe and cleaned it out. I don't know what was in there, but you can bet it wasn't the family heirlooms."

"I think you're jumping to conclusions," Harper told him. "Jago was no fool; he'd have been the first to realise just what sort of field day the press would have with him if his house happened to be burgled and his case notes ended up on a municipal rubbish dump."

"That's ducking the issue, Cedric, and you know it. I need all the help I can get, and you owe me."

"I'm not denying that," Harper said.

"Our writ only extends to the UK," Marsh continued remorselessly. "What we know about neo-fascist groups in the rest of the world doesn't amount to a row of beans."

"You'd like a special briefing?"

"And then some. The NSLA didn't materialise overnight; they had to be recruited, trained and organised, and it's possible some of their right-wing friends in Europe gave them a helping hand."

"You can see our files on neo-fascists any time you like."

"Thank you, Cedric. That makes us even."

"Until the next time," Harper said and put the phone down.

There were two reports on his desk, each tagged with a pink 'Immediate' slip. One was the transcript of the Hollands interrogation, the other a tracking report from the surveillance team detailed to keep him under observation. Deciding that neither document was particularly urgent, Harper summoned Gattis and gave him what information he had on Sergeant Preece.

"Do you think he could be Macklin?" Gattis asked, when he'd finished.

"He's the only candidate we've got."

"A pity we don't know his regiment."

"That's for you to find out, Iain. Get out to Army Security and ask them for the location of his present unit and the name of his commanding officer. Once you have that information, contact the CO and tell him you want to see Preece. Then go in there wired for sound and get his voice on tape."

"Right."

"And you'd better have a good cover story," Harper continued. "If Preece is the man we're after, I don't want him warning his friends off because he's smelled a rat."

"That shouldn't be a problem. I know a warrant officer in the Special Investigation Branch of the Military Police who owes me one. Between the two of us, we should be able to come up with a convincing legend."

"You'd better get on with it then."

"This is a rush job?" Gattis asked, smiling.

"Have you ever known one that wasn't?"

Harper waited until Gattis had left his office, then opened the tracking report and began reading it. He was just halfway down the second page when his PA brought him an 'update' which she had taken down over the phone. It read: Hollands caught 0817 train from Clapham Junction to Waterloo and made straight for Underground. Subsequent behaviour at Oxford Circus suggests subject is aware that he is being followed.

★　　★　　★

Two other passengers had got off the train at Northolt – a smartly dressed young woman who looked as though she might be an office worker, and a blond man in dark blue slacks, open-neck shirt and a windcheater. The woman had been a few paces behind Hollands when they'd passed through the barrier and had seemed a little disconcerted when he'd doubled back to ask the ticket collector where the nearest pay phone was. Wandering over to the news stand in the booking hall, she had bought a copy of the

128

Daily Mail, then made her way to the bus stop outside the station where she was now waiting, apparently engrossed in her newspaper. The blond man had been more subtle. Instead of hanging back, he'd strolled on towards the pedestrian crossing near the shopping precinct where he'd waited for a break in the traffic before crossing over to the opposite pavement. As a result, he was now roughly five yards behind Hollands and moving on a parallel course.

The itchy feeling that he was being followed had started soon after he'd left his flat. Although no one had loomed large on the horizon when Hollands had run a couple of checks as he'd walked across the Common, the prickly sensation between his shoulder blades had persisted. At Waterloo, he'd moved swiftly through the rush hour crowds in the concourse towards the Underground and had then sped down the moving escalator, a fistful of silver in his right hand ready to feed into one of the vending machines in the entrance hall. The terminus was served by the Bakerloo and Northern lines and he'd figured there was an even chance his unidentified tail would make the wrong choice, provided he had a good head start. In the event, a five minute delay on the Bakerloo northbound had scotched that ploy, but he'd had better luck at Oxford Circus.

The first westbound train on the Central Line had only been going as far as White City and had been closely followed by one to Ealing Broadway. By the time it too had pulled out of the station, relatively few passengers had been left on the platform and it had been that much easier to run his eye over the remainder. Timing it just right, Hollands had waited for the next train and then, at the last moment, had cut through the subway to the eastbound platform. The ruse was as old as the hills but the balding man in the knee-length raincoat had fallen for it. Unfortunately, the other members of the surveillance team had remained undetected until he'd got off the train at Northolt.

Hollands walked up to the phone box, took a quick glance over his shoulder as he opened the door, then went inside. The young woman was still waiting at the bus stop, her back now towards him. Across the road, the blond man had stopped outside a men's outfitter's and was gazing at the merchandise displayed in the window. Refusing to be rattled, Hollands reached for the local directory in the bin shelf, looked up the name Edwards and found they occupied a full column. 'I got a nice semi in Moat Farm Road,' Stanley had told him at the Christmas Eve party, and there was only one Edwards whose first name began with the letter 'S' living in that road. Leaving the phone box, Hollands walked into an estate agent's office at the far end of the precinct and asked the girl in the outer office if she could point him in the right direction.

28 Moat Farm Road was a typical pre-war suburban semi-detached, with two main bedrooms, bay windows, mock Tudor beams under the gables and a small boxroom over the front porch which estate agents loosely described as a third bedroom. A narrow concrete path ran arrow straight to the front door and was flanked on either side by even narrower flower beds planted with rose bushes and daffodils. The property was fronted by a stomach high, crenellated brick wall, backed by an overgrown privet hedge which obscured most of the minuscule front lawn. There was also a 'For Sale' noticeboard by the front gate announcing that Creasey and Jones were the sole agents. Diagonally across it, there was now a fresh-looking sticker with the magic word 'Sold' in luminous orange.

Hollands pushed open the gate, walked up the front path and gave the brass knocker a sharp rat-a-tat-tat. A few moments later, Edwards opened the door, a cigarette clinging to his bottom lip.

Hollands said, "I bet you didn't expect to see me standing on your doorstep, Stanley."

"That I didn't, Major. As a matter of fact, I thought it was the removal people."

"I heard you were moving house. Looks like I dropped in just in time to say goodbye and wish you the best of luck in your new home, wherever that may be."

"California," Edwards said. "I'm off first thing tomorrow morning."

"To live with your daughter and son-in-law in San Diego?"

"Yes. I'm going to give them a helping hand with their

diner or whatever they call it." Edwards opened the door wider, invited Hollands inside, then removed the cigarette and tossed it into the nearest flower bed before closing the door behind him. "I'm selling up, lock, stock and barrel – the furniture's going to the local auction room. Don't suppose it'll fetch much but at least it'll help pay the legal costs of selling this place. You fancy a cup of coffee, Major?"

"Only if you're having one."

"Might as well put the kettle on; the removal men will be here soon and they're bound to want one."

Hollands followed him into the kitchen, a narrow room spanning half the width of the house, which looked out to a back garden that was mostly lawn. "You're looking pretty fit, Stan," he said.

"So are you, Major. When did you get out of hospital?"

"Just over a fortnight ago. As of now, I'm on indefinite leave."

"You're not going back to the JIB then?"

"No, I've been replaced, Stan."

"Same thing happened to me, in a manner of speaking." Edwards filled a kettle under the cold tap, then put a match to the gas. "Only difference is, my job sort of folded up. They said it was all part of the government's policy to make the civil service leaner and less costly. Didn't bother me none; I got full severance pay right up to my official retirement date."

"And so you should have, considering what a hard time the Security Service gave you."

"Who told you that?" Edwards asked sharply.

"Lieutenant Commander Ingersole. He said they really leaned on you."

"He doesn't know what he's talking about, Major. They just wanted a few straight answers to a few straight questions and that's exactly what they got. If anyone was in trouble, it was Colonel Whyte. But for her stupidity, Redmond would never have been able to open all those safes."

"What are you saying?" Hollands asked him quietly.

"I'm telling you, she gave him the combination to her

safe and when Redmond opened it, he found God knows how many other combinations inside it. Our Miss Efficiency was a right little jackdaw. It didn't matter whether the information concerned her section or not, Colonel Whyte had to know everything that was going on so that she could impress the Director. Look at the hours she put in. When did you ever know her to leave on time?" Edwards paused for breath, then answered his own question. "About once in a blue moon. She was always there working at her desk long after everyone else had gone home. That's why she needed all those combinations so that she could get whatever file she wanted after office hours."

Hollands recalled that Lindsey had never had a very high opinion of the portly clerical officer, and it was evident the antagonism had been mutual. Yet there was more than a grain of truth in what Edwards had said. Lindsey was something of a workaholic and it was a fact that every time he'd been the branch security officer, she had always been the last person to leave the building. Nor could he forget that Lindsey had tried to obtain the combination of his cabinet from the duplicate held by the clerical staff and might have succeeded had he not warned her that it was contrary to security regulations.

"She was a very odd woman," Edwards continued, "and I wasn't the only one who thought so. Remember Maureen Akehurst?"

"Who?"

"Maureen Akehurst, the pretty little brunette in the typing pool. Asked for a transfer about fifteen months ago."

"That was before my time."

"So it was." Edwards measured a spoonful of instant coffee into two mugs. "Do you take sugar, Major?"

"No thanks."

"I don't know how you can drink it without. Me, I've always had a sweet tooth."

"You were telling me about Maureen," Hollands reminded him.

"Oh, yes. Well, she was a shorthand typist and Colonel

Whyte used her as a sort of personal assistant. Wasn't a day went by but what she called Maureen into her office for dictation, usually towards the end of the afternoon when everyone was thinking of going home. Kept her there long after office hours and she didn't get no overtime for it neither – the Treasury wouldn't allow it. Of course, Colonel Whyte made it up to Maureen – gave her days off in lieu, little presents, and took her out to dinner." Edwards leered. "She was very fond of Maureen, a bit too fond if you ask me."

Hollands stared at his coffee. He knew he shouldn't be listening to this garbage from Edwards and ought to put a stop to it here and now, but it was revealing to the extent that it showed how the Security Service had stitched them up. They had seemingly convinced Lindsey that he had co-operated with Redmond up to a point; Ingersole had told him that Edwards was suspect because of his adverse Irish connections; and now Edwards was implying that Lindsey had lesbian tendencies. In producing three scapegoats for the price of one, they had also effectively obscured the whole issue and kept the affair under wraps. The only thing Hollands found puzzling was why the Security Service had apparently gone out of its way to muzzle Lindsey.

"Did you mention this to the security people when they questioned you?"

Edwards cupped his ears, eyes and mouth in turn. "You know the old saying, Major. Hear no evil, see no evil, speak no evil."

"You haven't answered my question, Stanley."

"I didn't have to tell them anything, Major. They already knew all about her funny little ways."

Edwards was lying. He was the man who'd given Redmond the combination to his safe, and had come up with this smear when Lawrence and the other investigators had backed him into a corner. If there had been any substance to the allegation, Lindsey would have been moved out of the JIB long ago, her security status downgraded to zero.

"I'll give you a piece of advice," Hollands said grimly. "Unless you can prove Colonel Whyte was having an affair with Maureen Akehurst, you'd be wise to keep your mouth shut. If you don't, and the colonel gets to hear the story, she'll hit you with a writ for libel so fast your head will spin."

"I'm not frightened of her," Edwards said defiantly.

"You should be. Lawyers don't come cheap in the States and you could end up losing all the proceeds from the sale of this house. Then there's the question of damages. Two hundred and fifty thousand dollars? Half a million?" Hollands shrugged. "Your guess is as good as mine but I'm betting you'd have to commute the greater part of your civil service pension to cover them."

"I could refuse to do it."

"Sure you could and then maybe the Americans would deport you as an undesirable alien."

From the expression on his face, Hollands could tell that some of the enormity of his predicament had begun to sink in. Visibly shaken, Edwards found a packet of cigarettes, put one between his lips and lit it, his hands trembling. Totally demoralised, he stood there at the kitchen sink gazing blankly into the garden. The sudden loud rat-a-tat-tat on the front door almost made Edwards jump out of his skin.

"Jesus Christ," he said hoarsely. "Who the hell is that?"

"I expect it's the removal men," Hollands told him.

"Yes, that would be it."

"I'm glad we had our little chat, Stanley."

"You're leaving?"

"Well, I wouldn't want to outstay my welcome," Hollands said poker-faced.

As though in a trance, Edwards accompanied him to the door and stood there limply, his mind obviously elsewhere. When Hollands reached the end of the road and looked back, he was still standing there in the porch, seemingly oblivious of the removal men who trooped past him into the house.

Smiling to himself, Hollands made his way back to the station where he found the blond man waiting for him on the platform.

Chapter XII

The CIA and the Secret Intelligence Service had followed Major General V. I. Zavorin's military career with considerable interest for more than thirty years. He had first come to notice in December 1950 as an unidentified voice on the combat frequency allocated to the 5th Air Regiment of the People's Republic of North Korea. Attached to a fighter unit operating from an airfield north of the Yalu River, Zavorin had scored his first victory over Toko-Ri downing one of the F86 Super Sabres which had been providing top cover for the Corsairs attacking the bridges. Up until then, the US Signal Corps personnel monitoring the frequency had thought the strange voice on the net belonged to a slow-speaking and very dense North Korean who was barely capable of piloting his MiG 15. Seconds after the Super Sabre had ploughed into the hillside, they'd learned otherwise. Elated by his success, Zavorin had suddenly lapsed into Russian and had been swiftly rebuked by ground control.

Although he'd never made the same mistake again, the damage had already been done; his voice was on tape and had been instantly recognisable from then on. By the end of the Korean War, US Air Force Intelligence had credited him with a further five kills, a figure which had included two Gloster Meteors of the South African Air Force Squadron with the United Nations, and a Hawker Sea Fury from the carrier HMS *Glory*.

The voice had acquired a name shortly after Yuri Gagarin had become the first man in Space. Eager to make the most of this outstanding achievement, Moscow Radio had interviewed a number of cosmonauts under training, one of whom had been Major Vasili Ivanovich Zavorin. The broadcast had been monitored and recorded by the Government Communications Headquarters at Cheltenham who had ultimately dispatched a copy to the CIA, Langley, Virginia where, after the voices on the tape had been compared with those in the library, a positive ID had been made. Some five months later, the name had acquired a face when Zavorin's photograph had been featured in an article on Space travel published in the Soviet Air Force Journal.

From that high point of public notoriety, Zavorin had suddenly dropped out of sight and nothing more had been heard of him for a number of years. Then, in 1973, he'd surfaced again, this time in North Vietnam. If he'd failed to meet the highest standards of a cosmonaut, as some experts had surmised, Zavorin had rapidly demonstrated that he had lost none of his old combat skills with the passage of time. Supposedly an undercover military adviser, he had nevertheless flown thirty-eight unofficial combat missions between October '73 and his recall to Moscow in April of the following year, and in the process, had downed one F111, two Phantoms and four Sky-raiders. Not surprisingly, his departure from the theatre of operations had been greeted with something akin to a collective sigh of relief, so too had the subsequent news that he had been promoted to one star rank and taken off flying duties.

Western Intelligence however had not heard the last of V. I. Zavorin. In February 1978, a spy ship operating with the 5th US Fleet had identified him as the Air Defence Commander of Sakhalin, a factor which, for some experts, had explained the increased Soviet air activity over the Sea of Japan. Two years later, GCHQ Cheltenham had been able to confirm that Zavorin had been appointed to command the Murmansk Military District. They had also provided incontrovertible proof that he had personally ordered the downing of a South Korean Airlines Boeing 747 which had strayed into Soviet air space.

And now Zavorin was back in the news again. This time his voice had been picked up by electronic warfare operators of the US 6th Fleet who were monitoring the command net of the Syrian missile batteries deployed in the Bekaar Valley. His presence in Lebanon could only mean trouble of the worst kind and the intercept had been flashed to the Pentagon, the National Security Agency and the CIA. In accordance with the reciprocal agreement between the two countries, GCHQ and the Secret Intelligence Service at Century House in Westminster Bridge Road had then been advised of the latest update on the man who had been codenamed Electra. At Century House, the intercept had been analysed, edited and photocopied for inclusion on related subject files as a high grade but unattributable source. Then the original flimsy had been passed to the Automated Data Processing systems manager for coding and input prior to destruction.

The flimsy was delivered by hand of messenger shortly after two o'clock that afternoon. It was actioned personally by the systems manager who prepared the necessary input and punch cards and keyed the material into the computer. A cautious man, he then called for the information on the Visual Display Unit to satisfy himself that the entry had been accepted. Seconds later, a message appeared on the screen. It read: NOT ACCEPTED. NO PREVIOUS RECORD OF ELECTRA FILE. CHECK INPUT/PUNCH CARDS/CODING FOR ERRORS. The systems manager did just that, found there were no errors and tried again, only to find at the end of the second run that the computer still refused to comply with his instructions. Thoroughly alarmed by now, he asked the MIDAS computer for a complete print-out on Electra and got exactly the same negative response.

It just did not make sense to the systems manager. To his certain knowledge, V. I. Zavorin had been the subject of well over a hundred radio intercepts since he'd first come to notice, yet here were two different computers telling him that the Soviet major general was a non-person. Although he was prepared to believe that the SIS computer had developed a hiccup, he thought it was stretching things beyond the bounds of credibility to suppose the MIDAS computer had been similarly afflicted. There was only one logical explanation; someone had gone into both systems and had deliberately expunged the file. If that was so, then there was every possibility that more than one file had been destroyed. Just how they were going to discover precisely what material was missing when the previous 'in house' audit had failed to reveal any discrepancies was beyond him. In the circumstances, the systems manager did the only sensible thing he could do and reported the occurrence to his immediate superior.

⋆　　⋆　　⋆

Hollands opened the communal front door, stepped inside the hall and then picked up the mail lying on the black and white tiled floor that had arrived by second post while he was out. A circular for the occupants of the ground floor flat, a postcard from Geneva addressed to the people on the top floor and a couple of letters for him, one of which was in Caroline's familiar hand. He turned about, placed the mail belonging to the other residents on the hall table and slowly closed the door. The blond man in the windcheater who'd followed him back to the house, had suddenly vanished and there was no sign of a replacement.

Hollands went upstairs and let himself into the flat. Caroline's letter was full of hyperboles and exclamation marks that was a micro reflection of their tempestuous relationship. The whole tenor of her note was to make it absolutely clear that she was not prepared to change the arrangements for the children's Easter holidays merely because he'd been discharged from the Officers' Convalescent Home. But it was the sting in the tail, the bald statement that she was taking steps to ensure he saw even less of Richard and Judith in the future that made him reach for the telephone and put a call through to Richmond.

When Caroline answered, he said, "It's me – Dutch. I've just received your letter."

"Oh, yes?"

Two little words but they conveyed a wealth of arrogance, and he could picture Caroline standing there in the oak-panelled hall mentally preparing herself for a show-down, her eyes narrowing, jaw set in a determined line. The image got to him and fanned a spark of anger.

"So what's all this nonsense about Richard and Judith?" he demanded.

138

"I thought I'd made my position crystal clear. I'm not going to have the children upset again the way they were after Christmas. I know it wasn't your fault, you didn't choose to go into hospital, but you're accident prone and these things keep happening to you."

It was a well-rehearsed answer to a question he hadn't asked, but Caroline was in a mood to say her piece and nothing was going to stop her. Roger had rented a villa in Juan-les-Pins and they were off to the south of France at the end of the week for a whole fortnight. There could be no question of him seeing the children before they left unless he was willing to make a fleeting visit to Richmond, preferably on Thursday.

"Why not tomorrow?" Hollands asked.

"We're going to the Agricultural Show at Harrogate."

"Really? How long has that been on the cards?"

"Ages and ages."

"I find that hard to believe."

"Are you calling me a liar, Anthony?"

"No, I just think you're stretching the truth. I don't doubt you're going to Harrogate, but it's a spur of the moment thing and it's all part of this crazy notion that you can deny me access."

"A crazy notion? You'll be singing a different tune when you hear from my solicitors."

You mean dear old Daddy, Hollands thought sourly, and rose to the bait. "Give me one good reason why I should?" he said.

"How about Lindsey Whyte for starters? From what I hear, she has a very unsavoury reputation."

"Oh, my God," Hollands said wearily. "You're the second person today who's tried to sell me that piece of fiction."

"Well, I happen to know it's true, and I'm not having my children contaminated by a woman like that."

"And I'm supposed to be enjoying a torrid affair with her?"

"Yes."

"Who said so? Gattis?"

"Never you mind."

"Lawrence then?" It couldn't be anyone else. Lawrence had led the investigation and knew just how spiteful Caroline could be when the spirit moved her. It was Caroline who'd told him about the flat in Clapham and had made his financial position appear worse than it was. "It was Lawrence, wasn't it?" Hollands insisted.

"Perhaps."

"Well, don't bank on him to support you in court because he'll do the old vanishing trick before your father can serve a subpoena on him. I don't pretend to know what his motives are but he's using you to build a case against me and Lindsey Whyte."

"Don't be stupid, Anthony."

"Why don't you listen to me for once in your life? I was only discharged from Osborne House yesterday morning but you sent your letter direct to this address. That means Lawrence must have been on the phone to you before I'd even boarded the ferry at Ryde. Now why would he do that? Out of the goodness of his heart?" Hollands snorted. "For Christ's sake, Caroline, he doesn't give a damn about you, his one aim is to muddy the waters. Ten to one he told you about Maureen Akehurst."

"What if he did?"

"I've really got to spell it out for you, haven't I? Lawrence gives you some ammunition which you pass on to Daddy who tells you it's no good without any corroborative evidence and next thing we know you've got a private detective looking for Maureen Akehurst. Of course, in the end, everything will be settled out of court and in all probability the story won't appear in the newspapers, but a lot of people in the Intelligence world will get to hear about it and they'll nod their heads wisely because in their book, there's no smoke without fire." Hollands paused, waiting for Caroline to pour scorn on him. When she didn't, he said, "I guess all this must seem pretty far-fetched to you?"

"Well, Anthony," she said with a brittle laugh, "you always did have a vivid imagination, but you, of all people, ought to know that I don't like being manipulated."

"So what will you do?" he asked.

"Nothing. I've seen the bait and I'm not about to swallow it."

"I'm sure you're doing the wisest thing."

"Yes?" Her voice was full of doubt as though she was beginning to suspect he might have pulled a fast one.

"Is it still okay for me to see Judith and Richard on Thursday?" he asked.

"I suppose so."

"I'll see you then."

Hollands waited for her to hang up on him and slowly replaced the receiver. Within a matter of seconds, the phone rang and he presumed it was Caroline having second thoughts. Instead, he heard a series of blips followed by a loud ping as a coin dropped through the slot; then a languid voice informed him he was talking to his friendly watchdog.

"My what?" he said.

"Why don't you come to the window and see for yourself?"

Hollands picked up the phone and moved across the room as far as the cord would allow. Glancing at the call box some twenty yards down the road to his right, he saw that it was occupied by the blond man.

"Nice to see you again, Major."

"I wish I could say the same."

"If you look across the common, you'll see another friendly face."

"The balding man," Hollands said. "I notice he's swapped his raincoat for a yellow anorak."

"It's his way of disguising himself," the blond man told him solemnly. "His name's Henry, by the way."

"Is it really?"

"Henry's not the greatest shadow man in the world, Major, so we would appreciate it if you didn't go out of your way to lose him."

"What is this? An elaborate practical joke?"

"What do you take us for? A bunch of overgrown school kids?"

The phone went down with a definite clunk. As he left the call box, the blond man looked up at the house, then pointed to Henry and gave him a thumbs-up sign. Hollands recognised the ploy for what it was, a variation of the old three card trick with a live decoy up front. Unfortunately, he wasn't able to spot the genuine article.

★　　★　　★

The voices were clearly audible and there was no background noise; from a purely technical standpoint, the recording was therefore well nigh perfect. The only thing that bothered Harper was the fact that Gattis and the SIB warrant officer had done most of the talking while Preece had confined himself to a simple yes or no. And even on the few occasions when he had been forced to put a whole sentence together, he'd been very careful to say no more than had been absolutely necessary.

"The sergeant wasn't exactly forthcoming, was he?" Harper observed drily. "In fact, one gets the impression that he was downright suspicious."

"There was nothing wrong with our cover story," said Gattis.

"Quite." Privately, Harper thought it had been a shade too exotic. The Special Investigation Branch had obtained Preece's record of service from the computer and, matching it against their crime index, had discovered that in 1976 they had charged four members of his unit in Germany with illegal possession of cannabis. They had then decided to write a whole new scenario around the sergeant's former comrades. If it was to hold up, a good cover story had to be based on fact, and what could be more authentic than a well-documented case history? Trouble was, Preece had evidently thought the whole episode was just too much of a coincidence.

"I admit he sounds wary," Gattis went on, "but then the SIB has an unnerving effect on most soldiers. We'd also given him every reason to suppose his former comrades had implicated him in this latest bust."

"And he believed you were a detective inspector in the Drugs Squad?"

"I had a warrant card to prove it."

"A good stage prop always comes in handy."

"Preece found it convincing."

"What does the army have to say about Preece?" Harper asked, changing direction.

"According to his commanding officer, he's a good soldier. His Company and Regimental Conduct Sheets are clean and he was graded excellent in his last three confidential reports. Preece originally enlisted in the Royal Signals and was trained as a radio telegraphist before he transferred to the infantry in 1977. Seems he was then serving in a brigade signal squadron and was part of the rear link detachment attached to the 2nd Royal Green Jackets. Anyway, he got to like the Regiment and decided they were the mob for him. The Signals were sorry to lose him."

"Has he ever been positively vetted?"

Gattis nodded. "It was allowed to lapse when he transferred. The army is sending us his security file; all being well, it should arrive first thing tomorrow morning."

"What else have we got on him?"

"The usual details. Preece is twenty-nine, average height, average weight, has dark hair, grey eyes and a cleft chin. He's been married for five years, no children. At the moment, he's living in a house belonging to the Territorial Army at 5 Goldhawk Close in Hammersmith, but his wife, Janice, has an office job with an export/import firm in the City and they're hoping to buy a place of their own in the near future. Although Preece is actually with battalion headquarters in King's Cross, he attended two drill nights a week with 'Z' Company in Fulham from May to August last year when he was running a training cadre for their wireless operators."

"And some time during those summer months, Preece could have taken a wax impression of the keys he needed to get in and out of the drill hall."

"Could is the operative word, but where's the proof?"

"We're about to get it, Iain."

Harper set the tape running again, found the passage where Preece had finally come out of his shell, then called his PA on the intercom and told her to ring Hollands at his flat in Clapham. As soon as they were connected, he introduced himself briefly and hooked the phone into a voice amplifier so that Gattis could hear their ensuing conversation.

Hollands said, "Before we go any further, I'd like to know just who you represent."

"I thought I'd already made that clear," Harper said patiently. "I'm in the same department as Mr Gattis."

"I've only your word for it."

"I don't think it'll matter after you've listened to this."

Harper placed the tape recorder near the amplifier and depressed the play button. In a voice with overtones of the nasal, Midland accent, Preece said, "I remember their names all right, but I'm blowed if I can recall their faces now. But that's not surprising, is it? I mean, it all happened a long time ago and it isn't as if any of those guys were in my rear link detachment."

"Macklin," Hollands shouted, breaking in. "Jesus Christ, that's Macklin."

Harper switched off the Sony recorder and spoke into the amplifier. "We think so too," he said. "How would you like to meet him face to face?"

"Where and when?"

"Tomorrow morning. I'll get Drew to pick you up from your flat."

"Drew?"

"The blond man in the windcheater," Harper said and hung up on him.

From the resigned expression on his face, he knew Gattis had guessed what was in the wind and was pretty unhappy about it. "There's no need to look so worried, Iain," he said disarmingly. "I've no intention of breaking the law where Preece is concerned."

"So who's going to pick him up? Special Branch?"

"Eventually."

"What do you mean by eventually?"

"I mean after we've had a quiet chat with him at our little hideaway in Tetbury Gardens."

"You told me everything was going to be legal and above board."

"And so it will be."

"But we're going to detain Preece," Gattis said tersely.

"Yes."

"On what authority?"

"The Prevention of Terrorism Act," Harper said blandly. "You couldn't have anything more legal than that."

Chapter XIII

Preece went through the medicine cabinet in the bathroom and found a bottle containing half a dozen milk of magnesia tablets. His stomach had started acting up the previous evening and had got progressively worse during the night. Unable to face even a bowl of cornflakes this morning, he'd settled for a slice of dry toast and a cup of black coffee. "Rum and coke doesn't mix with sweet and sour pork," his wife, Janice, had told him over the breakfast table, but he knew the griping pains hadn't been caused by what he'd had to eat and drink last night. They had been triggered by a hunch that Gattis was no more a detective inspector in the Drugs Squad than he was a candidate for Sandhurst. Three and a half months after the event, the police had somehow made the connection and knew that he'd taken part in Silent Night.

Preece washed a couple of tablets down with a glass of water then went into the front bedroom. There were no interlopers in Goldhawk Close that he could see and the neighbourhood looked as quiet as the grave, the way it always did at this hour of the morning. In the circumstances, he should have felt reassured, but a nagging inner voice kept telling him they were out there somewhere, watching his every move. His stomach churning again, Preece backed away from the window and sat down on the bed. Gattis was bad news, but it had been yesterday evening's headlines in the *Standard* and in the *Daily Mirror* this morning that had really spooked him.

Bernard Jago. He'd never heard of the Jew-boy lawyer before his name had appeared in the newspapers and even then he wouldn't have paid much attention to it if the murder hadn't been attributed to the National Socialist Liberation Army. Now, his every instinct was to cut and run while he still had a chance, but that was easier said than done.

Including the loose change in his pocket, he had just over eleven pounds on him and his cashpoint card was hardly the open sesame to a small fortune. With Janice putting every spare penny into the Halifax Building Society, there was never more than a hundred in their joint bank account. He could raise the money for the air fare to Dublin and what was left out of the hundred pounds would be enough to tide him over until Janice could join him, but he wondered if running to Eire would be such a good idea after all. The Security Service, MI5 or whatever they called themselves, were a pretty hard-nosed lot and some of them might feel it would be more profitable to set him up as a target for the IRA than go to the bother of applying for his extradition.

"It's ten to eight, Gary."

Preece heard Janice call to him from the hall below and answered her with a grunt.

"I'm going to be late if you don't get a move on."

"Yeah, okay," he called back, "I'll be with you in a minute."

Galvanised into action, Preece stripped off his uniform and changed into a pair of slacks and a sports jacket. Wallet, loose change, cashpoint card, military ID: he checked the pockets of his service dress to make sure he hadn't overlooked anything, then opened the deed box which Janice kept in the wardrobe and took out his passport.

"For God's sake, Gary, how much longer are you going to be?"

"I'm coming," he said. "Right now."

Bundling his uniform into the wardrobe, Preece closed the bedroom door behind him and went downstairs. For all that she claimed to be in a hurry, Janice was still inspecting her appearance in the hall mirror. At the sound of his footsteps, she turned round to face him, her eyes widening.

"What made you change?" she asked.

"There didn't seem much point in dressing up like a soldier. All we're doing today is filing bits of paper."

"You knew that when you got up this morning."

"Yes, well, I changed my mind, didn't I?" he said irritably.

147

"You look as white as a sheet."

"Sweet and sour doesn't mix with rum and coke, remember?"

"No." Janice shook her head. "No, there's more to it than that. You're scared stiff about something." She glanced at the copy of the *Daily Mirror* tucked away inside her plastic shopping bag by the hall table. "It's because of that lawyer who was strangled, isn't it?"

"Don't be stupid; the night he got killed, you were drinking it up with me in the Sergeants' Mess."

"You're mixed up with this National Socialist lot, aren't you?" She hurled the accusation at him in a voice that was both angry and contemptuous.

Janice was petite and slender. Even in high heels, the crown of her head was only on a level with his shoulder and he could lift her one-handed, yet it was she who was the dominant partner. Sensuous as a cat, she could arouse him to fever pitch simply by the way she curled herself up on the couch. And sometimes, like now, her other feline qualities would surface and she would unsheath her claws and rip him to pieces.

"I'm waiting for an answer, Gary." Her eyes were baleful with a malicious glint that unnerved him.

"What if I am?" Preece blustered. "You started me down that road and your precious brother-in-law did the rest."

"Don't try to put the blame on me. You're just sick with fear and I'd like to know why."

Sick with fear was a gross exaggeration but he didn't bother to argue the point. Instead, he told her about the two police officers who had stopped him in the Fulham Road on Christmas Eve and how, nearly four months after the event, a Detective Inspector Gattis had suddenly showed up at battalion headquarters yesterday ostensibly to question him about a number of signalmen he'd known who'd been kicked out of the army years ago. Some things he didn't have to spell out. For all that Janice pretended that she'd never heard of the NSLA, she knew he'd taken part in Silent Night.

"You think the police are on to you?"

"They could be."

"Well, if they are, you'll know what to do."

"Will I?" he said.

"It's a question of loyalties," Janice told him. "You'll simply have to decide where they lie." She picked up the plastic shopping bag and opened the front door. "Of course, if you want my opinion, I think all your fears are in your mind. You've always been a worrier, Gary."

*　　*　　*

Drew was a triple 'A' man, arrogant, aggressive and abrasive. Those qualities had been self-evident to Hollands when he'd spoken to him on the telephone the previous afternoon, and he'd no reason to alter his opinion on further acquaintance. The only thing to be said in Drew's favour was the fact that he didn't seem to mind whom he offended.

Between Clapham Common and Waterloo Bridge, he'd been involved in two altercations, first with a van driver, then with a motor-cyclist. The van driver had merely pounded his horn when they'd cut in front of him, but the motor-cyclist had decided to teach Drew a lesson. At the next set of traffic lights, he'd pulled up alongside their Capri and had aimed a kick at the offside door. His movements had been slow and deliberate, like those of a heavyweight who'd had too many fights and was punchdrunk. Timing it to perfection, Drew had opened the door and slammed it against his leg, catching him across the shin. Not surprisingly, the stream of invective had been superseded by a howl of pain, but it hadn't ended there. While he was still struggling to retain his balance, Drew had hit the motorcyclist again, knocking him out of the saddle a split second before the lights had changed to green. Pausing just long enough to satisfy himself that the man was okay, he'd then put his foot down and left the rest of the traffic standing. The fact that at least one pedestrian had made a note of their number hadn't perturbed him in the slightest. As he'd subsequently explained to Hollands, the vehicle licensing centre at Swansea could spend the rest of time feeding the number into their computer without getting a listing for the Capri.

The tacit admission that he was driving around London

with false plates had been the one illuminating thing Hollands had learned from him. Thereafter, Drew had withdrawn into his shell again as though conscious that he'd committed a gross breach of security. After crossing Waterloo Bridge, he'd taken the underpass into Kingsway and turned right off Southampton Row. Half a mile farther on he'd swung left into Gray's Inn Road, then disappeared into a maze of back streets beyond the Gardens.

Unfamiliar with that part of London, Hollands couldn't place any of the landmarks. The occasional street sign indicated they were somewhere in the borough of Islington and he thought they were generally heading in a north-easterly direction, but with Drew following a zigzag route, he wasn't inclined to bet on it. A couple of left and right turns brought them into Tetbury Gardens and a decidedly upmarket neighbourhood. Swinging over to the wrong side of the road, Drew pulled up outside number 16.

"This is where you get out," he said in his usual offhand manner.

"Macklin lives here?"

"You've got to be joking; he couldn't raise the asking price for the doormat. This place belongs to us."

Hollands gritted his teeth. He might have guessed that Drew would take him literally. "So where the hell is Macklin?" he snapped.

"I'm about to collect him. Meantime, why don't you go inside and talk to the nice man who runs our department?"

Hollands got out and walked round the back of the Capri. Part of a terrace, the house had been built around the turn of the century and was on three levels – ground, first floor and garret. Considered eminently suitable by the Edwardians for a skilled artisan and his family, it had been seen in a very different light sixty years on. Scheduled for demolition along with several other streets in the immediate neighbourhood, Tetbury Gardens had survived, thanks to a property developer who'd made an offer the local council had been unable to refuse. Within weeks of an extensive facelift, a whole new socio-economic group had moved into the area – up-and-coming executives with young families and au pair girls in the attic.

Hollands tried the front door, found it unlocked, and walked into the hall. The décor was straight out of *Ideal Home* – a plush, fitted carpet, expensive wallpaper and the kind of elegant fittings synonymous with Harrods.

"Up here, Major Hollands."

The voice came from the landing above and sounded familiar. Looking up, he saw that it belonged to a trim, sprightly looking man who he thought was in his early or mid fifties.

"My name's Harper," the stranger said. "I spoke to you on the phone yesterday afternoon."

"And gave me to understand that Mr Gattis is one of your colleagues."

"Yes indeed."

"Drew tells it differently." Hollands climbed the stairs and shook his outstretched hand. "He says you're in charge of this department, whatever it's called."

"DSW," Harper said. "Subversion is our stock in trade; we're either busy fermenting it or else we're doing our best to stamp it out."

"You must have an unlimited budget."

"Don't be fooled by this place. It's a gift from the Sultan of Muscat and Oman in recognition of services rendered."

Hollands followed him into a room at the front of the house that had been furnished as a study with a leather settee, a free-standing bookcase, a mahogany writing desk and an upright chair. There was also a television set and video recorder pushed away into one corner. The green, dog-eared file with a security classification of Confidential had been deliberately placed in the centre of the uncluttered desk where he was bound to see it.

"37945600 Preece G. T." Hollands raised a quizzical eyebrow. "Macklin's?"

"Yes. It's quite interesting."

"May I read it?"

"By all means," said Harper.

The papers showed that Preece had been cleared by positive vetting before his nineteenth birthday and while he was still under training at Catterick. After the initial clearance, there had been several follow-ups at twelve monthly intervals and a full scale review at the first five year point. Throughout the file, all the referee and superior officer reports were pretty much of a muchness. Punctuated with such illuminating observations as 'loyal', 'totally reliable', 'discreet', and 'very security conscious', they depicted him as a man who could safely be allowed access to highly classified information. There was, however, a lone dissenting voice from a Foreman of Signals who had known Preece when he was a corporal serving in Germany.

"Has a deep and abiding hatred of the Left Wing and everything they stand for," Hollands said, quoting from the statement. "Thinks our immigration laws are too liberal and reckons it would be no bad thing if the Asians and West Indians were encouraged to return to their own countries. Professes to be a traditional Labour voter but talks and acts like a fully paid-up member of the National Front." He looked up from the file. "It makes you wonder how his PV clearance was renewed at the quinquennial review."

"The Foreman of Signals was an Anglo-Indian," said Harper. "The vetting officer thought he had a chip on his shoulder and was racially prejudiced."

"What do you think?"

Harper moved to the window and stood there, his back towards him, both hands deep in his pockets. "Right now, I don't give a damn whether Preece is a member of the National Front, the Seventh Day Adventists or the Friends of the Earth. You say he's Macklin and that's good enough for me. There'll be time enough to discover what makes him tick after he's led us to the others."

"You've got to break him down first," Hollands pointed out.

"I'm relying on you to do that." Harper turned about and faced him, a faint smile hovering on his lips. "With a little help from us," he added.

"Then I hope you've got something up your sleeve. If he's anything like Redmond, he'll be a hard nut to crack and my unsupported evidence may not be enough. You can bet Preece will have fixed himself up with an alibi, and it'll be my word against his."

"You're wrong there, Major Hollands. Luckily for us, he was stopped and questioned by a couple of police officers late on Christmas Eve."

"You know what I would do if I were Preece? I'd invite you to go ahead and charge me; then I'd brief my solicitor to find an eloquent lawyer who could persuade the jury I'd been framed."

"What if we said we could get you as an accessory to murder?"

"You're referring to Bernard Jago?"

"Yes."

"Can you make it stick?" Hollands asked.

"The trick lies in convincing Preece that we can."

A car turned into Tetbury Gardens and screeched to a halt outside the house. Moments later, the sound of muted voices floated up from the hall below.

"I think we should go and meet them," Harper said.

"Right."

"I'll leave you to introduce yourself to Preece: it'll be more dramatic."

"I'm a soldier, not an actor, Mr Harper."

"I'm not expecting an Oscar-winning performance," Harper said, and steered him towards the landing.

Preece was different, not at all like the image Hollands had formed in his mind. Instead of the small, bouncy individual in his early forties that the nasal voice had suggested, he found himself confronting a much younger looking man with a round open face, totally lacking in guile.

"Hullo, Macklin," he said casually, "my name's Hollands. I've been wanting to meet you for a long time."

Preece froze, one foot on the landing, the other on the step immediately below, the nervous half smile on his mouth rapidly fading to nothing. He turned to Gattis who was standing next to him on his left side, his throat working overtime before he finally managed to find his voice.

"Hey, what is this?" he said feebly. "I don't know this guy from Adam."

"Don't give us that shit," Drew said, thumping him in the back. "You must think we were born yesterday."

He jabbed Preece again and went on jabbing him in the small of his back as he herded him into the room next to the study. In what was obviously going to be a re-run of the old Mutt and Jeff routine, it wasn't difficult to guess who had been typecast as the hard-nose.

Chapter XIV

An interrogation room was never intended to be a home from home. It was usually stark and issued with the bare minimum of furniture. Some of the more sophisticated ones that Hollands had seen had been fitted with a two-way mirror and wired for sound, but the house in Tetbury Gardens was in a class of its own. Instead of a conspicuous mirror with a restricted field of vision, the interrogation room on the first floor was equipped with concealed video cameras which zeroed in on Preece and recorded his every word and gesture on to a cassette for posterity. And on the advice of a consultant psychiatrist who believed it wasn't necessary to furnish the place like a prison cell in order to turn a man around, there were pictures on the walls, a patterned Axminster carpet on the floor and comfortable armchairs to sit in.

The technical refinements and the psychology behind the décor were, however, wasted on Preece. Minutes after Drew and Gattis had begun their interrogation, he'd indicated that he was prepared to co-operate provided they observed certain well-defined parameters. He would not admit to being a member of the NSLA and he didn't want to know about Bernard Jago. As long as they accepted this limitation, he would tell them what little he knew about Silent Night. He repeated the offer in the same roundabout fashion and simultaneously turned towards the dividing wall as though he knew where the cameras were concealed. His face filled the TV screen in the study, the close-up magnifying his features so that the tiny beads of perspiration on his forehead were like peardrops.

"You want me to sit in on this part of the procedure?" Hollands asked.

"Yes. Having you there will remind Preece exactly what we've got on him, and it just might unnerve him."

When they entered the room, Preece immediately got to

his feet and stood to attention, head up, shoulders back, hands clasped with the thumbs in line with the seams of his civvy trousers. He was the well-trained, well-disciplined soldier, but there was something very obsequious about the whole performance and it didn't impress Harper.

He motioned Preece to sit down, waited until Drew and Gattis had left, then said, "All right, let's talk about Redmond."

"Who's he? The man who planned the operation?"

"Don't try to be clever with me, Sergeant. You know damned well he is."

"No. No, I don't and that's a fact. I never met Sunray from start to finish, didn't even speak to him on the phone."

"Sunray?" Harper repeated.

"We were using the standard appointments code," Preece told him. "Sunray is a commander at any level – platoon, company, battalion. Same rule applies to an Intelligence officer; he's always Acorn whether he's a lieutenant or a two star general." He paused briefly and looked in Hollands' direction as though seeking confirmation. "That's the way it was with us, we did everything by the book. You name it, we had one – Sunray, Acorn, Playtime, the guy who organised the transport . . ."

"Why did they call you Macklin?" Harper said, cutting him short.

"I don't know. Acorn never told me, but I guess he was someone pretty important."

"Congratulations, Sergeant, you've hit the jackpot. Macklin happens to be the name of the number two man in the Cabinet Office."

"Oh." Preece avoided Harper's gaze and focussed on the carpet instead. "Well, that's news to me," he mumbled. "Acorn just told me I was to pass myself off as the chief umpire and act like a senior army officer."

"What about Roach?"

"I've never heard of him. He could be Playtime . . ." Preece shifted uncomfortably in the chair. "It's like I said, we did everything by the book. We operated in separate watertight compartments and never met face to face. That's why our security was so good."

"Except for the link man," Hollands said. "You'd have seen him, not once but several times. Right, Sergeant?"

"Yes."

"So who was he?"

"Dukes, Harry Dukes."

"A tall man around six two and thin as a rake?"

"That's Harry," Preece said and smiled nervously.

"Known him a long time, have you, Sergeant?"

Preece nodded. "We're sort of related. Harry's married to my sister-in-law, Lorraine. As a matter of fact, he introduced me to my wife back in 1976. We met up at Aldergrove airport outside Belfast. There was a whole gang of us from different units on the way back to the UK for seven days R and R." He glanced at Harper, then added, "That's Rest and Recuperation."

"Thank you," Harper said gravely.

"Anyway, the RAF Hercules was delayed on account of poor visibility and the two of us got talking in the bar. We must have had a skinful by the time the plane showed up and I don't remember too much about the flight except that there was this great looking dolly bird waiting for Dukes when we landed at Lyneham. He told me there was another like her at home and next thing I knew, I'd accepted his invitation to spend part of my R and R at his in-laws' place in Southwark." Preece shook his head, then clucked his tongue for good measure. "That's really how we got to know one another. You see, Harry was in the Paras and we would probably have gone our separate ways if I hadn't taken up with Janice."

There had been another factor. When they weren't serving abroad or in Northern Ireland, the Para battalions were stationed in Aldershot, less than an hour's journey from London. That had made it easy for Dukes to get up to town whenever Preece had been on leave.

"I didn't mind Harry and Lorraine making up a foursome," he continued. "Truth is, he's a good man to have on your side in a tight corner."

"Having got you into one in the first place," Harper said caustically.

"You didn't have to go looking for trouble in

Southwark; the coons were usually out in force looking for whitey. Five of them jumped us one Saturday night in the forecourt of the tower block where Janice was living with her parents. Harry kicked the nearest one in the crotch, broke the nose of another with the heel of his palm and carved a third up with his own switchblade. After that, you couldn't see the remaining two for dust."

"You were lucky, Sergeant," Hollands said, goading him.

"The police didn't pick us up, if that's what you mean. But it wasn't for want of trying; they were crawling all over the place asking questions. You can bet it would have been a different story if the coons had done us over." The hate was there in his narrowed eyes, in the way his lip curled. "The blacks would have been up in arms screaming police harassment, and before you knew it, a whole busload of smart-arsed lawyers from that Civil Liberties organisation would have descended on Southwark to advise them of their fucking rights. These days, you've either got to be black or brown to feel at home in this country. I'm telling you, unless something is done about it, the Brixton riots are going to seem like a vicarage tea party. There'll be a complete break-down of law and order, something the Trots, the Maoists and the Reds would love to see."

"It's their primary objective," Hollands said in a deceptively quiet voice. "Anyone with half a brain knows they're Moscow's Fifth Column. Right, Sergeant?"

"They're the enemy within."

"Only you couldn't put a name to any of them, and that's why you decided to tap the MIDAS computer."

"I don't know anything about a computer. Harry merely said the information we needed was held by the Joint Intelligence Bureau and Sunray reckoned it was ours for the taking."

"Four men broke into Quebec House – Roach, Dukes, Redmond . . ."

"I keep telling you, their names don't mean a thing to me. Harry is the only one I ever met."

"Then we'll have to settle for him, won't we?" Harper said icily.

"Yes."

"Good. Just don't leave anything out."

Preece took a moment to marshal his facts into some kind of order, then rattled them off at machine-gun speed. No longer a regular soldier, Dukes had joined the TA less than a month after he'd been discharged from the army and was currently a member of the 21st SAS Volunteers. As a civilian, he'd had a variety of jobs ranging from a sales rep for a firm of office suppliers to a traffic warden. None of them had either been well-paid or suited his temperament. In keeping with his restlessness, Dukes had changed jobs yet again last October, becoming a despatcher for Rapid Transit, a small collection and delivery company in Kilburn who liked to think they were competing for business with the Post Office.

"Harry moved house about two and a half months later, said he wanted to live near his place of work, but that was just an excuse. If you ask me, Harry is all set to go underground."

"Are you saying he refused to give you his new address?" Harper said menacingly.

"Not exactly." Preece shifted again in his chair and looked everywhere but at Harper. "See, we had this brief note from Lorraine telling us they'd found a flat in the High Road but she never gave us the number and we still don't know whether the High Road is in Kilburn, Cricklewood or Willesden."

"So how do you keep in touch with him?"

"I don't; it's the other way round. Harry will ring me at home once in a while to see if we're okay."

"What if there was an emergency?"

"I'm supposed to phone him at the office during working hours. If he isn't in, I leave a message for him that Janice has suddenly been taken ill. Then I go to a pre-arranged phone booth and wait for him to contact me."

It didn't make sense to Hollands. Silent Night had been a textbook operation, planned and executed by professionals who knew their job backwards. But the emergency procedures which Preece had just described were so amateurish that it was hard to believe the same people could be involved. He wondered if there was anything to be gained from pursuing the point, but Harper was already on his feet and moving purposefully towards the door.

"Is that it then?" Preece asked.

"It is for the time being," Harper said.

The change-over was smooth; Gattis and Drew had been monitoring the interview on the TV and were waiting for them on the landing as they left the room. Entering the study ahead of him, Harper switched off the set and sat down at the desk.

"Shall I tell you something?" he said abruptly. "I'm beginning to understand why Lawrence was so keen to prove that Silent Night was an IRA operation. At least you don't have to consider motivation when the Provos are involved and Quebec House is exactly the sort of prestigious target they would go for. Of course, the KGB would like to get into the MIDAS computer, but somehow, I can't see them committing five deep-cover agents to a single high-risk assignment."

"And now the front runner is the NSLA and you're stuck with the strong probability that they're a splinter group of the National Front, the British Movement or the British National Party." Hollands shrugged. "A lot of people are going to find that equally hard to swallow. They may abhor the racist policies of the National Front but, to their way of thinking, at least they're patriotic and would never betray this country. Therefore they didn't attack Quebec House."

"Yes. Well, in my book, they're simply not up to it. Daubing slogans on the wall or dropping a petrol bomb through the letter box of an Asian family is more in their line." Harper reached for the phone and drew it nearer. "Still, if the worst comes to the worst, Special Branch can always charge Dukes with breaking and entering."

"It's their pigeon now, is it?"

"We don't have powers of arrest; Special Branch do." Harper lifted the receiver and began dialling. "Occasionally, one has to observe the legal niceties if only for Gattis's peace of mind."

*   *   *

Roach got off the Jubilee Line train at Kilburn and walked down the flight of steps that led from the high-level island platform to the entrance hall below. The offices and lock-up garages belonging to Rapid Transit were directly across the street under the arches of the viaduct. Turning right outside the station, he made his way along the High Road towards the café near the old Gaumont cinema.

The café was next door but one to a betting shop that was largely patronised by the Irish population of Kilburn. It had started out as The Black Cat and was now called Jimmy's Kitchen; in between, it had been known as The Taj Mahal and The Ace of Clubs. On a bright afternoon when the sun was shining directly on to the signboard above the entrance, it was possible to see the previous names beneath the latest coat of paint. Former owners had included a Chinaman who hadn't been able to speak a word of English and an Indian gentleman who'd sold up and returned to his native city of Agra, having sadly come to the conclusion that the Irish didn't appreciate his curry dishes. The latest proprietor was a Greek Cypriot called Andreas Metaxas, universally known as Jimmy.

Roach opened the door and walked inside. Despite an all-pervading smell of hot cooking fat which the extractor fans could never entirely dispel, the café with its formica-top tables was a popular eating place with the drivers of Rapid Transit. At a quarter to two that afternoon, however, there was only one other customer.

"Hi, Jimmy."

Behind the counter, Metaxas looked up from his newspaper and stared at Roach for a moment or so, then greeted him with a broad smile.

"Hello, Stevie," he said, giving him the wrong Christian name. "This is a nice surprise. We haven't seen you in how long?"

"Must be all of four months," Roach said.

"So what brings you here after all this time?"

"I had some business in London. Thought I'd look up one or two old friends while I was at it."

"It's always good to look up old friends," Metaxas said, philosophically. "You want something to eat maybe?"

"One of your bumper mixed grills – four gammon rashers, two fried eggs, grilled tomatoes, baked beans and chips."

"Tea or coffee?"

"Coffee." Roach started towards the men's room at the far end of the café. "No rush though. I need a wash and brush-up first; bloody train from Leeds was filthy."

The men's room consisted of a small urinal, a wash basin and two lavatories that dated back to the Iron Age. Entering the left-hand cubicle, Roach locked the door behind him, kicked off his shoes and stood on the wooden seat to get to the overhead cistern. He pushed his jacket sleeve up, undid his shirt cuff and folded it back. Then raising the lid, he reached inside the cistern and found the oilskin packet where Dukes had said it would be, wedged alongside the dome so that it wouldn't foul the ballcock.

Folded in three, the oilskin pouch was about twice the size of a lady's washbag and was fastened by two linen tapes. Inside the pouch was a leather shoulder holster and a model 1911A Colt .45 automatic. To Roach, the hand gun was as aesthetically pleasing to the eye as a Van Dyck, as exciting to the touch as the feel of satin underwear on a sexy-looking woman. He handled the pistol lovingly, totally fascinated by the blue-grey sheen of the gunmetal which had been highlighted by a thin film of lubricating oil.

He pressed the release catch, withdrew the magazine from the butt, and held it up to the light. Seven fat-bodied, copper-jacketed rounds seated rim in front of rim, the bulbous nose of the uppermost one filed down to a level plateau to convert it into a dumdum. Harry's visiting card, he thought, recalling the IRA gunman Dukes had shot in the Falls Road and the bewildered expression that had appeared on his face when he'd discovered his left leg had been crudely amputated above the kneecap.

Roach pushed the magazine home, jacked a round into the breech, then gently squeezing the trigger, eased the hammer forward, his thumb acting as a brake to prevent it striking the firing pin with sufficient force to detonate the percussion cap. If anyone had asked him to explain why he had loaded the automatic, Roach would have said that, for a moment, he'd imagined he was with the Special Patrol Unit again, back on the streets of Belfast in an undercover role. But even though Roach was aware that his reaction had been part instinctive, part romantic, he made no attempt to unload the weapon. Instead, he carefully placed the automatic on the lavatory seat, removed his jacket, and slipped both arms through the double yoke harness of the shoulder holster. Despite its size and weight, the .45 fitted snugly under his armpit and didn't create a noticeable bulge, provided the sports jacket was left undone.

Roach flushed the toilet and left the cubicle. After washing his hands under the tap, he buried the oilskin pouch amongst the mound of used paper towels in the waste basket, and returned to the dining room.

"That's what I call good timing." Metaxas waved a plump hand in a sweeping motion that covered the entire room. "Where do you want to sit, Stevie?"

"Over here," Roach said, and made his way to the table nearest the entrance.

"Okay, one bumper coming up."

The mixed grill that Metaxas placed in front of him filled the whole plate and he doubted if he would finish it before Dukes arrived.

★　　★　　★

At thirty-nine, Donald Neasden was one of the new breed of Whitehall mandarins who had not been to Oxbridge. A graduate of Bristol University with First Class Honours in Ancient History, Neasden had been groomed for stardom from the day he'd been accepted as a senior management trainee. Now, seventeen years later, he was deputy head of Personnel and Liaison at the Foreign and Commonwealth, with every prospect that he would be a Permanent Under Secretary before he reached fifty.

An administrative as opposed to a policy-making branch, Personnel and Liaison was involved in every facet of career planning and was responsible for briefing other government ministries and departments. Acting as a front man for the Secret Intelligence Service was one of the less agreeable duties Neasden was called upon to perform in the absence of his immediate superior. This had only happened once before and on that occasion he'd scarcely been landed with a crisis situation. This time he had, and it had brought him to the Department of Subversive Warfare.

Neasden checked the cover name of the department on the brass plate inside the narrow entrance to the corner building, then moved briskly to the solitary lift at the bottom end of the passageway. Closing the wrought-iron gate behind him, he pressed the button on the control panel; sounding like an asthmatic old man, the lift wheezed him up to the sixth floor where it suddenly came to an abrupt, spine-jarring halt.

Two people were waiting for him, a smartly dressed woman in her early forties and a Ministry of Defence police constable masquerading as a uniformed commissionaire. The woman waited until the constable had checked his ID card, then said, "I'm Mrs Swann, sir. We haven't met before but we've spoken."

The gentle barb went home and was an uncomfortable reminder to Neasden that he'd behaved rather badly. Running Harper to ground had proved exceedingly difficult and although it was scarcely his fault that her boss had been out of the office all morning, Neasden felt he owed her some sort of apology. "I'm sorry if you felt I was harassing you," he said, "but there's a flap on."

A slow but friendly smile appeared on her mouth. "There always is when this department is involved," she told him.

Neasden followed her along a poorly lit corridor and into the end room. Compared to his own office in Carlton House Terrace, it resembled a pigeon loft and he wondered how anyone could possibly work in such a dismal place. Heavy furniture of Germanic appearance, a faded blue-grey carpet on the floor that had probably been declared surplus to RAF requirement in the long, dim, distant past, and a couple of unidentifiable military prints.

"Waterloo and Balaclava."

"What?"

"The military prints," said Harper. "You seemed very interested in them."

"Oh, indeed I am," Neasden said hastily.

"But that isn't why you're here."

"No." Neasden assumed the careless wave was an invitation to sit down and cautiously lowered himself into a leather armchair. "No, you can blame Major General V. I. Zavorin for that."

"What's he done?"

"Vanished," Neasden said bluntly. "The ADP systems manager reported him missing yesterday afternoon. He tried to update Zavorin's file and the computer informed him it didn't exist. At first, the experts were reasonably confident that MIDAS had simply hiccuped because there was a bug in the system, then they began to have second thoughts, and now they're saying that a considerable number of memory cells have been destroyed."

"When is all this supposed to have happened?"

"No one can say precisely, but the systems manager remembers working on the Zavorin file in November last year and there are punch cards to prove it. Unfortunately, punch cards are destroyed six months after the date of input so it's impossible to ascertain exactly when the other missing files were last worked on. All we do know is that none of them were amended between the thirty-first of October and the first of April. In our opinion, that's a pretty solid indication that the wipe-out is directly connected with the attack on the JIB."

"I think your friends across the river are being just a bit naughty," Harper told him. "Every government department was required to carry out a hundred per cent check after Silent Night, and the SIS were quite adamant that there had been no leakage of information from their terminal."

Neasden fingered the knot in his tie, wondered how he was going to get through the next few minutes; he was on decidedly shaky ground and Harper was a lot shrewder than Century House had led him to believe.

"I'm afraid they asked MIDAS the wrong questions," he said lamely. "The ADP staff merely checked the defensive measures; when the computer made the correct responses, they didn't bother to look any farther."

"Until they were forced to."

"Quite."

"So how many files are missing in all?"

"Seventeen." Neasden took a deep breath, then said, "But there's no evidence of a concerted attack. The missing files appear to have been selected at random – different subjects, different geographic areas, different personalities. However, they do have one common denominator; most of the information on the data base was supplied by our transatlantic cousins."

"Another security leak by the Brits?" Harper shook his head. "Washington's going to love that."

"If they hear about it."

"What are you trying to say, Mr Neasden? That my department should back off and leave well alone?"

"No, of course not."

"I'm glad to hear it," Harper said grimly.

"On the other hand, we hope Subversive Warfare won't be too heavy-handed. I mean, we'd all feel pretty sick if the Americans decided to deny us access to their Signal Intelligence."

"And?"

"Well, everyone's quite happy with the present story – that the Provos had a go at Quebec House and ran off when the alarm was raised."

"Have you ever heard of Rapid Transit, Mr Neasden?"

"No, I can't say I have."

"I'm not surprised," Harper said. "They're a very small firm in Kilburn but they're about to become headline news, and when they do, the Provos theory will go down the tube."

"We believe that would be a pity."

"Who's we?"

"Ourselves and the Cabinet Office."

"I think I'd better have a word with the Secretary."

"He's up in Scotland, but Macklin's expecting you to call," Neasden said, and wondered why Harper appeared to find that amusing.

CHAPTER XV

Dukes kicked through the gears into second, made a left turn at the junction of Kilburn High Road and Cavendish Street, then swung right to park the BMW motorcycle in the alleyway behind the service entrance to Jimmy's Kitchen. As though performing a drill movement on the parade ground, he dismounted, heaved the bike on to its stand, and switched off the transmitter in the right-hand pannier. The despatcher at Rapid Transit would hit the roof when it finally dawned on him that he'd gone off the air, but Dukes wasn't inclined to worry too much about that.

He removed his dark blue crash helmet, tucked it under his arm, and walked into the restaurant. No one questioned his right to use the service entrance, least of all the kitchen-hand washing the greasy dishes. A Lebanese student and new to the job, he took one look at the visored helmet, blue coveralls and paramilitary anorak and decided the intruder was a police officer. So did the chef who'd seen him hobnobbing with Metaxas on many an occasion and believed he had an armlock on the Greek Cypriot. Andreas would have objected had he been around, but he was having his daily freebie with the Irish callgirl who rented the upstairs flat from him.

Roach was sitting alone at the table nearest the front entrance, his back towards him. The street door was locked and the hanging card in the window had been reversed to show that the café was closed until evening time. Dukes, however, was not the kind of man who left things to chance; raising the flap in the lunch counter, he started towards the men's room in the back.

"You needn't bother, Harry," Roach told him without looking round, "I checked it out myself."

"When?"

"About twenty minutes ago, after the last customer had gone."

"I guess that's all right then." Leaving his crash helmet on the lunch counter, Dukes walked over to the table, pulled out a chair and sat down beside Roach. "You pick up the hardware okay?" he asked in a low voice.

"Yeah, no problem."

"So now you're all set to go?"

"The spadework's all been done; it's just a question of deciding when."

"You don't sound like a man champing at the bit," Dukes said.

"Don't I?"

"No. Something's bugging you, I could sense it the moment I walked into the room."

Roach took a cigarette from the packet of Silk Cut he'd left on the table and lit it. He went about it slowly and very deliberately, taking time to marshal his thoughts. "When did you see Boden last?" he asked finally.

"Ten – eleven days ago. Why this sudden interest in Nick?"

"Because I want to know if you trust him."

"Trust him?" Dukes echoed. "What the hell is this?"

"You answer my question, I'll answer yours."

"Well, okay. Sure I trust him – I have to. If he'd wanted to, he could have had me put away for life years ago."

"What for?"

"Murder," Dukes said, helping himself to a cigarette. "At least, that's what the Director of Public Prosecutions would have called it."

July 1974: He and one of the battalion snipers had set up an observation post in a wood near the village of Crossmaglen. It had taken them four days and nights to get the bloody thing properly established and then, just when they were about to go operational, some frigging Irish poacher had blundered across them half an hour before first light when they'd been refurbishing the camouflage on their hide. They'd tried to explain to the Irishman why it was vital he kept his mouth shut but the sight of two blacked-up Brit soldiers had had an unnerving effect on him and Dukes had failed to get the message through. In the end, they'd been faced with a simple choice; either they let him go and hope he wouldn't set them up for the Provos or else they silenced him there and then. It had taken Dukes no time at all to make up his mind; Crossmaglen was bandit country and the battalion would have a couple of military funerals to contend with if they went for the soft option.

"Was Nick involved?"

Dukes shook his head. "He was the battalion Intelligence officer and my number two spilled his guts to him when he was debriefing us."

They had tried to kill the Irishman silently and that had been the difficult part because there was no way you could muffle the sound of a 7.62 mm self-loading rifle. Dukes had attempted to strangle him while the sniper pinioned his arms, but the poacher had proved a hell of a sight tougher than either of them had imagined and they'd had to finish him off with their eating utensils.

"You ever tried killing a man with a knife and fork?" Dukes asked softly.

"No, I can't say I have."

"Take it from me, it's a messy business."

It had been messy all right, but after thirty or more stab wounds in the face, neck, arms, chest and throat, the Irishman had finally stopped breathing. The sun had been well up over the horizon by then and they'd had to drag his body into their hide and wait until nightfall before they'd been able to bury him. Dukes was inclined to think it had been that nightmarish experience more than anything else that had unnerved the sniper and had led him to hit the bottle. The spineless tow-rag could have done for them both but luckily, one night he'd drunk himself into a stupor and had drowned in his own vomit.

"So Boden kept his mouth shut and that makes him okay, does it?"

"Nick's always been straight with me." Dukes crushed his cigarette in the ashtray. "I can't think of any reason why he should suddenly go sour on us."

"There's a first time for everything."

"Yeah?" Dukes noticed that the cigarette Roach was holding between his fingers had burned down to the filter tip without him being aware of it. "I think you'd better tell me what's on your mind," he said heavily.

"It's probably nothing."

"Suppose you let me be the judge of that."

"Well, okay then. I keep thinking about Silent Night and wondering how Boden managed to put it all together. I mean, he's been out of the Regular Army how long now? Four years?"

"Three and a half," Dukes corrected him.

"Three and a half, four years – what's the difference? So Boden's a reserve officer, but he's still on the outside with no access to the kind of classified information we needed. Where did he find Kardar, that computer whizz-kid? Who supplied the fake ID card and gave him all the inside dope on the Joint Intelligence Bureau? The Party?" Roach scowled. "Shit, most of the hard core I've met couldn't find their way to the local bus stop."

"We've got friends and sympathisers in Whitehall; that's how Nick got his information."

"And after Franklin was killed, was it the same people who got us out of a tight corner so that we could live to fight another day?"

"Yes."

"Bullshit." Roach flicked his cigarette stub at the ashtray and missed. "Apart from you and Boden, there is no organisation. We've no logistic backing and our equipment is a joke – a few sawn-off shotguns and a collection of kitchen knives. I need a handgun and I have to come all the way to London to pick up a World War Two relic. Then there's the people I'm supposed to work with. All we've got up in Leeds is a bunch of loud-mouths from the terraces of Elland Road football stadium. They're only good in a crowd and after they've put away a skinful of booze."

"Have you finished?" Dukes asked grimly.

"Except for one final question. Who's sitting on this mountain of information Kardar is supposed to have stolen from the computer?"

"Nick's got it."

"Have you seen the print-out?"

"It's being circulated on a need-to-know basis."

"In other words, Boden is doling it out a bit at a time." Roach shook his head. "Jesus, Harry," he said plaintively, "how naïve can you get? Can't you see he's making a big production out of nothing?"

"Are you saying Jago was a nobody?"

"No, of course I'm not, but he wasn't exactly one of your unknown Fifth Columnists, was he? I mean, let's face it, he had more than his fair share of publicity when he was alive. And it's the same with *my* target; the only thing I learned from the briefing was his home address and I could have got that from the electoral roll." Roach took another cigarette. Lighting up, he inhaled and blew a smoke ring towards the ceiling. "Fact is, Harry, I can't help wondering why the Special Branch bothered to classify that garbage."

"It isn't garbage. All right, so their names have appeared in the newspapers and there have been some pretty broad hints about them being fellow travellers, but what MIDAS gave us was positive confirmation."

"If you say so, Harry."

Dukes frowned as a thought suddenly struck him. "You've lost your bottle," he murmured incredulously.

"Balls."

"You've lost your bottle and you want out. Why can't you admit it?"

"Because it wouldn't be true. Sure, I'm worried; so would you be in my shoes if you saw the morons I'm supposed to work with, but I'm not about to back off. Whatever else may happen, the Labour Party in Wharfedale is going to have to find a new candidate to represent the constituency. You can depend on that, Harry."

"Now you're talking." Smiling now, Dukes punched him lightly on the arm. "Jago was just the beginning and we've got to keep up the momentum. Right?"

"Yes."

"Listen, if you need any help, just say the word and I'll be there."

"I can handle it on my own, Harry."

"Sure you can, but the offer's there." Dukes pushed his cuff back and glanced at his wristwatch. "I'd better check in with Rapid Transit before they start wondering what's happened to me."

"And I've got a train to catch," said Roach.

"I'll give you a lift to the station, it's on my way." Dukes left the table and walked over to the lunch counter. Retrieving his crash helmet, he tried the communicating door to the kitchen and discovered that someone had locked it while they'd been talking. It also became evident that that same someone wasn't inclined to pay any attention to him when he rattled the door handle and kicked the panel a couple of times. "Shit, wouldn't you just know it," he said disgustedly.

"Take it easy," Roach told him, "there's no need to get uptight about it. We can go out the front way, Jimmy has left the key in the lock."

*   *   *

The radio died suddenly, inexplicably and without any prior warning; one moment there was the usual background mush, then a split second later, total silence. The communications failure was, Hollands thought, symptomatic of the whole operation to date. There had been a jinx on it from the time Harper had decided to call in Special Branch. It had taken him a good half hour to locate Detective Superintendent Marsh and get him to a telephone, then before Harper had a chance to brief Marsh fully, the dead hand of the Foreign and Commonwealth Office had made itself felt and he'd had to return to his office. Thereafter, they'd been in a stop-go situation and Marsh had taken advantage of the enforced delay to modify the plan. By the time Harper came through on the land line, what should have been a simple arrest had become a four-car operation.

"First immediate action drill," Gattis said, and gave the radio several thumps. "I always find a little brute force works wonders."

"Always?"

"Usually." Gattis hit the radio once more for luck, then

conceded defeat. "How very inconvenient," he murmured in a voice that sounded only mildly vexed.

Hollands thought it qualified for the understatement of the year. He and Gattis were parked outside the old Gaumont Cinema in Kilburn High Road and were facing north, while Drew and Preece were some three hundred yards beyond the railway viaduct facing south on the forward slope of Shoot Up Hill. Marsh and the rest of the Special Branch team were round the corner in Maygrove Road directly opposite the entrance to Kilburn Underground station. Less than five minutes ago, Marsh had informed them that according to Rapid Transit, Dukes had checked out at one fifteen to collect a package from Heathrow for delivery to the Australian High Commission in the Strand. If he now spotted Dukes on the street, Hollands figured he'd have a hard time alerting Marsh and the others with a duff radio.

As though reading his mind, Gattis produced a short-range VHF set from the stowaway bag on the door. "I've got a walkie-talkie," he said.

"Is it compatible?" Hollands asked.

"I wouldn't know, but it's got four channels."

"Maybe you'd better try each one in turn." Hollands broke off, stared at the two men who'd just emerged from the café farther up the road. One, tall and thin, dressed like a traffic cop; the other, small and wiry. "We've hit the jackpot," he said quietly. "That's Dukes and Roach."

"Where?"

"My side, about ten yards beyond the road junction and coming this way."

"I've got them."

Gattis tossed the VHF set on to the dashboard, opened the glove compartment and reached inside for a .38 Police Positive. Then he told Hollands to stay put, got out of the car and advanced towards the two men on the pavement. Hollands grabbed the VHF set and started calling Marsh, first on channel alpha, then on channel bravo.

A young mother, wheeling her child in a pushchair, saw the revolver Gattis was holding behind his back and let out a piercing scream. Reacting to the situation Dukes and

Roach fanned out, then came to a dead stop and slowly raised their hands to shoulder height.

It was a token gesture; they did not appear to be frightened, nor were they. When Gattis signalled with his revolver that he wanted them to close in, they simply smiled and moved farther apart. They had looked into his eyes, recognised the bravado of his movements and knew that he wouldn't shoot. So did Hollands. He switched channels again, failed to raise anyone on charlie and desperately flicked to delta. A voice faint enough to be coming from another planet acknowledged his call and, in that same instant, Gattis leapt into the air and went over backwards. The double whipcrack from two handguns followed a millisecond later.

"This is Watchdog Two," Hollands said tersely. "My partner has just been shot."

He repeated the message, threw the nearside door open and slid out of the car into a crouching position on the kerbside. Gattis was down and needed help; and he had to hold Roach and Dukes in check until the others arrived. Hollands crouched lower, transferred the oblong-shaped VHF radio to his left hand and pointed it round the door, hoping that at a distance, it would be taken for something more lethal. Three hundred yards beyond the railway viaduct, Drew pulled out from the kerb and started towards him, hazard lights flashing, horn blaring.

Dukes spotted the man crouching behind the open door of the Austin Maestro to his left and zeroed in on the weapon he was aiming at him.

"Uzi," he shouted. "Watch it, the bastard's got a Uzi submachine gun."

The BMW motorbike was parked in the alleyway behind Jimmy's Kitchen but to reach it from this direction, he would have to turn right into Cavendish Street which meant his back would be a perfect target for the Uzi. He raised the .32 Webley revolver that had been his constant companion since the Jago execution, aimed at the crouching figure and squeezed off two shots in rapid succession. Then yelling to Roach to cover him, he made a dash for the entrance to the flats above Jimmy's Kitchen.

Roach didn't think to question his orders; he had been a professional soldier and in an emergency, still acted like one. Facing the target square on, he used a double-handed grip to steady the heavy automatic and opened fire at a little over twenty-five yards' range. The first round was short and richocheted off the pavement, the second hit the door dead centre, the third drilled through the side window and severely wounded a pregnant woman who was waiting at the bus stop a quarter of a mile down the road.

Drew hugged the crown of the road and forced the oncoming traffic to give way. There had been no time to fasten the seat belts and out of the corner of his eye he could see Preece bracing himself. He tripped the indicator to show that he was turning right and flashed the main beams. A sizeable gap between a bread delivery van and a double decker bus offered him the chance he'd been waiting for and, whipping from top straight into second, he put the wheel hard over and flattened the accelerator.

The Ford Capri mounted the kerb with a sickening jolt that broke the front shock absorbers and blew the offside tyre. The tail slewed to the left and Drew found himself heading straight for a launderette three doors up from Jimmy's Kitchen. As he fought to regain control of the car, a short wiry-looking man in a sports jacket who'd been running towards the café, suddenly skidded to a halt and wheeled round to open fire at an oblique angle. The windscreen shattered with a loud report and Preece grunted as though startled by the noise. Travelling at a muzzle velocity of eight hundred and thirty feet per second, the flat-nose bullet entered his head midway between the left ear and eye and blew out the right side of his face, spattering the interior with fragments of bone and a great deal of blood. His vision limited by the opaque windscreen, Drew stamped on the brakes and steeled himself for the inevitable impact. When it happened, his arms weren't strong enough to arrest the forward and upward motion of his body and his head slammed into the sun visor, knocking him unconscious.

Fire and movement were second nature to Dukes. The threat from the right flank was virtually non-existent; the officer crouching behind the Austin Maestro seemed to be having problems with his Uzi submachine gun and his partner had obviously had it. The major threat now came from the direction of the launderette; swivelling round to his left, Dukes pumped a couple of rounds into the rear end of the Ford Capri to provide covering fire for Roach as he ran towards the entrance. As soon as he was in position, Dukes squeezed past him, climbed the flight of steps to the flat above the café and rang the doorbell. Getting no reply, he used his crash helmet to smash the rippled glass above the letter box; then reaching inside, he unlocked the door and pushed it open. Metaxas and his Irish whore were still in the bedroom and made no attempt to stop him as he stormed through to the kitchen.

Hollands broke cover and started running towards the betting shop as fast as his gammy right leg would allow. Although Roach was still crouching in the passageway beyond the restaurant, he figured the risks were minimal. In fourteen years' service, he had yet to see the marksman who could hit a moving target at forty yards. It was also a fact that Roach didn't have eyes in the back of his head and was looking the other way towards the launderette. As he raced across the pavement to the betting shop, Hollands saw him withdraw into the narrow passageway and guessed that Dukes had told him to pull back. Changing direction, he ran over to Gattis.

A brief glance was enough to satisfy him that there was nothing he could do for Gattis. He had been hit twice, once in the abdomen with a large calibre bullet that had made an ugly-looking entry wound and again with something much smaller that had left a neat round hole slightly below the heart. His face was pinched, his lips a bluish colour, and there was no expression in the light brown eyes. The .38 Police Positive was lying where it had fallen, some eighteen inches from his outstretched hand. Picking it up, Hollands went after Roach and Dukes.

As he entered the passageway, a large sliver of wood from the door frame nicked his left ear and the blood began coursing down his neck. In that same instant, there was a deafening explosion and looking up, he saw Roach on the landing above. Reacting to the situation, Hollands went down fast into a semi-prone position on the steps and opened fire with a double tap, then realigned the revolver and squeezed off another two shots. All four rounds found the target; hit in the left thigh, stomach, chest and throat, Roach did a swallow dive off the top step and executed a forward somersault before ploughing into Hollands.

Dukes unlocked the kitchen door, ran down the concrete steps to the yard below and went out into the alleyway. Straddling the motorbike, he switched on the ignition, kicked down on the starter and opened the throttle. Within minutes his description would be relayed to every police officer on the beat, every patrol car in the Metropolitan area. He would have to ditch the BMW somewhere in the myriad of back streets and find himself another set of wheels. Thereafter, he'd go to ground, wait until dark and then get in touch with Boden.

He looked up at the flat, hoping against hope to see Roach, but there was no sign of him and he knew he couldn't afford to wait any longer. Heeling the gear lever into first, he opened the throttle wider and released the clutch. The bike shied and snorted like an angry stallion, then the rear wheel found purchase on the soft earthen surface of the alleyway and he took off like a rocket.

Hollands pushed the dead man out of the way, climbed the steps to the flat above and went inside. A door opened off the hall and a half-naked woman in a quilted housecoat gave him a mouthful of abuse in an Irish brogue as he edged towards the kitchen.

The back door was open and the alleyway deserted. Above the hubbub of noise coming from the High Road, Hollands could hear the urgent warble of an ambulance and the even more strident bleep of several police cars.

Chapter XVI

Marsh got out of the car and elbowed his way through the small crowd of spectators who'd already begun to gather on the pavement. As near as he could make it, only two and a half minutes had elapsed since Hollands had come up on the air, yet it seemed a goodly percentage of the local population had arrived on the scene ahead of Special Branch.

Gattis was in a comatose state and by the sound of it, the ambulance was stuck somewhere in Maida Vale which came as no surprise to Marsh considering how the traffic was snarled up in both directions. He looked round for a police constable but there wasn't a single one in sight which he thought was about par for the course. Rounding on his detective sergeant, he told him in no uncertain terms to get it sorted, then stalked over to the launderette.

The Ford Capri had demolished the shop front to the right of the entrance and had ended up inside the premises, its forward momentum finally arrested by a row of Bendix washing machines, several of which had been reduced to scrap metal. The whole floor was awash in two inches of water and what was left of someone's laundry was looking less than Persil white. A couple of abandoned shopping baskets provided mute evidence of a hasty evacuation by customers and staff alike.

There weren't too many signs of life inside the car either. Preece had toppled sideways and was lying across the seat, his neck resting on the handbrake so that he appeared to be gazing up at the roof even though half his face was missing. Drew was slumped over the steering wheel, his chest bearing down on the horn ring. A constant stream of blood was oozing from a wound above the left eye but at a cursory glance, Marsh didn't think the injury was fatal. Walking on tiptoe, he picked his way round the Ford

Capri and opened the offside door as far as the crumpled mudwing would allow. Then, turning sideways, he squeezed the upper part of his body through the narrow gap and raised Drew into a sitting position. Although it was doubtful if Drew felt any the better for it, Marsh consoled himself with the thought that at least he'd stopped the horn blaring.

In the ensuing silence, he could hear his detective sergeant in full voice establishing some kind of order. By the time Marsh rejoined him on the pavement, the medics had arrived, the traffic was flowing again and most of the spectators had been moved on.

"You seen Major Hollands?" he asked.

The detective sergeant shook his head, then jerked a thumb towards the passageway adjoining the café. "No, but we've got another dead body over there, so perhaps he went on up to the flat above looking for the other gunman."

"What do you mean, another dead body?"

"Gattis has just pegged it."

"Shit." Marsh said it again, but it didn't make him feel any better.

Turning about, he walked over to the passageway, his sodden feet squelching inside his black lace-up shoes. The dead man was lying at the bottom of the steps, his head at an unnatural angle which suggested his neck had been broken. Inspecting the body with a semi professional eye, Marsh reckoned two of the four bullet wounds would have proved fatal in any case and wondered what the pathologist would put down as the cause of death. Then a female voice shrill with anger claimed his attention and he went on up to the flat above to investigate.

The woman had long, silky, black hair that reached halfway down her back and was wearing a quilted house-coat, fishnet stockings and red, high-heeled pumps. Her anger was directed at a plump, olive-skinned man at the far end of the hallway who was having trouble zipping up his fly. Her language, delivered in an Irish brogue, would have caused a few raised eyebrows even in Billingsgate fish market. In the midst of telling him what a gutless barrel of lard he was, it suddenly dawned on her that they had company. Breaking off, she whirled round to face Marsh.

"I'm a police officer," he told her and produced his warrant card in case she had any doubts.

"About fucking time." The woman raised a skinny arm and pointed to the front door. "Where were you when they broke into the bleeding flat? Sitting on your arse drinking tea in the canteen?" The housecoat parted company above the sash round her waist to reveal a gold crucifix nestling between melon-shaped breasts. "You should have stayed and had another cup; one of the bastards is still here."

"Then you've got exactly ten seconds to make yourself scarce."

"Who do you think you're talking to?"

"A scrubber." Marsh pushed her out of the way and beckoned the man to come nearer. "What's your name, sunshine?" he asked.

"Metaxas. Andreas Metaxas."

"One of her punters, are you?"

"He owns Jimmy's Kitchen," the woman told him. "And this flat."

"Ah, well, that explains everything," Marsh said acidly. "You just dropped in to collect the rent." He clucked his tongue at Metaxas, then jabbed a finger into his midriff. "Of course it could be said you're living on her immoral earnings."

"That's not true, sir."

"Really? Well, suppose you finish dressing and we'll talk about it later." He jabbed the Cypriot even harder, burying his index finger in a roll of fat. "Meantime, I'm holding you responsible for your girlfriend's behaviour. One peep out of her and I'll have you both for causing a breach of the peace. Understand?"

"Yes."

"Good. I've got a lot of respect for a man who's quick on the uptake."

Marsh shouldered past him, went into the kitchen and found Hollands on the back step. He was leaning against the guard rail, the VHF radio in his left hand, the .38 Police

Positive held loosely by his side, the barrel pointing at the ground.

"I think I'd better have that." Marsh took the revolver from him, broke it open and ejected the live rounds and empty shell cases into his left palm. "Ballistics will have to make a comparative test, but I guess you already know that."

"It was standard procedure in Northern Ireland." Hollands rubbed his jaw. "The dead man on the steps is Roach, but I don't know if that's his real name. Dukes came up here, broke into the flat and went out the back way. He must have parked his motorbike in the alley."

"Very likely."

"I tried calling you on the VHF but I couldn't get a word in edgeways after the initial contact report, and now I don't seem to be transmitting a carrier wave. The bloody thing went flying when I dived for cover after Roach opened fire on me. I don't suppose that did it a lot of good."

"It's not a particularly robust piece of equipment."

"Still, I expect you've already got an update on his description from Rapid Transit."

Marsh hadn't thought to ask for one when he'd questioned the office manager, but he wasn't going to admit that. "They weren't too sure what Dukes was wearing," he said, fishing.

"Dark blue coveralls, anorak and crash helmet," Hollands said tersely. "His paratroop jump boots were black and there was a fur trimming around the collar of the anorak. I think Dukes will ditch the gear as soon as he can; he must be feeling pretty conspicuous."

"So are you, Major."

"What?"

"Conspicuous," said Marsh. "Or at least you will be if some nosy reporter buttonholes you. This is supposed to be a police operation and I'd like to keep it that way. Save a lot of embarrassing questions."

"I can see that it would."

"That's why I want you to stay in the background." Marsh glanced over his shoulder to satisfy himself they were still alone, then edged a pace nearer. "Do you know where the Department of Subversive Warfare is?" he asked.

Hollands nodded. "Carfax House, top end of Whitehall near the Admiralty Arch."

"Good. Now I'd like you to leave this flat by the back way, collect the Austin Maestro and get over there. Meantime, I'll phone Harper to let him know you're coming."

"Right."

"Better get moving then."

Hollands went on down the steps to the yard below, walked out into the alley and made his way back to Kilburn High Road via Cavendish Street. The keys were still in the Maestro but the law had arrived in force and one of the cops wanted to know where the hell he thought he was going. Hollands figured Marsh could explain that a lot more convincingly than he could and steered the constable towards the detective superintendent. Thereafter, the constable was only too eager to see the back of him.

★　　★　　★

Dukes squeezed the BMW motorbike into a vacant slot at the kerbside and cut the engine. Pond Avenue looked decidedly promising; amongst other advantages, it was a quiet backwater off the Harpenden Road in Willesden and far enough removed from Kilburn for him to feel that he wasn't in any immediate danger. There was one special plus factor; all the houses had been built around the turn of the century when a garage was unheard of and today's residents were obliged to leave their cars out on the street.

Dukes dismounted, removed the short wave radio from the pannier and started walking. The VHF transceiver was bigger than the standard police issue, but only an expert would know that and he doubted if there were too many of those around in Pond Avenue. To any busybody who might be watching him, he was simply a police officer going about his business checking the tax disc on every vehicle. If the worst came to the worst, he would jemmy open a side vent, but what he was really hoping to find was a car that hadn't been properly secured.

The owner of the Vauxhall Cavalier was the kind of absent-minded person who made a car thief's job easy;

three out of four door catches were flush with the panelling but the offside rear was sitting up like a miniature toadstool. Nonchalantly, Dukes walked round the back, opened the rear door and released the catch on the driver's side. Then he got into the car, reached under the dashboard and rejigged the circuit to bypass the ignition switch. The warning light came on and he set the choke for a full rich mixture. There were a couple of eight-to-ten year olds back down the avenue but they were too preoccupied kicking a ball around to pay any attention to him when he raised the bonnet and pressed the solenoid on the starter motor, nor did any of the neighbours appear to notice him when he pulled out from the kerb and drove away.

Dukes removed his crash helmet, then steering one-handed, he slipped out of the anorak. Beneath the outer garments, he was wearing a checked shirt and a pair of faded jeans. Removing the overalls was not without its hairy moments but somehow he managed to ease them off over his jump boots without wrecking the car in the process.

★   ★   ★

Harper sat immobile. In the unnatural stillness of the room, he was vaguely conscious of the constant hum from the traffic in and around Trafalgar Square and of the pigeons jostling one another on the ledge outside the octagonal porthole window above and behind him. But his senses seemed to be blunted by a feeling of total shock.

There had been other fatalities over the years, but none had touched him in quite the same way or with such intensity. Harper supposed it was because Gattis had been special, in the sense that he had seemed singularly resistant to the idea of joining the department and it had taken all his considerable powers of persuasion to talk him round. Some months later, in a moment of confidence, Gattis had told him that much of the opposition had stemmed from his wife, Mary, who had been reluctant to leave her native Glasgow. Supremely assured of his own infallibility, Harper had promised him that, given time, Mary would become as much a Londoner as anyone born within the sound of Bow bells, and had been proved utterly wrong.

Mary had never adopted London, had merely tolerated it because Iain liked his job and she was old-fashioned enough to believe that a wife's place was by her husband's side. She was, however, a long way from being a doormat and in their married life together there had always been an element of give and take. Whereas other members of the staff went abroad for their holidays Iain and Mary invariably spent theirs in Glasgow. Now that special relationship had been brutally terminated and no matter how illogical it might seem to a neutral observer, Harper felt he was responsible for what had happened.

The secure telephone broke the oppressive silence with a strident jangle that made him flinch even though he'd been expecting the Cabinet Office to return his earlier call. Taking his time about it, Harper lifted the receiver and grunted a lukewarm hello.

"We've been giving a lot of thought to this rather disturbing incident," Macklin told him, after checking to make sure they were both on scramble. "And frankly, we're not at all happy about the situation."

Three men had been killed, an innocent bystander had been seriously wounded, Drew was thought to have a fractured skull and Macklin called it a rather disturbing incident.

"These vexing problems have a habit of arising from time to time," Harper said acidly.

"I'm sorry, Cedric, that was very thoughtless of me. Naturally, everyone is shocked and horrified by what has happened." Macklin was suitably contrite. "I imagine Mrs Gattis is eligible for the usual widow's pension but please don't hesitate to call on us should you have any difficulties with the Treasury."

"Thank you."

"Not at all." Macklin cleared his throat. "At the risk of sounding callous, there are a number of questions that need to be answered before we can think of making a statement to the press. So let's begin with the dead gunman."

"Roach?" Harper interjected sharply. "What about him?"

"Are you quite sure he was a member of the NSLA?"

"Absolutely. In fact, you can safely assume he was one of their leading lights."

"I see." There was a longish pause, then Macklin said, "I don't think we should make that public. It would involve us in too many explanations about Major Hollands, Sergeant Preece, Dukes and Roach. Before we know where we are, every left-wing politician with an axe to grind will be gunning for the armed forces, demanding they should be purged of the fascist elements within their ranks. Can you imagine what that would do to their morale?"

A lot would depend on how the purge was conducted, but Harper didn't bother to make the point. The question was purely rhetorical, a means of preparing him for the expedient solution the Cabinet Office had dreamed up.

"We have to keep it simple," Macklin continued. "Roach was a member of the Provos, Major Hollands is in charge of the army's Counter Terrorist Intelligence Team and Preece was a serving soldier who'd come forward with certain information concerning an IRA active service unit operating in London. I think the press and the public at large will buy that. If any reporters want to interview Hollands, we can always fend them off with the judicial inquiries routine."

"Why don't we transfer him to the SAS while we're at it? Their reputation for cloak-and-dagger work is second to none, and you'd have the press eating out of your hand, grateful for any crumb of information."

"That's a thought."

It was impossible to tell from his voice whether Macklin had taken the suggestion seriously or was merely being equally facetious. Like Neasden, he was one of the new breed of Whitehall mandarins and Harper didn't know him well enough to make up his mind one way or the other. In the circumstances, it seemed only prudent to sound a warning note.

"Of course, you may feel that an SAS involvement would be counter productive," Harper said hastily. "It might engender the kind of interest and speculation you're trying to avoid."

"Quite. There are too many uncharted minefields as it is without creating another."

"You're referring to Bernard Jago?"

"Well, it could be said that if Roach was a member of the NSLA, there was a fair chance that he either murdered Jago or was party to it."

"In which case, the IRA involvement would then begin to look highly suspect," Harper said, finishing the hypothesis for him.

And naturally, the Cabinet Office couldn't have that. The IRA involvement had to stand up because what had happened in the Kilburn High Road was directly attributable to Silent Night. If British Intelligence now admitted that some other subversive organisation had broken into Quebec House, the Americans might well conclude that despite previous claims to the contrary, the intruders had succeeded in tapping the MIDAS computer after all.

"Bang goes the special relationship," Harper murmured to himself.

"What?"

"Neasden believes there's a real danger we would be denied access to US signal intercepts if the truth got out."

"Donald is absolutely right," Macklin said irritably. "Why do you suppose I was so anxious to ensure Dukes was arrested with the minimum of fuss?"

And look what happened. Macklin didn't actually say it but the implication hung in the air and it was enough to put Harper on the defensive.

"The information Preece gave us wasn't a hundred per cent accurate and we had a run of bad luck, starting with a communications failure."

"Between you and me, Cedric."

"Meaning?" Harper asked him quietly.

"Meaning that from now on, you will not make a move, initiate a new line of inquiry or take any executive action without first clearing it with this office. Do I make myself clear?"

"Abundantly."

"I don't wish to be offensive, Cedric, but right now a period of masterly inactivity in your department would not come amiss."

Somehow Harper managed to control his temper, some-

how he managed to replace the phone without damaging
the cradle. The in and pending trays on the desk clamoured
for his attention and Hollands would be arriving very
shortly, but the work could wait and so could Hollands.
He had to see Mary Gattis first.

★ ★ ★

Boden checked the rear view·mirror to make sure no one
was coming up behind him, then tripped the indicator and
branched off Kew Road into Old Deer Park Gardens. Halfway along the street he changed down into second and
turned into the gravel driveway of a detached residence with
bow windows that looked out on to the Mid Surrey Golf
Course. At little more than walking speed, he drove round
to the garage at the side of the house, put the headlights on
full beam and signalled the photo electric cell to operate the
up-and-over doors. Shifting into first, he then ran the Porsche inside, switched off the engine and killed the lights.

As he got out of the car, a familiar voice called to him
from the shadows.

"Harry?" Boden spun round and peered into the darkness beyond the garage. "Is that you, Harry?"

"It's not my ghost, Nick."

Boden walked towards him and fastened the louvered
doors. "What are you doing here?" he asked.

"You mean you haven't heard? It should have made the
headlines by now."

The six o'clock newscast on Capital Radio – three dead
after a shoot-out in Kilburn. Suddenly, Boden made the
connection and the adrenalin began to flow. "Jesus Christ,"
he said breathlessly, "you're one of the Provos gunmen
they were talking about."

"Is that the story the media's putting out?" Dukes sucked
on his teeth. "Sounds like a cover-up to me. What do you
think?"

"I think we're wasting time. How long have you been
here?"

"About ten minutes. Don't worry, no one's seen me. I
waited until it was dark before I approached the house."

"I suppose that's something to be thankful for." Boden

187

jerked a thumb over his shoulder. "You'd better go on round to the back of the house and I'll let you into the kitchen."

"The tradesmen's entrance."

"What's wrong with that?"

"Nothing," said Dukes. "Just don't keep me waiting on the doorstep. I might get the wrong idea."

Boden didn't like his attitude but he let it pass. Leaving Dukes, he walked round to the front and let himself into the house. He put the hall lights on, made a slight detour to draw the curtains in the sitting room, then went into the kitchen and opened the back door to Dukes.

"Go on through to the lounge," he told him curtly. "First on the right off the hall."

"Somehow I get the feeling you're not best pleased to see me, Nick."

"Balls. Whatever gave you that idea?"

"The sickly look on your face."

Boden locked the door and followed Dukes into the other room. Opening the drinks cupboard, he took out a bottle of Johnnie Walker and two glasses. "I take it whisky's still your favourite tipple?"

"With a splash of lemonade."

"The newsreader said there were two IRA gunmen, one of whom had been killed." Boden added a dash of lemonade to a large double and handed the glass to Dukes. "Who was he referring to?" he asked flatly.

"I guess it has to be Roach. He stayed on to see me after he'd collected the shooter. There were things he wanted to discuss with me." Dukes avoided his gaze, looked anywhere but at Boden. "I didn't run out on him, Nick."

"Just made a tactical withdrawal."

"You could say that."

"So tell me about it."

"I stole a car in Willesden, dumped it a good half mile from the Underground station at Queen's Park, then caught a Bakerloo train to Paddington, doubled back to Hammersmith on the Metropolitan and switched to the District Line. There is no way they can pick up my tracks."

"I wouldn't bet on it," said Boden.

"You think I don't know my job? Listen, I got the ticket from a vending machine, not the booking clerk, and I got out at Kew Gardens, one stop up the line from here."

"You ever tell Lorraine about this place?"

"No."

"Have you ever mentioned my name to her?"

"I might have," Dukes said defensively. "What the hell is this anyway? Some kind of Spanish Inquisition?"

"If I'm going to help you, I'd like to know how long we've got before the police latch on to me."

If they had succeeded in tracing Roach and Dukes, it could only be a question of time before they eventually caught up with him. Although, as far as Boden knew, neither man had been vetted, their personal files contained all the annual confidential reports they'd received while they were in the army. If Special Branch ever got around to it, a check would show that he'd written two on Dukes, one on Roach. In itself, that didn't prove anything, but it would put him in the frame.

"Did Roach know where I live?"

"Not unless you told him."

"What did he tell you, Harry? That's the important thing. I mean, why did he want to have a chat with you? Was he worried about something?"

"Like what?"

"I don't know, Harry; that's why I'm asking you. Maybe the police were breathing down his neck."

"No chance."

"Either he led them to you or else someone fingered the pair of you."

"You're the only one who could have done that, Nick. Look at the way the original team was organised and put together. Roach recruited Franklin, I recruited Preece, and those two guys never met you, didn't even know your name. Good for security, you said. But whose? You don't have to be a genius to work out the answer."

"You forget I recruited Kardar."

"And promptly detailed Roach to wet-nurse him."

Boden stared at him, wondered how much he knew or

had guessed. "You'd better give me the rest of it, Harry," he said quietly.

"Richmond's a desirable neighbourhood and this is a pretty big house, Nick. Must be worth well over a hundred grand."

"It belonged to my parents."

"Yeah, so you told me a while back, but it's the 'For Sale' notice by the entrance that worries me. I don't remember seeing it when I was here ten days ago." Dukes finished his whisky and held the glass up to the light. "Kind of a sudden decision, isn't it?"

"Not really, I've been thinking about it for some time." Boden relieved Dukes of his empty glass and fixed him another drink. "You said it yourself, this is a big house, too big for me."

"The Porsche must have set you back a few quid."

"I've had the car for five months now, Harry, and you've seen it before. I bought it secondhand, and yes, it did cost me a few quid, but I'm a damned good insurance broker and I make a lot of money." He smiled as though faintly amused. "Honest to God, you make it sound as though I'm planning to leave you in the lurch."

"It wouldn't be the first time that thought has crossed my mind. I keep remembering how you were leading from the front when we had to get out of Quebec House in a hurry. Then Roach said something this afternoon which made me wonder just how many stormtroopers we've actually got in the NSLA and whether we really do have any influential sympathisers in Whitehall. It got so that I began to think you'd pulled the wool over our eyes about Silent Night."

Dukes had stumbled upon the truth but couldn't bring himself to believe it. He wanted Boden to convince him that he'd got it all wrong. The plea was there in his voice even though the overtones were menacing.

"If you feel like that, Harry, why did you come running to me?"

"Who else would I go to for help? In spite of all the doubts, I remembered you'd saved my hide once before and figured you'd do it again, not out of loyalty but because

I've had an armlock on you ever since Crossmaglen."

Dukes was half right, half wrong. It had been a mistaken sense of loyalty to his subordinates that had prompted him to suppress the facts when Harry's number-two had broken down and confessed to murdering an Irish farm labourer turned poacher who had stumbled across their observation post. In a guerrilla war, the enemy wasn't readily identifiable and they'd had to make a split second decision. The way Boden had seen it, you didn't sell your men short because they'd made a bad one. But Harry was right in one respect; from that day on, he'd been in a position to twist his arm.

"You've gone very quiet, Nick."

"I'm thinking."

"Well, I hope you've come up with a bright idea, we can certainly use one."

"I've got a place in La Rochelle we can use as a temporary bolthole until we see which way the wind is blowing."

"Brilliant," Dukes said heavily. "Thing is, I didn't have time to pack and I forgot to bring my passport."

"We can soon fix that."

"You and who else?"

"Our old friend, the Exercise Director." Boden finished his whisky and set the glass down on the drinks cabinet. "One of those non-existent sympathisers in Whitehall you were on about."

★   ★   ★

Harper stepped out of the lift into the dimly lit corridor, closed the trellis gate behind him and made his way towards the pool of light and the low murmur of voices coming from his PA's office. The desk officers and clerical staff had long since departed; only Mrs Swann, the MOD constable disguised as a uniformed commissionaire and Hollands remained. Although reasonably sure they weren't talking about him, Harper cleared his throat noisily before walking in.

"I'm sorry, Mrs Swann." He smiled apologetically, opening both arms like a priest welcoming his congregation. "I thought I'd be back long before this."

His PA smiled sympathetically. "You can't rush these things," she said. "How is Mrs Gattis?"

"Not too good, I'm afraid. The doctor's given her a couple of sleeping tablets and the neighbours are looking after the children and generally keeping an eye on things until her parents arrive from Glasgow."

"Good. Is there anything else I can do?"

"Nothing comes to mind at the moment." Harper eyed the buff-coloured folders arranged in two uneven piles on the top shelf of the security cabinet. "Where did all those come from?" he asked her.

"The Record Office at Hayes. Apparently Mr Gattis had asked to see the personal documents of an ex-soldier named Roach who came from the north of England, had some experience of mountaineering and was possibly a qualified electrician. Hayes played it safe and sent us the documents of every Roach they had who wasn't actually drawing an old age pension. Major Hollands suggested we should eliminate anyone who was over thirty-five; that's why there are two piles."

"And?"

"We're left with sixteen possible contenders," Hollands told him, "none of whom exactly fill the bill. There are no qualified electricians among the mountaineers, potholers or fell walkers, and all the electricians are interested in other sporting activities. If the police can give us the forenames or initials of the dead man, we'll begin to see a little daylight. Get Records to send the file on Harry Dukes with a view to examining the annual assessments on both men and we really could be in business."

"Because you think that at some stage in their respective careers they had the same reporting officer?"

"Yes. I have a hunch he'll be the man who passed himself off as Redmond."

"I'd go along with that. But there's nothing more we can do tonight, is there?"

"No."

"Then I suggest we allow Mrs Swann to get off home and finish our conversation in my office."

Hollands had got the bit between his teeth and could

see the way ahead. Telling him the Cabinet Office was determined to erect a few detour signs along the route was not a task Harper relished; despite the age difference, they were too much alike, endowed with the same single-mindedness that made them unwilling to compromise. Harper just wished he'd known the 'I' Corps officer long enough to take him into his confidence. As it was, he could only give him the official line and drop the odd hint.

"Have you been listening to the news?" Harper asked, waving him to a chair.

Hollands nodded. "The media would like us to believe that Roach was a member of the IRA."

"How do you feel about that?"

"I've never killed anyone before; if there had to be a first time, I wish it had been a PIRA gunman."

"Then your wish has been granted, for that happens to be the official line. You'll also be interested to learn that you're in charge of the army's Counter Terrorist Intelligence Team."

"I've never heard of such an organisation."

"Neither have I," Harper admitted, "but you've got to admit it sounds authentic. Incidentally, Sergeant Preece was one of your informants."

"What is this? A whitewash job?"

"It has also been suggested you should make yourself scarce for a day or two," Harper continued remorselessly.

"You'd like me to get out of London?"

"Would that be difficult?"

"No. As a matter of fact, I was planning to drive up to Yorkshire tomorrow. I'm supposed to be spending the day with my children."

"Make it a week."

"A week?" Hollands stared at him thoughtfully. "I've heard it said that's a long time in politics."

Harper smiled. "This could be our chance to find out if it's true."

Chapter XVII

Hollands turned left outside Charing Cross station and made his way towards Carfax House on the south side of Trafalgar Square near Admiralty Arch. If a week was a long time in politics, it was apparently an eternity in Harper's world. Five days after being told to make himself scarce, Harper had tracked him down through an irate Caroline to the Wheatsheaf Hotel six miles from the Leach household. "First you're only coming for the day, then you're staying a week and now, just as Richard and Judith had got used to having their father around, you're off back to London." Caroline had acted as though he were a free agent and had some say in the matter, but he hadn't attempted to contradict her. Five years of marriage had taught him that once Caroline had made up her mind about something, it was a waste of breath arguing with her.

The commissionaire on duty in the narrow entrance hall at Carfax House asked if he could be of any assistance, then promptly directed Hollands towards the solitary lift at the other end of the passageway when he told him that he had an appointment with Mr Jordan of Natural Resources. Jordan was the blanket cover name for the duty officer, Natural Resources the innocent label for the Department of Subversive Warfare. A television camera picked up Hollands as he walked towards the lift; when he alighted at the sixth floor, Drew was waiting for him, alerted by the commissionaire.

"I wasn't expecting to see you again quite so soon," Hollands told him. "When did you get out of hospital?"

"The day after I was admitted. They took a few X-rays, decided my skull hadn't been fractured, and allowed me to go."

Drew stopped by the PA's office, pointed to the end room and got an affirmative nod from Mrs Swann. He tapped on the door before opening it, then stepped to one side.

"You first," he said and waved Hollands into the office.

Harper was sitting behind a remarkably neat and uncluttered desk. All three trays, in, out, and pending, were empty; the pen and ink stand was positioned at the centre point in front of a large unstained blotting pad. The buff and green coloured folders stacked one on top of the other in the middle of the desk looked out of place. Opening the buff-coloured one, Harper removed a military identity card and pushed it across the desk.

"Do you recognise this man?" he asked.

Boden, Nicholas Spencer. Hair fair, eyes grey, height five foot eight, weight one sixty-two pounds. The description made little impact but the snapshot in the top right-hand corner held him mesmerised.

"That's Redmond," Hollands said finally.

"You're sure?"

"I'm not likely to forget his face in a hurry. How did you trace him?"

"The way you suggested – by examining the personal files of Roach and Dukes to see if there was a connecting link."

"So when are you going to pick him up?"

"That rather depends on Drew and how quickly he can get Boden's address from the Department of Health and Social Security at Newcastle-upon-Tyne. Until you identified him, we weren't even sure we'd got the right man."

"I'd better get cracking," Drew said.

"You certainly had," Harper told him.

The ID card told its own story; had Boden still been on the active list, it wouldn't have been lodged with his personal file.

"When did he leave the army?" Hollands asked.

"Three and a half years ago. The only address he ever gave the Officers Documentation Office at Stanmore was care of 'F' Section, Lloyds Bank Limited, Cox's and King's Branch, 6 Pall Mall, London. Boden told the army that he'd got a job with the UNO Aid Commission to Ecuador and would write and let them know his permanent address as soon as he was settled, but of course he never did."

"Looks as though he was trying to disappear."

"That's not as easy as it sounds," Harper said. "Unless you're prepared to live the life of a vagrant, you can't remain completely anonymous. If the Inland Revenue doesn't catch up with you, the Department of Health and Social Security certainly will."

"Is there anything of interest in Boden's security file?" Hollands asked.

"Have a look for yourself."

The minute sheets inside the front cover were a condensed summary of the whole file and served as an index to the more important enclosures. Approximately six months before Boden had applied to retire prematurely, the wheels had been set in motion to have him positively vetted for a Grade 3 staff job in Headquarters Northern Army Group. Nothing had come of it because PV had been denied on two counts. One of his previous superior officers had gone on record stating that he believed Boden had made a number of fraudulent travel claims but had been unable to prove it, while another had stated that he had a total inability to recognise a moral principle, never mind the strength of character to abide by one. During the subject interview, Boden had solemnly assured the investigating officer that, while not inexperienced, he had never made anyone pregnant or had an affair with a married woman. Photocopies of enclosures on the security files of a major in the Ordnance Corps and a junior NCO in the Women's Royal Army Corps had cast more than a shadow of doubt on his statement. The WRAC lance corporal had alleged that a Para lieutenant called Nick had refused to pay for an abortion after he'd made her pregnant, and the major's wife had written a spiteful letter to Boden's commanding officer describing in graphic detail just where, when and how they'd fornicated. No disciplinary action had been taken against Boden; the WRAC girl had been widely regarded as the garrison bicycle and the major's wife was a highly neurotic woman who'd confessed to having an extra-marital affair on a previous occasion and was receiving psychiatric treatment.

"Dishonest, unscrupulous and a proven liar." Hollands closed the file and placed it on the desk. "You certainly wouldn't allow a man like that to have constant access to

Top Secret material, but as far as we're concerned, the investigation doesn't tell us what makes him tick."

"Why should it? The people who conducted the inquiry uncovered a number of adverse character traits which were sufficiently damaging to convince them that Boden would be an unacceptable security risk. They didn't need to dig any deeper, nor did they have any reason to."

"And shortly after they'd completed their investigation, Boden resigned his commission." Hollands smiled lop-sidedly. "I wonder if someone told him he hadn't made the grade?"

"I think it's more likely he was told there was no future for him in the army. I suspect the fraudulent travel claims were only the tip of the iceberg, and that his commanding officer knew he had sticky fingers but couldn't prove it."

"Are you saying that Boden's just a small-time crook and that there was no political motive behind Silent Night? He planned and led the assault on Quebec House because money talks and someone had made him an offer he couldn't refuse?"

"Something like that."

"What about Dukes and Roach?" Hollands demanded angrily. "Were they only in it for the money too?"

"We know Dukes wasn't; we have Preece's word for that and his testimony was pretty convincing. I think we can assume Roach was a genuine one hundred per cent bigot like the other two." Harper shrugged his shoulders. "Of course, it's possible that Boden shared their prejudices at some stage, but first and foremost he's an opportunist with an eye to the main chance. That's why he was prepared to double-cross them."

"How?"

"The man who broke into the MIDAS facility expunged a considerable amount of ultra-sensitive data on the Soviet Armed Forces." Harper picked up both files and deposited them in the out-tray. "Somehow, I don't see Dukes and Roach offering their services to the Kremlin."

"I'm with you there."

"What complicates matters even more is the fact that the information they sabotaged was supplied by the Americans."

"That could prove embarrassing," Hollands said quietly.

"Yes, I'm glad you understand why this affair must be handled discreetly."

Discreetly: the adverb of discreet, meaning judicious, prudent, circumspect, not speaking out at an inopportune moment. After the contact in the Department of Health and Social Security had come across with Boden's address, it seemed to Hollands that at least one other definition had escaped the Concise Oxford Dictionary. As defined in Whitehall, it meant Harper had to brief the Cabinet Office and seek their approval before he could act on the information. It then took him the rest of the morning to obtain the necessary search warrant and arrange for Special Branch and the local police to be present when they swooped on the house in Richmond.

"One has to observe the legal niceties occasionally," Harper told him, dredging up a familiar-sounding explanation.

*　　*　　*

The legal niceties produced an over-reaction by the uniformed branch of 'W' District the like of which had not been seen before by the residents of Old Deer Park Avenue. The two patrol cars and the transit van parked outside the entrance to number 36 were merely the overflow from the small mechanised army jammed nose to tail inside the gravel driveway. The house itself was ringed by an inner cordon of police constables who, if they weren't actually standing shoulder to shoulder, were practically within touching distance of one another. An Alsatian sniffer dog and his handler were rummaging about inside the garage, their joint efforts supervised by a youngish-looking inspector. There was, of course, no sign of Boden.

"Very impressive." Harper cast a professional eye over the cordon and turned to Marsh. "When are we expecting the Queen?"

"You're right," Marsh said irritably, "this is bloody ridiculous. I'll have a word with Boy Blue and tell him he can stand most of his people down."

"It would be helpful if they interviewed the neighbours,"

Harper said. "I'd like to know who saw Boden last and when."

"Anything else?"

"Yes – the press photographer who snapped me as I was getting out of the car."

"Don't worry, Cedric," Marsh told him. "Your picture won't appear in the newspapers."

The back door of the house was bolted top and bottom and there were Chubb locks on all the windows, but they were only a minor obstacle. One of the Special Branch men found an old tyre lever in the garage and went to work on the glass. By the time he'd finished hammering the pane, a hippo could have passed through the yawning hole.

Boden hadn't left in a panic. From the state of the wardrobe and chest of drawers in the master bedroom, it looked as though he'd simply packed what he needed into a suitcase and had then calmly walked out of the house. Downstairs in the living room, they found the pigeon holes of the drop-leaf writing desk crammed with receipted invoices, bank statements, insurance policies and old cheque-book stubs, none of which could tell them anything they didn't already know about Boden.

"I don't believe any man can lead a totally anonymous life." Harper swept a wad of bank statements on to the floor in a rare gesture of petulance. "Everyone keeps something – old letters, newspaper cuttings, snapshots and the like."

"And Boden isn't an exception," Hollands said. "His friends just came in and cleaned the place up after he'd gone."

"His friend, Dutch. There is only one, and I doubt if he had to do any tidying up. When we eventually catch up with him, I think we'll find that Boden had been getting ready to disappear for quite some time. Perhaps even before he broke into Quebec House."

"Oh yes, I keep forgetting – he did it for the money, didn't he?"

"There's enough evidence in his security file to suggest he did."

"All right," Hollands said, "if that's the case, who hired him?"

"The KGB."

"The KGB? Well, why not? Everyone knows they're a very philanthropic organisation. Some nonentity they've never heard of gets in touch with them and says, 'Look, I've had this great idea' and after they've listened to his scheme, they give him their blessing and a pot of gold to go with it."

"Of course they didn't," Harper said patiently. "And Boden wasn't exactly a nonentity."

"What?"

"I ran a security check on him before I showed you his military ID card. The Security Service opened a dossier on Boden some eight months after he resigned his commission. They have him listed as a regional organiser for the National Front. According to their source, he broke with the Party in May last year because he didn't see eye to eye with the leadership."

Hollands stared at Harper incredulously. "Let's get this straight," he said eventually. "Are you implying that someone in the Security Service acted as a go-between for the KGB and hired Boden to break into Quebec House?"

"It's the only explanation that makes sense to me." Harper raised a hand to silence him before he had a chance to open his mouth. "And don't ask me who the broker is because I don't know. He could be one of the current or previous desk officers in 'K' Section or someone who could go through their card index on subversives and call for a particular file without arousing suspicion. This same man would also have a working relationship with 22 SAS. I need hardly add that Boden will certainly know him by sight."

"Find Boden and he'll give you the broker?"

Harper nodded. "That's the conventional approach."

"The one we've already started on, Major." Marsh lit a panatella cigar, aimed the spent match at the empty grate and managed to drop it on the carpet. "The Plods will get the description and make of his car from the neighbours and pass it to the vehicle licensing people at Swansea. They will then go through their sort sequences until they come up with the registration number."

And once they had the number, they would circulate it to every other force in the UK. That was standard police procedure, patient, unspectacular but very thorough.

"And who knows what else we'll learn about Boden after we've traced the cleaning woman and had a little chat with her."

"Assuming he employed a daily help."

"Take a good look at this place, Major. You ever met a bachelor who could keep a house looking so neat and tidy?"

Marsh had a point, but there was another line of inquiry he hadn't mentioned yet. "What about Lorraine Dukes and Janice Preece?"

"We've got a couple of very hard young women there," Marsh told him. "Mrs Preece shed a few tears when we told her that her husband had bought it but they were the crocodile kind. Those two sisters believe in looking after number one; tell them it's in their interest to keep their mouths shut and suddenly they're deaf and dumb. How else do you suppose we got away with that cock-and-bull story about the Provisional IRA when you had that shoot-out in Kilburn?"

Marsh had neatly side-stepped the question, showing an adroitness few politicians could equal, but Hollands wasn't going to let him get away with that. "But are you going to see them again?" he persisted.

"I'm going to ask them what they know about Boden." Marsh moved a pace nearer the hearth and flicked his cigar ash into the grate. "Trouble is, they may be tempted to invent a few facts just to keep us sweet."

His tone of voice said it all. Special Branch were merely going through the motions because the Cabinet Office had intimated they wouldn't be too upset if the police were unable to find Boden.

"Then there's the unconventional approach," Harper said quietly, "the artificially stimulated chain reaction."

"The what?"

"Moscow planted a delayed-action bomb when they hired Boden to sabotage the MIDAS facility. Unless it's disarmed in time, there won't be much left of the SIS, and the exchange of information between ourselves and the US Intelligence Agencies will come to a grinding halt. Colonel Whyte doesn't know it, but she is the fuse which has been pre-set to detonate the bomb. I'd like you to render the device harmless by a controlled explosion."

Drew and Marsh appeared to understand the allusion, but it didn't make any sense to Hollands. "Do you mind explaining that again in plain English?" he said.

"In plain English, I'd like you to ask Colonel Whyte what she was doing between two and four thirty on Christmas Eve."

Christmas Eve, the office party. Hollands recalled that he'd slipped away early to make a private phone call and Lindsey had stopped by his office some time later to tell him she was going out. "Colonel Whyte wanted something to read," he said slowly, "and asked if I'd listen out for the phone in the duty officer's room while she bought herself a paperback."

"Mr Edwards tells a different story; he reckons she'd arranged to meet Maureen Akehurst."

"You don't want to believe that garbage."

"Who said I did?"

"Then why are you sending me to Rome?"

"That's easy," said Harper. "I'm going to force the broker out into the open with a few well-chosen lies in the right quarter."

Hollands waited expectantly, confident there was more to come but as the silence lengthened, it became evident the old need-to-know principle was in vogue. "Do you have Lindsey's address in Rome?" he asked after a while. "Or is that a state secret too?"

"Of course it isn't. She has an apartment at 279 Via Appia Nuova."

"Thanks."

"What for? I'm setting you up as a live target."

"I guess I'll have to watch my back," Hollands said ruefully.

"No," Drew told him, "I'll be doing that."

Hollands turned slowly about and eyed the blond man

appraisingly. "Then I've got nothing to worry about, have I?"

* * *

Mikhail Semenovich Putilin was thirty-seven and though a native of Leningrad, was regarded by his near neighbours in Putney as a well-mannered, thoroughly nice little man. An employee of the Narodny Bank in King William Street, he had spent just over eight years in London which he and his wife, Ludmilla, had come to regard as their second home, or so he liked to tell everyone.

It was chance remarks like these that had led Special Branch and the Security Service to give him a grey card halfway through his second tour in August '79. Apart from the fact that Putilin had done nothing to arouse their suspicions during those early years when he'd been under constant surveillance, there had been other favourable indicators. In the first place, unlike the staffs of the Trade Delegation and the Soviet Embassy, he was not required to live inside the Russian enclave at Highgate, a sign of his lowly status which therefore made him relatively harmless. Secondly, his wife was a Latvian from Riga, and the Security Service was very aware that there was no love lost between the Balts and the Russians.

The grey card was not, however, the equivalent of a clean bill of health; it merely signified that the authorities were reasonably sure Putilin was not a member of either the KGB or the GRU, the Military Intelligence Directorate of the Soviet Armed Forces. In practical terms this meant that although the Security Service continued to monitor all conversations on his private telephone, he was no longer kept under physical surveillance.

But MI5's counter espionage section had got it wrong. Mikhail Semenovich Putilin was in fact a junior lieutenant in the KGB. Despite his rank and the long and costly training he'd received, he was just a minor piece on this particular chessboard and his role was to act as a cut-out between the case officer and the source. Akin to a sacrificial pawn, it was accepted that he would be the one who would be declared persona non grata by the Foreign and

Commonwealth Office if anything went wrong and the source was blown. In effect, he existed to protect the more important chess pieces; hence he was the logical choice to make contact with the Englishman.

The Englishman was different and therefore dangerous. Moles were invariably hand-reared and carefully nurtured over the years while they burrowed in deep; they did not come forward out of the blue to offer their services as the Englishman had done. Suspecting a trick, the KGB Resident had instructed Putilin to act as the front man and had then sat back to await developments. Contrary to his expectations, events had shown that the Englishman was genuine and not the agent provocateur he'd imagined him to be. Codenamed Lake, he was the most valuable acquisition since Philby and was looked upon as a future Director General of the Security Service. Lake was in fact the man who had conceived, planned and directed Exercise Silent Night.

Yesterday morning Putilin had left a visiting card at one of the dead letter boxes he used to communicate with Lake. The visiting card, a tiny blue chalkmark on the window box of a newsagents, had told the Englishman he was required to phone a certain public call box in Newport Place between 1308 and 1312 hours that same day. In accordance with standard operating procedures, Putilin had answered the phone call and had arranged to meet Lake the following evening at 1930 hours in the lounge bar of the Red Lion in Lewisham.

As was his customary practice, Putilin got to the RV first; as was invariably the case, the Englishman arrived dead on time. Making straight for the bar, he ordered a couple of small beers and carried them over to the table where Putilin was sitting.

Lake was in his mid thirties, a rather plump, dark-haired man with an amiable disposition. Men liked him for his bubbling enthusiasm, jovial manner and irrepressible good humour; most women felt a strong urge to hug him like a soft cuddly toy.

"So how are things with you?" he asked Putilin cheerfully.

"Not so good." Putilin toyed with his drink, wondered how he was going to tell the Englishman in veiled speech that Moscow was getting impatient. "Head Office think they should be seeing a better return for their money," he said eventually. "After all, two hundred and ten thousand pounds is a lot of money and they haven't had much in the way of a dividend yet."

"Really?" Lake seemed genuinely astonished. "I thought their accountant, Mr Josef Kardar, had given them a preliminary report?"

"That was over four months ago and there has been no movement since then. The market has remained static."

"Where's the harm in that?" Lake smiled easily. "The longer the wait, the bigger the dividend."

"Head Office wants to see some action now," Putilin said.

"Don't we all, but I don't know what I can do about it."

"Now there we have a very big difference of opinion. Head Office is convinced you can send the shares tumbling on Wall Street."

"They must be out of their tiny minds," Lake said affably.

"You've got a week in which to make it happen." Putilin racked his brains for a banking metaphor that would leave the Englishman in no doubt where he stood with Moscow, then said, "If the market continues to be quiet, Head Office is going to unload their stock."

"You mean they're actually planning to dump me?" Lake said and laughed incredulously.

"It's one way of making a quick killing."

"Your people are being very short-sighted and not a little stupid. Why kill the goose that can lay golden eggs?" Lake leaned forward over the table and tapped his chest. "I'm the best long-term investment they've ever had, Michael. Maybe you'd better remind them of that before it all ends in tears."

The smile was still there on the Englishman's lips but Putilin thought some of his old bounce and confidence was missing.

Chapter XVIII

The study centre was sandwiched between an antique bookshop and a small picture gallery in Bloomfield Place off New Bond Street. The number above the entrance had been erased, which meant that officers from other government departments who'd been detailed to attend one of the periodic instructional courses run by the Security Service often experienced some difficulty in finding the place. Harper also walked past it before he realised the narrow doorway was not the side entrance to the antique bookshop. Retracing his steps, he pushed open the door, walked inside and told the young woman behind the reception desk that he had an appointment to see Mr Lawrence, the chief instructor.

Neil Lawrence was thirty-four and a rising star. A graduate of New College, Oxford where he had read Politics, Philosophy and Economics, he had made a name for himself while still at university. Entry into the Security Service was usually by invitation; Lawrence had applied to join MI5 towards the end of his second year and had been accepted even before the results of his finals had been known. He had dark curly hair, a round face that was already beginning to acquire a double chin and an infectious smile. His youthful appearance and ebullient manner were, however, deceptive. Those who, on first acquaintance, made the mistake of thinking him immature and treated him like an overgrown schoolboy, rapidly discovered that he had a nimble brain and a turn of phrase that could make them look extremely foolish.

Lawrence had been through the mill and had received a thorough grounding in every aspect of the trade. After six months' basic training, he had gone to the vetting section, then moved to the Irish Desk. His next job had been with 'K' Section where he had been responsible for targeting potential subversives, following which he had been seconded to the Secret Intelligence Service to work in protective security. Though less demanding than his previous appointments, his current post as chief instructor and deputy commandant of the training school was regarded as a very important rung on the promotion ladder. It was a job that left the incumbent with plenty of spare capacity; consequently, Lawrence had been the logical choice to lead the inquiry into Silent Night.

"We've met before," Harper reminded him as they shook hands. "About ten months ago at the seminar on international terrorism."

"I remember the occasion well," Lawrence said warmly. "We shared the same table at lunch." He smiled as though recalling a pleasant memory, then said, "It's good to see you again, Cedric."

"No hard feelings then?"

"About the investigation?" Lawrence shook his head. "Someone needed to look at the evidence with a fresh eye. We started off with the preconceived idea that Quebec House had been targeted by the IRA and we set out to prove it. Truth is, we never dreamed a bunch of neo-Nazis would have the organisation or the know-how to pull it off. As a matter of fact, I still find it hard to believe."

"You're not the only one," said Harper, "which is why I wanted to pick your brains. Boden may have been a regional organiser for the National Front, but he was bought and paid for by the KGB."

"Can you prove it?" Lawrence asked.

"We've been looking at his finances. All Boden inherited from his parents was a large house in Richmond and a taste for a life-style way above the income he made as an insurance broker. Until last September, he was running an overdraft, then suddenly his current account is in the black. That's one side of the coin; when you look at the sort of damage done to the MIDAS computer, it's evident that Silent Night was a KGB operation. Furthermore, they're the only organisation who were able to provide Boden with the back-up he needed."

"You're alluding to the help he obviously received from an unknown number of people on the inside?"

"Yes."

"I doubt if he got it from Colonel Whyte, Major Hollands or Mr Edwards."

"You surprise me," Harper murmured. "Reading the report, I got the impression that your investigators had gone out of their way to prove they were all vulnerable to pressure."

There was a long pause while Lawrence mulled it over. In the ensuing silence, the background rumble of the traffic in New Bond Street was clearly audible.

"You'd have done the same in my place, Cedric," he said eventually. "We were faced with a major security incident and we had to satisfy ourselves that Edwards, Hollands and Whyte were as pure as the driven snow. So we dug a lot deeper than is usually the case when we're asked to vet a civil servant or a member of the armed forces. Take Edwards for example; we went to the roots of his family tree and found that a second cousin on his wife's side was doing ten years in the Maze for the attempted murder of an RUC inspector."

The Security Service had also discovered that his American son-in-law was a regular contributor to Noraid. If Silent Night had been an IRA operation as had been presupposed, then the alien connections provided grounds for thinking the Provos had obtained most of their information from Edwards. Lawrence, however, maintained that he had never been entirely convinced of this.

"Edwards only had a few months to do, Cedric. No one goes out on a limb when they are that close to an index-linked pension."

"And Hollands?"

"He may be hard up at the moment, but his bank manager evidently thinks he's a good risk and is prepared to allow him a sizeable overdraft." Lawrence busied himself with the paperknife on the desk, moving it from the right side of the blotting pad to the left before finally placing it near the telephone. "This may sound a little cynical, but whenever I come across a vetting file which is completely unblemished, I can't help thinking someone did a very sloppy job."

"Everyone's got something to hide?" Harper suggested.

"I wouldn't go as far as to say that, Cedric, but you can always find the odd wart if you look hard enough." He raised his eyes and gazed at him speculatively. "However, I don't think you came here to discuss the vetting system with me?"

"No, you're absolutely right." Harper cleared his throat. "As a matter of fact, my people have come up with a very interesting theory. Far from being a slick operation, they think Silent Night was a monumental cock-up."

"There was a time when I thought so too, Cedric, but then we had this memo from the Cabinet Office last Friday asking us to confirm that we hold a back-up for every file on the MIDAS computer. That tells me the operation must have been successful."

"Oh no," Harper said emphatically. "It failed because the opposition didn't have access to the departmental roster and therefore had no way of knowing that an American officer would be on duty the night Boden took over the JIB. The fact that Colonel Whyte had been an eye-witness concentrated everyone's minds wonderfully. Even before your investigation had got under way, she had already been brainwashed into accepting it as an IRA operation. That was the start point of the greatest security clamp-down since D Day, and you can bet the Ministry of Defence moved heaven and earth to ease her out of the JIB before any ugly rumours reached her ears. Nothing could have been more ironic; the KGB wanted the Americans to catch us out in a massive cover-up but we were too quick off the mark and a damned sight too thorough. Not a whisper got out and there was nothing their mole could do about it unless he was prepared to sacrifice himself."

"Yes, Cedric, it is an interesting theory. Who thought that up?"

"Major Hollands."

"A bright young man."

"Yes, he is," Harper agreed cheerfully, "which is why I'm sending him to Rome to question Lindsey Whyte."

"What about?"

"The lesbian relationship Edwards says she had with Maureen Akehurst. He'll need to be very diplomatic because we've been told not to go near Colonel Whyte and there'll be hell to pay if she makes an official complaint."

"I'm glad I'm not in your shoes, Cedric," Lawrence said drily.

"Well, it's too late for regrets now; Hollands is already on his way to Rome. Still, I daresay I'll survive with a little help from my friends." Harper leaned forward in the chair, both elbows resting on his knees, a suitably grave expression on his face. "Boden may have been hired by the KGB but they didn't recruit him; he was selected on their behalf by a mole."

"So?"

"Well, according to the army's vetting unit, someone in MI5 has asked to see Boden's security file on three separate occasions since he resigned his commission." The lie Harper had rehearsed in private sounded utterly convincing even to his sceptical ears, and he delivered the punch line with considerable aplomb. "Naturally, I'd like to know the name of the man or woman who was moved to take such a profound interest in him."

"And you'd like me to make a few discreet inquiries?"

"You took the words right out of my mouth," Harper said blandly.

*　　*　　*

They travelled separately to Rome; Drew on a scheduled British Airways flight from Heathrow, Hollands on a Dan Air charter departing from Gatwick an hour and a half later. On arrival at Ciampino airport, Hollands took a cab to the Hotel Atlante on the Via Vitelleschi near St Peter's Square. He checked in, unpacked his things and spent the next hour reading the abridged version of the Berlitz guide and Falk street plan of Rome which he'd picked up at the airport. Then he called the nearest Hertz agency and got them to deliver a Fiat 127 to the hotel.

Harper had told him that Lindsey Whyte was now commanding a small but ultra-sensitive communications and security group charged with monitoring the wireless frequencies of Warsaw Pact Forces from the Black Sea to the Baltic. Answerable to the CIA and the Pentagon, the communications and security group was a mix of civilian and military specialists. The uniformed element, numbering less than a hundred officers and enlisted personnel, were responsible for manning an intercept station in the foothills of the Apennines on the outskirts of Rome. Divorced from the intelligence gatherers, the civilian linguists and special analysts operated from the US Cultural Exchange Office in the Via del Corso and the English Language bookshop on the Via della Vite. Lindsey Whyte worked irregular hours and divided her time between all three locations; that she never returned home much before eight was the only certain thing about her movements.

With plenty of time to kill, Hollands passed the early part of the afternoon quartering the city to familiarise himself with its geography. He did the whole tourist scene – the Vatican, St Peter's, the Colosseum, the Roman Forum, the Spanish Steps and the white marble monument of King Victor Emmanuel in the Piazza Venezia which looked like something off a wedding cake. He moved further afield, took in the Europa Viale District, the modern residential quarter which was to have housed the Roman World Exhibition in 1942, then drove slowly back to the hotel.

It was a pleasantly warm afternoon; the temperature was just touching seventy-one degrees Fahrenheit, visibility was good and the pollen count was tolerably low. Hollands was not suffering from travel weariness or the heat; on the contrary, he was wide awake, fully alert and vigilant. But although he looked hard and often, he failed to spot Drew following him. There was, however, a small package waiting for Hollands back at the hotel.

"Two advance copies of your latest novel with the compliments of your Italian publisher," the desk clerk told him. "The young lady who delivered the package said you were expecting them."

Hollands thanked him and took the parcel up to his room. About the same size as a box of twenty-five cigars, it felt a little too heavy for a couple of books, even supposing they were hardbacks, and he didn't recognise the spidery handwriting on the brown wrapping paper. Letter bombs came in all shapes and sizes but he couldn't see, feel or smell anything that was remotely suspicious. Still not entirely satisfied that the package was harmless, he took out his penknife, made a neat incision and like a surgeon removing a plaster cast, slowly pulled the wrapping paper apart.

The parcel contained two books. The first third of one novel was still intact but the rest, as well as most of the book underneath, had been hollowed out to provide a safe repository for a canvas hip holster and 9 mm Beretta automatic together with a spare clip of ammunition. Although he'd been told that the Department of Subversive Warfare would be seeking help from their Italian counterparts, Hollands just wished the Carabinieri had chosen a less theatrical way of delivering the hardware.

Chapter XIX

Boden left the bar in the Rue Thiers and walked towards the quayside. The flat he owned in La Rochelle was in the old quarter on the eastern side of the inner harbour near the fortified ramparts that had protected the town from a seaborne invasion ever since the seventeenth century. From the spacious living room, he had an unrestricted view of the marina on the far side of the basin, where his own converted ketch was moored.

The flat and the boat were comparatively recent acquisitions financed in part by the down payment on Silent Night which he'd received from the man he knew as Lake. The balance of the purchase price had been funded by the Crédit Nationale by way of a million franc loan to a Mr George Davies, the alias Boden had used when he'd originally negotiated the whole deal. Had everything gone according to plan, the cover name would have enabled him to quit the NSLA and quietly disappear, but now it was doubtful if it would do more than buy him a little time. Sooner or later, Special Branch were bound to connect him with Dukes, and it was equally reasonable to assume they'd initiate a search request through Interpol headquarters at St Cloud. Once that had happened, every police force in Europe would be looking for them.

Boden let himself into the flat and strolled into the living room to find Dukes still sprawled in the armchair by the window where he'd left him an hour ago. The number of empty Stella Artois beer cans on the windowledge had, however, more than doubled in his absence and there were now a lot more cigarette stubs in the ashtray.

"Hello, Nick." Dukes focussed on the folded copy of the *Daily Telegraph* under Boden's left arm. "What are they saying about us?"

"Nothing. We don't even rate a mention in the Stop Press."

"Yeah?" Dukes eyed him suspiciously.

"Yeah." Boden tossed the newspaper into his lap. "Take a look for yourself."

He went on through to the kitchen, filled the electric kettle under the tap and plugged it in; then he measured two teaspoonfuls of Nescafé into a mug. Dukes was beginning to grate on him, setting his teeth on edge every time he opened his mouth to voice yet another doubt. His fear was contagious, and that was stupid because they still had a lot going for them. Harry had a new identity and the papers to prove it, thanks to Lake. Immigration had barely glanced at his passport when they'd boarded the Sealink ferry at Dover and the French authorities at Calais would have been hard pressed to show less interest. As for the Porsche, Scotland Yard would get the registration number from Swansea without too much difficulty and eventually they would discover that he had taken the car abroad, but it could be weeks before the Police Judiciaire in Paris traced the vehicle to the Rue de la Chine in the Twentieth Arrondissement where he'd reluctantly abandoned it.

"How much longer are we going to stay cooped up in this hole, Nick?"

Boden took a deep breath, held it as long as he could, then slowly exhaled, dissipating his anger in the process. "I'm about to have a cup of coffee," he said in a level voice. "You want to join me?"

"No thanks. All I want is a few straight answers."

"What would be the point of hiding anything from you? We're in this together, aren't we?" Boden unplugged the kettle, filled the mug with boiling water and added a drop of cream. "Look. We've got to stay put until I hear from Lake that he has made all the necessary arrangements. There aren't too many places we can run to, Harry. Bolivia, Chile, Peru and South Africa; they're about the only countries where we'd be reasonably safe, and you just can't walk into a travel agency and ask to be booked on to the next flight to Johannesburg or wherever. It takes time and money to organise an escape route."

"Yeah, well I guess you should know; you must have had plenty of practice at it."

"Why don't you come right out with it, Harry?" Boden said, raising his voice. "I was planning to double-cross you and the others all along. Isn't that what you're accusing me of?"

"If the cap fits," Dukes said woodenly.

"The hell it does! Preece was the one who sold us out and we both know who recruited him, don't we?"

"So everything's down to Gary and I've you to thank for saving my hide, is that it?"

"Yes," Boden said, then had a sudden flash of inspiration and hastily back-pedalled. "No." He shook his head. "No, that isn't quite true. It's Lake you should thank; I gave him the facts and he did the rest. And I don't just mean the blank passport he obtained for you. I'm talking about the artist's impression of the motorcyclist the police were anxious to question which appeared in all the UK newspapers twenty-four hours after we'd arrived in France. Who do you suppose was responsible for that misleading piece of information?"

"The eye-witnesses who saw me in Kilburn High Road. Lake had nothing to do with that."

"Preece blew the whistle on you."

"So what? There were no snapshots of me at home. I burnt the family album like you told me to; it was one of the points you covered at the briefing for Silent Night."

"You've overlooked something," Boden said forcefully. "Remember the military identity card you handed in when you left the army? It carried your photograph, and the police could have got it from your personal documents only Lake got in first, called for the file and destroyed the ID card. And do you know why he was able to do that without arousing suspicion? Because he's a desk officer in MI5, that's why."

He had allowed his fertile imagination to run riot but it was logical enough to sound like the truth and he could tell Dukes believed him. Then the telephone rang and both men flinched as though a gun shot had broken the tense silence.

"I'll get it," Boden told him. "Ten to one it's a wrong number."

But it wasn't, and he found himself listening to a familiar voice. Their conversation was brief and largely one-sided, a virtual repeat of the one he'd had on Christmas Eve except that, on this occasion, it was Boden who wasn't allowed to get a word in edgeways.

"That was Lake," he said, and reluctantly turned about to face Dukes who'd come up behind him.

"Yeah? What did he want?"

"Everything's fixed. We're on our way to South Africa."

"Has anyone told Lorraine?"

"Not yet," Boden lied, "but don't worry, she'll join you out there."

"Good." Dukes nodded several times, then said, "We're going to have to pay a price for it though, aren't we?"

"You don't get anything for free in this world, Harry."

"So tell me the worst."

"There are a couple of people we have to take care of in Rome."

"Is that all?" Dukes grinned. "For a moment I thought it was going to cost me an arm and a leg."

*   *   *

Hollands glanced at the quartz clock in the dashboard, saw that it was almost a quarter to eight and instinctively switched his gaze to the apartment house on the opposite side of the road from where he was parked in the Via Appia Nuova. Lindsey had one of the flats on the second floor overlooking the street and although he was pretty sure he hadn't missed her, it was still something of a relief to see that no lights were showing in the end rooms to the right of the entrance.

He knew the make, colour and registration number of her car and the locations of her various offices. The English Language bookshop, the US Cultural Exchange Office or the wireless intercept station outside Rome; it didn't matter where she had been working, in the end all the roads led to the Via Appia Nuova and she would park her car in one of the bays fronting the apartment house. It certainly didn't occur to him that Lindsey would arrive by public transport and from the wrong direction on a bus heading into town.

The bus stop was only some fifty yards from the apartment house and she had almost reached the front entrance before he spotted her. Reacting swiftly, Hollands scrambled out of the Fiat, locked the offside door and crossed the road. He came up behind her, his footsteps muffled by the rubber-soled shoes he was wearing so that she wasn't aware of his presence until he cleared his throat noisily; then she almost jumped out of her skin.

"Hullo, Lindsey," he said, smiling.

"Dutch." She stared at him dumbfounded, her eyebrows raised in astonishment. "This is a hell of a surprise," she said breathlessly. "What on earth are you doing in Rome?"

"Part business, part pleasure; both concern you."

"That's a pretty smooth line."

"It happens to be true." He glanced up and down the street but there was no sign of Drew. "May I come in?" he asked. "There are one or two questions I have to ask you about Silent Night."

"Are you in trouble, Dutch?"

"We both are," Hollands told her.

Lindsey took the news calmly. Producing a key from her handbag, she opened the street door and walked inside.

"My apartment is on the second floor," she said. "But I guess you already know that."

The architect who'd designed the building had evidently decided it wouldn't be grand enough to warrant a lift and had settled for a staircase instead. There were two apartments on each landing, each consisting of two bedrooms, a bathroom, separate WC, a kitchen and a lounge-diner. The kitchen was at the back of the building where there was an external fire escape to a narrow alleyway. Lindsey directed him into the lounge-diner, snapped on the lights and drew the curtains, then made straight for the bar in the near corner facing the windows.

"I reckon I deserve a stiff drink," she said. "It's been one of those days. You want to join me? I'm going to fix myself a very dry martini but I can offer you Scotch, gin or brandy."

"Scotch would be fine, thank you."

"On the rocks, soda or water?"

"I'll try it on the rocks," he said. "It's been a warm day."

Hollands glanced round the room while Lindsey went out into the kitchen to fetch some ice. The furniture was modern, armchairs and sofa in beige-coloured vinyl, the seats low to the ground, the arms wide and flat. The dining table and chairs in the alcove were simulated maple and he counted four pictures hung at strategic points, seemingly to relieve the bare walls. There were no ornaments or other items of bric-à-brac that would have given the apartment a less sterile, more lived-in appearance.

"One of these days I'll have to get around to unpacking the rest of my things," Lindsey said, as though reading his thoughts. "Only the pictures belong to me, everything else came with the apartment." She half-filled a tumbler with crushed ice, topped it up with whisky and waved him to a chair. "So how's the world treating you, Dutch?"

"Not too bad."

"Does that mean you and Caroline have patched up your differences over the children?"

"There's still a tug of war going on. I drove up to Yorkshire to see Judith and Richard on Thursday of last week. Caroline had said it was the only time I'd be able to see the children during the school holidays because she and Roger had rented a villa in Juan-les-Pins over Easter. When I got there, I discovered they weren't going away until the end of this week."

"How did she explain that away?"

"She said she must have got the dates mixed up." Hollands raised his glass, looked at the amber-coloured fluid. Lindsey had taken over and was deliberately stalling him. He was the last person she had expected to see in Rome and she needed to prepare her defences. "They got rid of me too," he said, abruptly changing the topic of conversation.

"What?"

"I'm no longer with the JIB. You, me and Edwards . . ." He smiled lopsidedly. "We all failed the Persil test so they moved us on."

"I don't know what you're talking about." Her voice was calm and just a touch contemptuous.

"You told the MI5 people I was in a financial bind and was up to my eyes in debt."

"No, I didn't. I said I had reason to believe you were hard up. There's a subtle difference."

"Yes? Where did you get your information from? My bank manager?" Hollands made a face and deliberately injected a note of anger. "I'd like to know what the hell my financial affairs had to do with you. It was none of your business."

"We were working in a highly sensitive department, I was your superior officer and it was my job to know these things. I'm sorry if that sounds pompous but it happens to be true. And just for the record, I didn't have to go behind your back to get my information; there were lots of little things you said which gave me the impression you had to watch every penny."

Lindsey's voice was still matter-of-fact but he thought it significant that she had stopped using his nickname.

"Even so, I bet you couldn't wait to tell MI5," he said, needling her.

"It was a full-scale security inquiry and they asked me what I knew about your life style. I'm sorry if they gave you a hard time but there was no way I could hold anything back."

"Did they give you a hard time over Maureen Ake-hurst."

"No, why should they?"

"You two are supposed to have been lovers." Hollands shrugged. "At least, that's the story Edwards gave the inquiry."

"I think I would enjoy strangling that man."

Hollands believed her. But there were no signs of embarrassment, only a cold hard look of implacable hostility.

"For what it's worth," he told her, "I thought the little bastard was lying too."

"Thanks a lot," Lindsey said acidly. "You can't begin to guess how much that means to me."

"It doesn't alter the fact that Maureen has lesbian tendencies, does it?"

"No."

"You want to tell me about her?" he invited.

Lindsey hesitated, then grimaced wryly. "Why not? I've nothing to hide."

Her story was very similar to the one Edwards had given the Security Service. She had asked Maureen Akehurst to work late on several occasions, and once, when they'd stayed on at the office until eight, Lindsey had taken her out to dinner, but it had been more of a snack meal than the à la carte at the Savoy Grill. It had been shortly after this so-called dinner date that Maureen had begun to make it obvious in lots of little ways that she was available.

"You never met her, did you?" Lindsey said.

"No, she'd left the JIB some months before I was posted in."

"She was a pretty little thing, a brunette with cornflower blue eyes and she kept giving me what Hollywood likes to call meaningful looks. I think she travelled both routes because I noticed she gave Ralph Ingersole the same kind of signals. Of course, proving someone's a lesbian is damned nearly impossible unless you catch them in bed with another woman and anyway, I was in an awkward position – American exchange officer, British civilian employee."

"I can see it might have led to a lot of unpleasantness," Hollands agreed.

"So I went to the Director and asked his advice, and he had a word with Lawrence, who's a friend of his, and Maureen was quietly transferred to a non-vetted post in Customs and Excise."

"Did Edwards know what was going on?" Hollands asked.

"I'm pretty sure he didn't; it was all done very discreetly." Lindsey frowned. "Maybe Lawrence dropped a few hints when he was questioning him."

"Anything's possible."

"If he thought it would stand him in good stead, Edwards wouldn't hesitate to tell his superiors what he thought they wanted to hear." Lindsey finished her dry martini and went over to the bar to pour herself another from the shaker. "I don't know though, perhaps I'm being unfair to the man; after all, what good would it have done him to suck up to Lawrence?"

Hollands remembered the ostentatious display of Top Secret files that had been lying on the table when Boden had interrogated him and thought the clerical officer had every reason to fawn on Lawrence. In all probability, Edwards had given Boden the combination to his safe and had been desperate to put the blame on someone else. Then suddenly it occurred to Hollands that perhaps Stanley had unwittingly done more than anyone else to wreck the whole concept of Silent Night. Lawrence had been forced to bring up the Akehurst episode because he had previous knowledge of the affair and had to cover himself in case the Director of the JIB decided to come clean about it. If Lawrence had mentioned the allegation to anyone else, he would have been met with a blank look of incomprehension and a potentially dangerous situation would have been quietly defused. Unfortunately for him, Edwards had used his imagination and had given him a fictitious but detailed account of a lesbian relationship between Maureen Akehurst and Lindsey Whyte. Lawrence had started something he'd been unable to control and, like it or not, he'd been forced to record Edwards' testimony because there had been no way he could have suppressed it without laying himself open to all kinds of accusations. And that unwanted piece of evidence had prompted the Director to act decisively; he had given Lindsey an outstanding report and had then eased her out of the JIB.

"An ominous silence," Lindsey said quietly. "I guess you think I've got it in for Edwards?"

"No, not at all. I was just wondering how to break the news that you could be in danger."

"I'm already aware of that. I was given a full security briefing on the threat posed by the Red Brigade the day I took up the Rome assignment. That's why I'm never in uniform and why I vary the route between this apartment and wherever I happen to be working. Tonight I left my car near the Ponte Lungo subway station and doubled back here on a bus."

"It's not the Red Brigade I'm worried about," Hollands

221

informed her. "You and I are deliberately being set up as a couple of clay pigeons."

"You're having me on, aren't you, Dutch?" The smile became hesitant, then died altogether. "No, I can see you're not." Lindsey finished her drink and set the empty glass down on a table. "Two questions," she said calmly. "Who wants to kill me and why?"

They had finally reached the crunch point and he stuck to the brief Harper had given him, fleshing out the cover story with a few half truths about Boden, Dukes and Roach to make it sound more authentic. He also succeeded in confusing her which was the whole idea.

"Let's see if I've got this straight," Lindsey said, after he'd finished. "Silent Night was definitely an IRA operation but there has been a new development. Your people believe the KGB has put a hit team on to me because they're aiming to make it look as though the British Government is engaged in a massive cover-up?"

"That's about the size of it."

"So what am I expected to do?"

"Nothing," said Hollands. "You carry on as usual and put your trust in the security forces. Our information is that the KGB will either make their move in the next forty-eight hours or not at all."

"I assume someone has briefed the US Defence Department?"

"I certainly hope so."

"I could wish for a more positive assurance," Lindsey said drily.

"I'm here to guarantee you live to a ripe old age."

"Keep it up, Dutch, you're a great comfort."

It was the second time in as many minutes that she had used his nickname. A thaw had set in and the cold front that had existed between them had melted away.

"It gets better." Hollands stood up and unbuttoned his jacket so that she could see the 9 mm Beretta in the hip holster, then went over to the nearest window and drew the curtain aside. "There's a whole army of Italian plainclothes men out there who've been detailed to protect you."

"You're right, it does get better." Lindsey crossed the

room and stood beside him, her left thigh almost touching his. "Only trouble is, I can't see a single one of them."

"They're out there."

"I'll take your word for it, Dutch."

Hollands released the curtain and turned to face her. The green silk dress she was wearing clung to her body like a second skin, emphasising every contour. In all the time they had served together in the JIB, he had never once made a pass at her, but now that Lindsey had ceased to be his superior officer, he no longer felt inhibited. Slipping an arm around her waist, he drew Lindsey close and kissed her long and hard.

"Hey," she gasped, and placed the palm of a restraining hand against his chest, but her protest was half-hearted and he didn't take it seriously.

*   *   *

Marsh shucked off his raincoat, hung it on the hook behind the door and went over to his desk. It had been one of those days when it had been uphill work all the way and it looked as though it was going to continue in much the same vein. The message the clerical assistant had scribbled on the memo pad was almost indecipherable, but he gathered Harper had been calling on and off all afternoon and could be contacted at his home in West Byfleet any time after eight.

When Harper answered the phone, Marsh asked him to switch on the secure speech facility and waited while he stooped down to check the black box on the floor of his study.

"I'm ready when you are," Harper told him eventually.

"I hope you've got a pencil and paper handy," said Marsh. "I've got a shopping list here as long as your arm."

"You can forget the Poles, the Czechs, the Bulgars and the rest of the satellites; I'm only interested in the Soviets."

Marsh thought of the hours he'd spent buttering up the engineer in British Telecom who was responsible to the Home Office for audio surveillance and was tempted to give Harper a piece of his mind, but only for a moment.

"Do you think that's wise, Cedric?" he said diplomatically. "I mean, this wouldn't be the first time the KGB has used another Intelligence service to do their dirty work."

"Silent Night was always a KGB operation and it happens to have gone wrong. I doubt if they would trust any of their little brothers to put it right."

"You know best, Cedric." Marsh cleared his throat. "My informant tells me MI5 are keeping tabs on a left-wing bookshop near King's Cross station. According to him, the owner receives some very odd phone calls and the people in Curzon Street think it could be a message centre."

"I'm not interested," Harper said curtly. "The man I'm after is a sleeper. If he did come to their notice, MI5 will have given him a grey card a long time ago. Furthermore, he'll be living outside the circle."

"What circle?"

"The Russian enclave at Highgate."

"I see." Marsh turned over several pages in his notebook, then said, "There is only one man in that category. His name is Mikhail Semenovich Putilin and he works for the Narodny Bank in King William Street."

"Then you'd better put him under close surveillance. From now on, I don't want him to break wind without my knowing about it."

"I'll have to clear it with the Security Service first."

"Why not give the Russian Embassy a call while you're at it?"

"You're asking me to go out on a limb putting this Russian under surveillance."

"Yes, I am."

"I hope you know what you're doing, Cedric."

"So do I," Harper said cheerfully and hung up on him.

Chapter XX

Hollands tapped on the door, heard a grunt that sounded like an invitation to come in, and walked into the bedroom. Still half asleep, Lindsey was lying on her stomach, her face turned towards the window, both arms hugging the pillow.

He cleared his throat noisily, then said, "I thought you'd like a cup of coffee."

Lindsey opened both eyes and raised her head just high enough to peer at the alarm clock on the bedside table. "What time do you make it?" she asked.

"Seven fifteen."

"Oh God, I'm usually in the office by seven thirty." She rolled over on to her back, then sat bolt upright, massaging her temples. "I think my head is trying to tell me I had one drink too many last night."

"Have you any aspirin?"

"There should be a pack in my handbag. Failing that, I know there's a bottle in the bathroom cabinet."

Hollands left the mug of coffee on the bedside table, fetched the handbag from the chair where Lindsey had dropped it, and gave it to her. The duvet had slipped down to reveal her naked breasts and he found himself wondering whether this casual air of intimacy was merely the aftermath of a frenzied sexual encounter or the beginning of a much deeper and more lasting relationship.

"I didn't hear you get out of bed, Dutch," she said casually.

"You were fast asleep."

"I must have been." Lindsey went through her handbag until she found a small pack of tablets, then she popped a couple into her mouth and reached for the mug of coffee to wash them down. "On the other hand, you look as though you were awake most of the night."

"I was keeping an eye open in case we had any unwelcome visitors."

"I thought the Carabinieri were supposed to be doing
that?"

"One can't be over-insured," Hollands told her.

"Provided it doesn't interfere with my job."

"Yes, well, that's something I'd like to discuss with you.
The Carabinieri have asked whether you would consider
restricting your movements for the time being. To be
specific, they'd rather you gave the wireless intercept
station a miss for a couple of days on the grounds that you
don't have to be a tactical genius to find a good ambush
position in the Apennines."

"They have a point." Lindsey pushed aside the duvet,
padded across the room in her bare feet and slipped into
the towelling bathrobe that was hanging from a hook on
the door. "I guess I could re-arrange my work schedule
and run things from the bookshop."

"We'd appreciate it if you would."

"Consider it done. Now, if you don't mind, Dutch, I
think I'm going to stand under the shower and freshen
myself up."

"Yes, of course. And while you're doing that, I'll arrange
for the Carabinieri to collect your car from the Ponte Lungo
and give it the once-over."

"There's no need to do that, I had it serviced less than a
month ago."

"This will be a different kind of service," Hollands said
drily. "The mechanic will be wearing body armour."

"No kidding?" Her eyebrows rose fractionally, but
otherwise she was ice cool. "Does that mean we'll be using
your car?"

"No, the Fiat stays where it is as a decoy. We leave by
the fire escape and cut through the alleyway into the Via
Bobbio where there'll be an unmarked car waiting for us."

"I guess you know what you're doing. Give me ten
minutes and I'll be with you. Okay?"

Hollands nodded. "Mind if I use your phone?" he asked.

"Be my guest," Lindsey said and smiled.

Hollands went into the living room, dialled the contact

number Mrs Swann had given him and got much the same sort of co-operative reaction from Drew after he'd finished telling him what he wanted him to do. Everyone was being helpful, everything was going smoothly; somehow he couldn't help wondering if that happy state of affairs would last much longer.

*   *   *

A slight change of course brought the morning sun to bear on Boden's face, the glare rousing him to the extent that he was painfully aware of a crick in his neck. Opening both eyes, he stared uncomprehendingly at the blank screen a few inches in front of his nose. Still not fully awake, he instinctively reached out to switch off the television and brushed his fingers against a cold surface. Like a blind man identifying an object by a sense of touch, it slowly dawned on him that the TV screen was in fact a window and it felt cold because they were at an altitude of close on forty thousand feet, heading south in an Air Italia Boeing 727.

Boden peered at his wristwatch, saw it was almost twenty-five minutes to eight and stifled a yawn. La Rochelle to Paris by bus and train, a cab to Charles de Gaulle and the first available flight to Rome; no two ways about it, they had covered a lot of ground in the last sixteen hours. He glanced at Dukes, fast asleep in the adjoining seat and wished him dead. But for Harry, he would never have contacted Lake again; but for Harry, he wouldn't be going to Rome.

He should have severed his connections with the UK back in February when the Bank of Geneva had confirmed that the balance of the money he was owed for Silent Night had been paid into his numbered account. If he'd done that, Dukes wouldn't have known where to find him, but of course he'd decided to hang around until the house in Richmond was sold because the estate agent had told him the property would fetch upwards of a hundred and fifteen thousand and, no matter how much was lodged in Switzerland, you don't walk away from that kind of money. He had also been assured that the house would be snapped up days after the advertisement had appeared in the local paper, but the quick, discreet sale hadn't materialised and in sheer desperation, he'd agreed to the 'For Sale' notice in the driveway.

The noticeboard had been a mistake; it had alarmed Dukes and had done more to arouse his suspicions than any other single factor. It had led him to question everything Boden had ever told him about the aims and composition of the NSLA. "What's the fighting strength of this army?" Dukes had asked him over and over again. "Are there enough of us to form an infantry battalion or are we so few in number that we couldn't even muster a lousy rifle platoon?" In truth, he'd been aiming too high; before Silent Night they couldn't have found a section of ten men. Afterwards, of course, it had been a very different story and various action groups had mushroomed up and down the country; but you couldn't tell Harry that.

Boden dipped into his jacket pocket, took out a packet of Gitanes and lit one. The operation had supplied the necessary momentum and everyone had wanted to jump on the bandwagon just as Lake had said they would, which only went to prove how good a judge he was of human nature. "Power and money, that's what you want, Nick, and if a choice has to be made between the two, you'll go for the money every time." He remembered Lake telling him that not long after they'd met, when he was still a regional organiser for the National Front.

Lake knew him well, better than any mother, father, sister, brother, wife or lover ever could. Boden just wished he knew him half as well, but Lake was a secretive type who never gave much away. Lake was working for the KGB, that much had become obvious when he'd disclosed the real purpose of Silent Night. And he had to be a pretty big wheel in the Intelligence world, otherwise Moscow would never have agreed to finance the operation. Nor would they have provided a computer expert like Kardar unless they'd been satisfied that he was a good investment. He had access all right; the British Telecom map was proof of that, so was the safe hide north of the Strand which they had used on Christmas Eve.

The hide had been constructed in 1940 for a small clan-destine unit. It was similar to scores of others that had been established by the War Office in Kent, Surrey and Sussex for the purpose of waging guerrilla warfare against the Wehrmacht should the UK have gone the way of France and the Low Countries. Sited beneath the cellar of a public house, the hide consisted of an oblong-shaped room equipped with double tier bunks for six, an ammo store and communication facilities which included a telephone that had still been in working order the night Boden and the others had moved in. A ventilating shaft from the underground telephone network served as one entrance, a narrow tunnel leading to the main sewers under Covent Garden provided an alternative escape route.

Forty-four years later, the location of the hide was still a closely guarded secret. Boden had described it in his notebook because, along with the ex-directory telephone number, it was one of the few clues to Lake's real identity, something he hadn't been able to discover for himself. The notebook would however enable MI5 to identify him and he'd made sure Lake was aware of its existence. It was the one all-risks insurance policy Boden carried.

There was a sudden flurry of activity in the galley at the rear of the cabin; a few minutes later, a dark attractive air hostess roused Dukes from a peaceful slumber as she began to pass out the breakfast trays.

"How long have I been asleep?" he asked, yawning.

"Ever since we took off from Charles de Gaulle," Boden said and stubbed out his cigarette.

"You sound grouchy, Nick, like a man with a whole lot of problems on his mind."

"Your antenna is picking up the wrong signals, Harry. Everything's jake."

"You're sure?"

"I'm positive." Lake had told him the hardware would be waiting for them at Vittori's on the Via Porta Portese in the Trastevere district and he'd also been given Lindsey Whyte's address.

"So when do we get into Rome?"

"Zero eight thirty," Boden told him. But only one of

them would leave the Eternal City; he had Lake's word on that.

★   ★   ★

Putilin got off the District Line train at the Embankment and walked up two flights of stairs to the main concourse above. The phone call he'd received from Lake the previous evening had led to a sleepless night. Although the Englishman hadn't pressed the alarm button, Putilin knew he would never have got in touch with him direct unless there was some kind of emergency. Worried in case his own cover had been blown, Putilin had kept a wary eye open from the moment he'd left his home in Putney. So far, he'd no reason to believe he was being followed, but this was the morning rush hour and only a rank amateur would stand out in such a crowd.

Turning left outside the station, he walked under Hungerford Bridge and made for the public telephone at the bottom end of Northumberland Avenue. At exactly eight fifty-eight, he entered the call box next to the cab shelter belonging to the Greater London Council. Two minutes later the phone rang; answering it, he scrambled the area code and last four digits, then waited for the caller to correct the deliberate error.

"We'll dispense with veiled speech," Lake said. "I'm going to use plain language because I don't want there to be any misunderstanding. Boden's on the way to Rome and I've told him to contact your friendly gunsmith in the Via Porta Portese."

Ernesto Vittori, radio and TV repairs, arms storeman for the Fascist terrorist groups operating in the Lazio Province and KGB agent provocateur. Putilin recalled how they had used the Italian to enhance Boden's reputation. In the run up to Silent Night, they had put him in touch with Vittori to arrange an arms deal. It had been a propaganda exercise from beginning to end and only a minuscule quantity of arms had actually reached the UK but the charade had made Boden a big man in the eyes of the more extreme elements of the National Front. But this time round, Lake obviously had some other purpose in mind.

"What for?" Putilin asked, reacting instinctively.

"Because there are two people in Rome I'd like him to deal with, and I don't see Boden obliging me unless he and his friend are armed."

"It's out of the question."

"I'm not asking you for your opinion," Lake told him arrogantly. "You're just the messenger boy."

Less than forty-eight hours ago, the Englishman had been worried and uncertain what to do, but now his old confidence and bounce had returned with a vengeance and Putilin didn't like it. When he tried to re-assert his authority, Lake cut him short.

"Why are you so determined to sabotage this operation?" he demanded.

"Don't be ridiculous, that's the very last thing I want to do."

"That's not the way I see it. Moscow's invested over two hundred thousand in this project and you're quibbling about a couple of lousy handguns just when they're about to see a handsome return on their money. Believe me, if this goes right, the special relationship between Great Britain and the US will die with Hollands and the American girl."

The Englishman was riding his favourite hobby-horse again. Great Britain was the fifty-first state of the Union, a puppet of the most militaristic nation on earth. Destroy the special relationship that existed between the two countries and the world would become a far safer place. Putilin didn't profess to understand this argument, but that was immaterial; it was sufficient to know that it had convinced the Englishman that, as a true patriot, he should offer his services to the Soviet Union.

"Let's hope you're right," Putilin said weakly.

"I have every confidence in Boden. However, he won't zero in on the target unless he's satisfied we've organised an escape route for him. Besides the small arms, Vittori has to supply him with the address of a safe house."

"You're asking for the impossible."

"One final point," Lake continued remorselessly. "Tell your people we'll all sleep a lot easier in our beds if Boden and Dukes are never seen again."

"But . . ."

"No buts, Mikhail Semenovich. All your superiors have to do is make a phone call to Rome and I've already told them how to neutralise our electronic surveillance. When I ring you again at half past twelve this morning, I expect to hear that everything is at 'condition green'."

Putilin felt duty-bound to lodge a strong protest, but it fell on deaf ears for the Englishman hung up on him before he really had a chance to get started.

*   *   *

The muted trill finally woke Hollands and rolling over on to his left side, he reached out for the telephone and lifted the receiver. The desk clerk wished him a cheerful good morning, then inquired if he was expecting a Mr Drew. Hollands said he was and asked the desk clerk to send him up to his room. Yawning, he replaced the phone and got out of bed. In the bathroom, he filled the basin and sluiced his face in cold water but the shock treatment failed to revitalise him. When he looked into the mirror, there were still dark shadows under his eyes which, coupled with the stubble on his chin, gave him a villainous appearance.

A sharp rat-a-tat-tat on the door put paid to the notion that he would feel a lot fresher after he'd had a shave. Drying his face on a hand towel, he asked his visitor to wait a minute, then returned to the bedroom and retrieved the Beretta automatic from under the pillow. He cocked the external hammer, moved the safety catch to fire and quietly moved into position. The amateur hid behind the door to obtain maximum cover from view; the pro checked the hinges to see which way it opened and positioned himself where he could see the target without being seen in turn. Reaching across, Hollands released the door catch and invited his visitor to come in. When Drew crossed the threshold, he was standing behind and to one side of the blond man, the automatic levelled at his head.

"You're getting a bit paranoiac, aren't you?' Drew said tersely.

"I don't believe in taking chances. I didn't know you were going to call on me." Hollands made the Beretta safe and tucked it into the waistband of his slacks. "After all, you haven't been exactly visible up till now."

"So why tell the clerk to send me up?"

"Because I prefer to lay an ambush rather than walk into one."

"That's more than can be said for your girlfriend. About an hour after you dropped her off at the bookshop on the Via della Vite, she borrowed a car from one of her colleagues and drove out to the wireless intercept station."

"Jesus Christ . . ."

"Relax," Drew told him, "she hasn't come to any harm. The Carabinieri were right behind her."

Hollands closed his eyes. He should have known that Lindsey would go her own sweet way.

"I can see you've had a fun time." Drew walked over to the mini-bar and helped himself to a cigarette from the packet on top of the fridge. "You look just about out on your feet."

"I've been up all night."

"I bet you have. What was she trying to prove? That there was nothing going on between her and Maureen Akehurst!" Drew saw the cold expression in his eyes and held up a hand as though to ward off a blow. "On second thoughts," he said hastily, "forget I said that." Reaching into his pocket, he took out a key ring. "These are yours."

"Thanks." Hollands caught the bunch of keys in one hand and tossed them on to the bed.

"It's a red Fiat 127. The registration number's Z5961068 and it's parked round the corner from the hotel."

"What happened to the other Fiat?"

Drew shrugged his shoulders. "Search me. The Carabinieri towed it away; what they did with it is anyone's guess." He looked round for an ashtray, spotted one on the low coffee table and stubbed out his cigarette. "I guess it's time I was getting back to their headquarters."

"You do that."

"And you stay by the phone so that I can tell you where and when to pick up Colonel Whyte." Drew started towards the door, then snapped his fingers and turned about. "Oh, by the way," he added, "if it's any comfort to you, we've clamped a magnetised homing beacon to the underside of the chassis. And we'll be able to hear every word you say because we've bugged the interior of the Fiat."

"Terrific."

"I knew you'd be pleased. Of course, the chances are the homing beacon will drop off the first time you hit a bump in the road, and the radio doesn't work too well in a built-up area."

Chapter XXI

Harper paid off the taxi outside Marylebone station, walked through the concourse, then returned to the forecourt to find Marsh waiting for him in a pale blue Renault 16 parked in rear of the cab rank, exactly where he'd said he would be. Opening the nearside front door, he got in beside him and was somewhat put out when Marsh started up, shifted into gear and drove off towards Baker Street before he had a chance to fasten his seat belt.

"In training for the Le Mans twenty-four hours, are we?" Harper inquired sarcastically.

"You're on your own, Cedric."

"What are you talking about?"

"I'm walking away from Putilin. Commander Special Branch called me into his office just before lunch for one of those man-to-man, straight-from-the-shoulder talks. In other words, I was told to mind my own business and stop poking my nose into things which didn't concern me. Seems the Director of the Security Service had been on to the Home Secretary complaining that the Metropolitan Police were jeopardising one of their operations."

"Any idea who snitched on you?"

Marsh shrugged his shoulders. "Your guess is as good as mine."

"How about your friendly engineer in British Telecom?"

"No. We've known each other for a long time. He wouldn't deliberately go out of his way to drop me in the shit."

Harper thought he could well have done so inadvertently. Someone, possibly one of the assistant secretaries in the Home Office Criminal Department, might casually have asked him if Putilin was showing signs of becoming more active and he may have indicated that Detective Superintendent Marsh evidently thought so. Just who had set the ball

235

rolling was, however, the really intriguing question.

"Have you talked to any of the officers who were shadowing Putilin this morning?" Harper asked.

Marsh nodded. "He left his house at the usual time and caught a District Line train to the city which he's been doing ever since he arrived in London, but today was different. Today, Putilin broke his journey at the Embankment and spent roughly ten minutes in one of the phone booths near the river at the bottom of Northumberland Avenue. Then he continued on his way to the Narodny Bank in King William Street as though nothing had happened."

"It was a meet," Harper said. "The mole must have rung Putilin at home yesterday evening and passed a coded message telling him where and when the meet was to take place."

"I'd go along with that." Marsh turned right into Oxford Street and continued on towards Marble Arch.

"I'd like to hear the tape of that conversation."

"Nothing doing, Cedric."

"If the mole is who I think he is, I'd recognise his voice."

"The answer's still the same," said Marsh. "I'm not going to ask my Telecom engineer to do me another favour. It's more than my job's worth and I'm in enough trouble as it is."

"You want to nail the men who strangled Jago, don't you?" Harper twisted round to face him. "I also seem to recall you saying you wouldn't rest until you smashed the NSLA."

"We've already buried one of the killers; his name was Roach. Of course, I can't prove he actually murdered Jago, but he'll do for the time being." Marsh jockeyed for position in the usual snarl-up around Marble Arch and filtered into Park Lane. "And I don't need your help to smash the NSLA either. I'm going to destroy the organisation from within; Mr Leslie William Tyler isn't aware of it yet but he's about to become supergrass of the year."

Harper wondered if he was being serious. Leslie William Tyler of Willowdene, Burleigh Crescent, West Harrow – the jobbing builder who'd reported that his Dodge Transit van had been stolen from outside his house during the night of December sixteenth. Eight days later, the same vehicle had been involved in a fatal traffic accident in the Old Kent Road. Marsh wouldn't be allowed to lean on Tyler because that would be tantamount to admitting that Silent Night was not the IRA operation Whitehall had claimed it was.

"You're an ambitious man," Harper said quietly, "so I'll make a bargain with you. Stick with me, and I'll give you the mole who made the whole lousy business possible."

"So who do you think he is, Cedric?"

"Neil Lawrence."

"Lawrence?" Marsh swerved, drifted into the next lane and caught an angry blast on the horn from the driver of a sleek Jaguar XJ6. "You've got to be joking."

"Think about it." Harper began to tick off the salient points on the fingers of one hand. "Lawrence was able to find someone like Boden because he cut his teeth with 'K' Section where he was responsible for targeting potential subversives. Secondly, he was loaned out to the SIS to advise them on protective security, which means he probably devised the safeguards for the material they were going to store in MIDAS."

Harper warmed to his theme, developing it with a cold, remorseless logic. Lawrence had worked with the SAS; furthermore, he had the means to tap into the army's computerised manning records to obtain a profile on any serving officer or soldier. The profile would also indicate exactly where the subject was serving at that precise moment in time, which had been an enormous help to him when he was searching for an officer whom Boden could impersonate. He had also been in a position to supply Boden with an MOD pass and a fake military ID card because MI5 were responsible for liaising with other government departments on security matters, and specimen examples of the various official documents in current usage were held by the training school.

"It's all just too hard to swallow," Marsh told him. "Next thing I know, you'll be telling me that, having planned the operation, Lawrence then made sure he was placed in charge of the subsequent investigation."

"No. That was the last thing he wanted. It put him in the limelight and he was forced to act as though he was determined his team of investigators would leave no stone unturned. In his anxiety to protect himself, Lawrence was altogether too successful and the activities of his investigators spurred Whitehall into action. There was a cover-up all right, but it was highly effective. Worse still, Lawrence was consulted at every stage and there was no way he could exploit the situation without pointing an accusing finger at himself. That's another reason why Silent Night was such a monumental balls-up."

"It's an interesting theory, Cedric. Question is, do you have any hard evidence to support it?"

"Not yet, but with your help I can get it."

Marsh didn't say anything, merely smiled enigmatically. Edging his way across the stream of traffic flowing into Piccadilly, he went on round Hyde Park Corner, ignored the turn off into the Mall which Harper expected him to take, and headed into Knightsbridge. Then he turned into Hans Crescent and whipped into a vacant parking slot opposite one of the side entrances to Harrods.

"You don't give up, do you, Cedric?"

"It's not in my nature. Lawrence lives in Blackheath . . ."

"I don't want to know."

"He bought one of those workmen's cottages built around the turn of the century which have been tarted up and are now called town houses . . ."

"No." Marsh shook his head vigorously.

"26 Pagoda Vale. You'd better make a note of the address."

"No."

"You don't mean that," Harper said.

"Yes, I do. The word's gone out, Cedric – you're being quarantined. No one, but no one, in Whitehall is going to lift a finger to help you." Marsh unclipped his seat belt, leaned across Harper and opened the nearside door. "The way things are, it's dangerous even to be seen in your company."

"That's ridiculous."

"They know Hollands is in Rome, Cedric. They know you've set him up with the girl as a pair of moving targets, and they don't like it."

The collective pronoun included the Foreign and Commonwealth. Shortly after returning to his office, Harper received a call from the deputy head of Personnel and Liaison. Neasden was chillingly polite; what he had to say was brief and equally chilling. Acting on the instructions of the Cabinet Office, the Permanent Under-Secretary had spoken to his opposite number in Rome. In an attempt to avoid a major diplomatic incident, he had apologised for the fact that, in approaching the Carabinieri for assistance, certain law enforcement officers had acted without the authority of Her Majesty's Government. In due course, a formal application for the arrest and subsequent extradition of Nicholas Spencer Boden and Harold Dukes would be submitted through the appropriate channels.

It was, of course, the Foreign Office way of asking the Italian authorities to withhold their co-operation until such time as they received an official request in writing. Realising it was also a recipe for disaster, Harper called Rome and spent the next half hour talking to his old friend the Minister of the Interior whom he'd first met during the war. In some respects, it was virtually a repeat of the conversation they'd had two days previously, but on this occasion he went to great lengths to explain why it was in both their interests to ensure that Hollands and Lindsey Whyte were kept under constant surveillance, no matter what the Minister might have heard from the Foreign Office.

*   *   *

The Trastevere District of Rome consisted of a maze of cobblestone streets, a solitary hotel and the city's jail which, for some unknown reason, was called the Queen of Heaven. The oldest quarter of Rome, it was always crowded, invariably noisy and extremely colourful, especially during the Noiantri Festival which the Trasteverini held every July to celebrate the fact that they were so very different from those foreigners across the Tiber. The

Trasteverini, as they never tired of telling people, were a race apart, the true descendants of the Etruscans, a claim that most historians dismissed out of hand, though not within the hearing of the local inhabitants.

Ernesto Vittori was not a Trasteverini but as he'd been living in the quarter since the end of World War Two, he was treated like a native by the locals. Vittori was sixty-one and pear-shaped. Bald, except for a few strands of jet-black hair which had been trained round the crown of his head like a laurel wreath, he had a sad-looking face as though he found the world and the people who lived in it a perpetual disappointment.

His shop on the Via Porta Portese was a mirror image of the man himself, a bit down-at-heel and in need of renovation. The radio and TV sets displayed behind protective metal grilles in the windows either side of the entrance were yesterday's models, their antiquity vouched for by the sun-faded price tags and the layers of dust they'd collected. The retail business was, however, merely a sideline; Vittori earned his living from servicing and repairing electrical goods of every make and description.

The shop was empty when Boden arrived with Dukes in tow, but it was still the lunch hour and officially the premises were closed until three o'clock. There was a hanging card in the window to that effect, but Vittori was expecting them and the street door had been left unlocked. Even so, they were not exactly greeted with open arms. Deliberately ignoring Dukes, the Italian offered Boden a limp handshake, then led him into the workroom at the back.

"Now," said Vittori bluntly, "what is it you want from me?"

Boden's eyes narrowed angrily. "I thought our mutual friend had already told you. We're here to do a removal job, you've been asked to lend us a helping hand."

"Perhaps my English is not so good." Vittori allowed himself a faint smile that died before Boden could make up his mind what it signified. "I was referring to the type of goods you require. I carry only a limited range of merchandise on the premises. If you should want a rifle

240

with a telescopic sight, I would have to send out for one."

"We're going in close, Ernesto; a couple of pocket-size revolvers or automatic pistols will do us. Something around a 9 mm or .38 calibre with a four and a half inch barrel – that's roughly twelve centimetres . . ."

"It would be handy if we could keep the noise down too," Dukes added.

"We shall have to see what we can do, won't we?"

Vittori dragged one end of the workbench away from the wall; then crouching down, he used a large screwdriver to raise one of the flagstones high enough for him to get his fingertips under the rim, preparatory to lifting it clear. Reaching into the cavity, he brought out an olive green container designed to hold half a dozen 81 mm mortar bombs and placed it on the bench. As of now, the box contained five Beretta automatics, two of which were the 7.65 model, a Walther PPK, two Luger P38s and four Spanish copies of the Colt .38 Police Positive.

"Please." Vittori waved a hand, inviting them to inspect the goods on offer.

Dukes picked up one of the Lugers, removed the magazine from the butt and snapped the toggle action back, cocking the trigger mechanism. He aimed the pistol at the fanlight above their heads and squeezed the trigger. Cock, aim, fire; cock, aim, fire; he repeated the drill over and over again to gauge the pressure and the amount of slack on the trigger.

"You got a silencer for this little beauty?" he asked eventually.

Vittori shook his head. "Only for the Berettas."

"Jesus Christ, why didn't you say so before?"

Somewhere close by, a Lambretta burst into life and silenced Dukes before he got into his stride. By the time the motor scooter moved off, he'd simmered down and was in a more equitable frame of mind.

"We'll take the 9 mm version," Boden said hastily. "You couldn't ask for a neater handgun."

"How much ammunition?"

"I don't see us needing more than a clip apiece." Boden cleared his throat. "Our mutual friend said you might know somewhere nice and quiet where we could stay for a while?"

"It's possible." Vittori rubbed his jaw. "When do you want to move in?"

"Tonight."

"The people who will be looking after you are very poor. You will have to pay them something, you understand?"

"Sure." Boden patted the money belt around his waist. "Would they like a down payment on account?"

"That would be a nice gesture."

"Unfortunately, most of my money is in French francs."

"They're very acceptable," Vittori told him.

Boden unbuttoned his shirt, slipped a hand inside and extracted a wad of one hundred franc notes from one of the pouches on the belt. Moistening a thumb and forefinger, he peeled off six 'C' notes, then had second thoughts and made it up to a thousand.

"That's more than generous of you, signore." Vittori pocketed the money, found a scrap of paper in one of the drawers of the workbench and wrote down a phone number. "You remember these figures," he told Boden. "Fix them in your head. Okay?"

"No problem."

"Okay, when you're ready, you phone the number, tell the man where you are and he will come and pick you up."

"How will I recognise him?" Boden asked.

"You must arrange that between yourselves."

"Is that all we're getting for our money?" Dukes said belligerently. "A lousy phone number? Shit, you must think we were born yesterday."

Vittori struck a match, took the slip of paper from Boden and held it over the flame, then dropped it into a small empty tin of crabmeat that served as an ashtray. "I think your friend is trying to insult me," he said quietly. "He is hinting that I am a liar."

"It may have sounded like that but Harry didn't mean it, did you, Harry?"

"No," said Dukes, "it just sort of slipped out."

"You should learn to be more trusting." Vittori laid a hand on his shoulder and squeezed it, seemingly in a friendly way. "Believe me, the phone number exists and we shall take good care of you."

There was no hint of malice in his voice but Boden was quite certain in his own mind that a terminal contract had been made at a knock-down price.

★　★　★

Regardless of whether it was spring, summer, autumn or winter, the siesta lasted from one to four and was scrupulously observed by office workers, shopkeepers, doctors, dentists, bartenders and most of Rome's six thousand policemen. Some galleries and museums remained open, restaurants generally allowed their lunchtime diners to linger on until three o'clock and first-aid posts throughout the city never closed. The British diplomatic staff observed the local custom and remained incommunicado until four o'clock when they re-opened for business. The Americans, in keeping with their traditional go-getting, hard-working image, were open all hours.

Few people put in more time than Lindsey Whyte. A pattern established in London was now being repeated in Rome. Although Hollands had asked her to finish early for once, it was beginning to look as though she wasn't going to oblige him. He wondered why he should find that surprising when Lindsey had always shown a marked aversion to having her life organised by a third party. Instead of running things from the bookshop, she had visited the wireless intercept station and from there had driven to the US Cultural Exchange Office where she had been ever since, except for an hour-long visit to the American Embassy in the middle of the afternoon. Exasperated by her lack of co-operation, Drew had phoned the Hotel Atlante and told him to get over to the Cultural Exchange Office on the Via del Corso before she disappeared on yet another jaunt.

In the movies, finding somewhere to park was never a problem but in real life it was a vastly different story. On this occasion, Hollands had gone round the block four times before a space had become available some fifteen yards up the road from the Cultural Exchange Office.

The evening rush hour had started shortly after he'd arrived, the noise level rising in direct proportion to the density of the traffic in a wild, undisciplined cacophony of single and double-tone horns. The traffic lights were only a guide, the normal rules of the road didn't apply, and the traffic police in their distinctive blue uniforms and white pith helmets were of course conspicuous by their absence. For most Italian motorists, the homeward journey was accomplished with the aid of a strident horn and the not too infrequent use of a pair of stout bumpers.

The nightly stampede had just passed its zenith when Hollands saw Lindsey in the rear view mirror. He didn't have to sound the horn or get out of the car to meet her; emerging from the building, she made straight for the Fiat, a clear indication that she had been watching him from her office. It had been a long day, the temperature high enough to give a foretaste of the hot summer to come and most people seemed a bit frazzled around the edges, but not Lindsey. She still looked very cool and fresh in the white linen two-piece and blue silk blouse. Appearances were, however, deceptive; as she drew nearer, he could see that her jaw was set in a determined line, and knew there was a storm in the offing. It broke the moment Lindsey got into the Fiat and slammed the door.

"We seem to have a communication failure," she began icily. "Last night you led me to believe that your people had briefed the Pentagon. This afternoon, I saw our Military Attaché and the resident CIA officer, neither of whom expressed the slightest concern. And you know why?"

Hollands knew what was coming and switched on the car radio. He'd no idea where Drew had planted the transmitter and he had to neutralise it before Lindsey said something which was strictly for UK ears only.

"Because Washington has been deliberately kept in the dark – that's why."

"It's often been said that attack is the best means of defence." Hollands searched the waveband, found a frequency where there was a lot of interference from a neighbouring station, and turned up the volume. "You're working yourself into a rage because you've got a guilty conscience. Who was going to re-organise her schedule so she could run things from the bookshop, then took off the moment my back was turned?"

"Either tune that radio in or turn it off," Lindsey told him loudly.

Hollands ignored her request and started the Fiat, then pulled out from the kerb. Before he could stop her, Lindsey reached across and switched off the radio.

"I don't know why the Pentagon sat on the information," Hollands said, beating her to the punch. "It's not a question I can answer. All I do know is that you're not making my job any the easier."

"I can make it a lot more difficult."

"Are you threatening me?"

"You bet I am. I've been thinking about the story you gave me last night and it doesn't stand up under examination."

"Everyone's entitled to their own opinion."

"Don't patronise me, Dutch. Either you tell me exactly what is going on or I shall call the resident CIA man in Rome and give him what little I know. It may not amount to much but I can always fill in the gaps with the odd hunch or two. For instance, I figure the KGB were behind Silent Night right from the start, and the only reason you people have been playing it close to the chest is because you've got something to hide."

Lindsey still had some way to go but she was getting there, and it was only a small step from one conclusion to the next. If the British were being tight-lipped, it was because the KGB had had inside help and they were still reeling from the after-effects of the Bettaney affair. Burgess, Maclean, Philby, Blunt, Prime and Bettaney; the list of Soviet agents read like an extract from *Who's Who in the Intelligence World*.

"You've gone awful quiet, Dutch."

"I'm thinking."

"Yeah? Why? There's only one decision to make."

"Yes, perhaps it is time we put our cards on the table . . ."

"You don't hear me denying it," Lindsey told him.

"I'll have to clear it with London first. Okay?"

"I guess it's your ball game, Dutch."

It had never been that, but at least he'd won himself a brief respite and could try and get the ground rules amended. He wondered how much of their conversation Drew had overheard and instinctively checked both the rear view and wing mirrors. Drew was riding around in a beige-coloured Fiat 130 which he'd spotted earlier on when he had been driving round the block looking for somewhere to park, but there was no sign of the vehicle now.

*   *   *

Boden gazed at the luminous face of his wristwatch. Ten, perhaps fifteen minutes from now they would hear the key go into the lock, and moments later Lieutenant Colonel Lindsey Whyte would be dead. So would Major Anthony Hollands, assuming he was with her.

"Get both of them if you can," Lake had told him, "but if that's not possible, I'll settle for Whyte. She's the one who'll make the newscasts in America and provide the kind of political mystery that investigative journalists love to unravel. And once that begins to happen, Washington is going to wake up to the fact that there was a whole lot more to Silent Night than they've been led to believe."

Lake had talked as though they shared a common purpose but, in reality, their individual motives had been, and still were, widely disparate. What counted was the fact that the information Lake had supplied about the prime target had been Grade 'A' and sufficiently detailed to dictate where and when the hit should take place. The only problem Boden had had to resolve was just how they were going to break into the apartment house.

In the event, this had proved almost ludicrously easy. There had been absolutely no sign of a police presence in the neighbourhood when they'd arrived shortly after dusk, and the fire escape into the alleyway behind the block had looked decidedly promising. Posting Dukes as a look-out after they'd parked the car in the Via Bobbio, Boden had made his way up to Lindsey Whyte's apartment on the second floor and, breaking a pane of glass, had let himself into the kitchen. The noise had been minimal and there had been no reaction from the occupants of the apartments on the floors above and below. A few minutes after he'd broken into the kitchen, Dukes had pressed the appropriate call button outside the front entrance, and he'd tripped the electronically controlled lock, permitting him to enter the apartment house.

There were two reasons why Boden had decided to wait for Lindsey Whyte in the lounge-diner. Firstly, the room was at the front of the building overlooking the Via Appia Nuova, which meant they would spot her as she approached the apartment house. And secondly, there was every possibility that immediately after entering the flat, she would walk straight into the room to switch on the lights and draw the curtains. Except that nothing would happen when she tried the switch because he had removed all the light bulbs and she would be left standing there in the doorway, a perfect target silhouetted by the hall light behind her.

Boden glanced at his wristwatch again. "Any time now," he muttered to himself.

"I reckon you're right." Dukes backed away from the window. "A small red Fiat's just arrived. Two people inside . . . a man and a woman . . . they're parked across the road from here near a street light."

★   ★   ★

Hollands scanned the apartment house from top to bottom, his eyes lingering on those seemingly unoccupied rooms where no lights were showing. His gaze came down to street level, probed the dark shadows in the lee of the building, ranged over the cars parked out front and took in every tree planted like sentinels at regular intervals along the pavement. Beside him, Lindsey stirred impatiently.

"How much longer are we going to sit here admiring the view?" she asked.

"Just another minute or two."

Hollands twisted round, leaned across her and looked up, his eyes searching the rooftops on the right-hand side of the road where a sniper with a starlight scope could have been lying in wait for them.

"Nothing," he muttered, "absolutely zero."

"Can we go now?"

"What's the hurry?"

"There isn't any; I just feel this is kind of stupid. I mean, if there is a gunman out there, we sure as hell are presenting him with a nice fat target."

"Only if he's on the same elevation. If he's above us, he'll have to go for an oblique shot, knowing there's less than a fifty-fifty chance of a lethal hit."

"That's what I like about you, Dutch," she said, "you're such a little ray of sunshine."

The rush hour had peaked some time ago and from then on the traffic had been rapidly tailing off. Where there had been a continuous stream of vehicles, there were now small assorted groups moving in convoy, seemingly drawn together by a common herd instinct. A Ferrari sports coupé, a Mercedes with CD plates, a couple of trucks, a bus, and Drew, sitting next to the driver of a beige-coloured Fiat tagging on behind. Hollands recognised the blond man as the small convoy overtook them and watched the vehicle make a left turn into the Via Bobbio. He waited until the car had disappeared from sight, then opened the door and depressed the catch.

"We're satisfied the coast is clear now, are we?" she asked.

"Give it a rest, Lindsey."

Hollands got out of the car and closed the door behind him. Then, joining Lindsey on the pavement, he grabbed her arm above the elbow and hustled her across the road towards the apartment house.

"Okay if I have my arm back now?" she asked when they reached the main entrance.

"Why not?" Hollands grinned. "I've got two of my own."

"Plus a few tentacles," Lindsey murmured, recalling the previous evening. Then, opening her handbag, she took out a bunch of keys and unlocked the street door.

"Which is the one to your apartment?" Hollands asked.

"Why?"

"Because I think I ought to go in first."

"My hero," she said, handing him the key.

★   ★   ★

Drew waited until the Carabinieri sergeant had reported their location, then got out of the car and walked back to the alleyway behind the apartment house. The day was ending as it had begun – badly. Just about everything that could go wrong had gone wrong. The sergeant had had a hard time finding somewhere to park in the Via del Corso and, in the end, they'd had to settle for a slot round the corner from the American Cultural Exchange Office. Hollands, who'd arrived later, had been faced with the same problem but eventually he'd been lucky enough to find a slot just up the road from the US Intelligence Centre. Unable to see Hollands from their location, they'd had to rely on the transmitter that had been planted in the rented Fiat, and that had worked fine until he'd switched on the car radio. Thereafter, everything had gone to pot. In addition to the interference, tall buildings had frequently screened the signal emanating from the transmitter and when Hollands had moved off, they had found themselves boxed in. The sergeant had reacted very calmly to this setback, confident their homing device would allow them to trail Hollands, but either the damned thing had dropped off or their receiver had gone on the blink. Fortunately, he'd driven Lindsey Whyte straight home, otherwise they might never have found him again.

The sergeant eyed the fire escape, then glanced questioningly at Drew and almost sighed aloud when he announced they'd better take a look. A feeling that they were probably wasting their time ceased to have any validity the moment Drew noticed the broken window pane.

★   ★   ★

The hinges were on the right and the door opened inwards. Inserting the key, Hollands quietly unlocked it, then, positioning himself next to Lindsey with his back to the wall, he threw the door open. The sudden movement should have spooked any gunman waiting for them in the hall, but nothing happened. Across the landing, he could

249

hear the excited semi-hysterical voice of some Italian TV personality hosting a quiz show. He glanced at Lindsey, but she avoided his gaze and looked up at the ceiling, resisting an inclination to burst out laughing.

"We'll still go through the motions," he said flatly.

"If you say so. The switches are just inside the hall on the right; trip the far one and you put the lights on in the lounge-diner." Her eyes went to the Beretta automatic he was holding in his right hand. "On second thoughts, maybe I'd better do that. Give me a nod when you want them on."

Hollands slipped into the hallway and side-stepped towards the lounge. Halfway along the hall, he gave Lindsey a thumbs-up sign, but no crack of light showed beneath the door when she flicked the switch.

"The bulb must have blown," he told her.

"It's more likely to be the fuse, Dutch. There are two bulbs in the ceiling light."

A blown fuse would have been the obvious and logical explanation in normal circumstances but there was this itchy sensation in his scalp and amongst the fine hairs at the base of his neck. He'd felt it on a previous occasion in that split second before the Hillman Avenger parked outside the Europa Hotel in Belfast had been ripped apart by twenty-five pounds of plastic explosive. He shouted to Lindsey to get down and simultaneously got the same advice in return as the penny also dropped with her.

The door splintered under a fusillade, each shot punctuated by the distinctive hollow cough of a silencer. Keeping well down, Hollands aimed at the door and opened fire. He was shooting blind and the odds against him scoring a hit were astronomical, but that was beside the point. The whole idea was to deter the gunmen from entering the hall and hold them off until help arrived.

*   *   *

Drew had just succeeded in opening the kitchen window to its fullest extent when he heard the exchange of fire. Abandoning all thought of trying to effect a silent entry, he squeezed through the gap and jumped down from the draining board. The serving hatch to the dining alcove was directly opposite him and he was able to see into the lounge beyond. Two men were firing into the hallway – one tall, thin as a beanpole, the nearer one a good head shorter – their physical characteristics registered, and he placed them even as he told them to freeze.

Boden did just what he was hoping for and turned towards the hatch, presenting him with the broad expanse of his head and shoulders to aim at. It was like a shooting gallery except there was no bull, inner, magpie or outer ring and the target was illuminated by the ambient glow from the street instead of a direct spotlight. Drew squeezed the trigger twice in rapid succession, the pistol rock-steady in his double-handed grip. Both rounds struck Boden in the heart within half an inch of one another and knocked him backwards into an armchair. As his lifeless body slipped to the floor, Dukes reacted in a way that was wholly out of character; whirling round, he raised his hands shoulder high.

It was the last thing Drew expected, the last thing he wanted. Behind him, the Carabinieri sergeant jumped down from the windowsill and he had just a split second to make up his mind. In the event, Dukes made the decision easier for him by providing the kind of excuse an eye-witness could accept without too many qualms. Suddenly realising he was still holding the Beretta, Dukes opened his right hand to release the automatic. The apologetic smile was still there on his mouth when Drew shot him in the head.

*   *   *

Hollands froze in the aim, suddenly aware the exchange of fire had ceased. He glanced over his shoulder to make sure that Lindsey was all right, then quickly looked to his front again. In the ensuing silence he heard Drew call to him that it was all over and immediately removed the magazine from the butt and pulled the slide back to eject the round from the breech. He squeezed the trigger, put the safety catch on and got to his feet. When he walked into the lounge-diner, Drew was crouched beside Boden, going through the money belt he'd evidently found around the dead man's waist.

"The Carabinieri had a tip-off," said Drew. "A reliable source informed them the Red Brigade were planning to kidnap the commanding officer of the US Signal Corps Intercept Station in Rome, like they did that one-star general a year or so ago . . ."

He was talking for Lindsey's benefit, laying down the guidelines they would eventually give the Italian press, but she wasn't buying it.

"First, it's all down to the IRA, then the KGB are taking a hand, now it's the Red Brigade who are up front. One thing I will say for you British, you don't lack imagination."

Drew unbuttoned another pouch on the money belt and took out a small pocketbook. "Do us all a favour, Major," he said languidly. "Take the lady aside and tell her what makes the world go round."

Hollands placed a hand under Lindsey's elbow and eased her out into the hall. The front door was still wide open but the landing was deserted and, across the way, the frenetic TV quiz show continued to hold the neighbours enthralled. As far as the residents on the other floors were concerned, the noise of gunfire had obviously been contained within Lindsey's apartment. All the same, Hollands thought it prudent to close the front door before he steered her into the bedroom.

"This is when you give me the facts of life, is it, Dutch?" she asked.

"Not exactly."

"But you're going to set me straight – if that's the right word?"

"Boden, Dukes and Roach are dead, and we'll get the man who manipulated them. And who knows, he may even lead us to the computer whizz kid who broke into the MIDAS system."

"Big deal."

"What more do you want?"

"The truth, for God's sake," Lindsey said impatiently.

"No matter what it costs?"

Something in his voice brought her up short and she

gazed at him thoughtfully for some moments. Then she said, "Okay, Dutch, I think maybe you'd better spell it out for me."

"I'll support you all the way," Hollands said quietly, "if you want to accuse British Intelligence of a cover-up. I'll tell your people that you're absolutely right. But it won't stop there. The CIA will want to know why you kept these suspicions to yourself for so long and you'd better have a good excuse ready because they'll dig deep. They'll be looking for a character defect and after they've exhumed your marriage and dissected it from A to Z, there's a good chance they'll get around to Maureen Akehurst."

"You can knock that lie on the head, Dutch."

"Of course I can, but you know how their minds work."

In their world, there was such a thing as guilt by association. Once the CIA learned about Maureen Akehurst, they would begin to see Lindsey in a new light, mainly because of the way she had dealt with a potentially embarrassing situation. The American exchange officer/British civilian employee would cut very little ice with them; they would think Lindsey had acted discreetly because she had something to hide and people who had something to hide were always vulnerable to pressure. No matter how slight the risk might be, the State had to be protected and there was one highly effective means of doing just that. Within a very short space of time, Lindsey would be denied access to all classified information and that would finish her career.

"I like my job, Dutch. I don't want anyone advising me to look for another," she said, in tune with his thoughts.

"Of course you don't."

"So give me one good reason why this particular bundle of dirty linen shouldn't be washed and aired in public?"

"Because it would only benefit the KGB."

"Then I guess I'll have to buy that."

Lindsey had been left with very little choice other than to participate in a cover-up and while the reason he'd given her happened to be true, they both knew she had seized on it just a shade too eagerly.

CHAPTER XXII

The year was barely six months old, yet this was the second time the Geordie from Tyneside had come down south, and that in itself was pretty remarkable because he was not a migratory bird of prey and rarely left his home territory.

Back in April, it had been cold, wet and windy and he'd spent the evening driving around the Surrey countryside near Hedley Court with a tall, miserable son-of-a-bitch called Harry who'd hardly exchanged a civil word with him. This time it was different; this time it was a pleasantly warm June evening and he was sitting astride a Yamaha 250 behind a tasty redhead in black leather. The scenery was also different – south-east London and the A2 trunk route through Blackheath.

The girl pulled out, overtook a Leyland truck on Deptford Bridge and went on up the Blackheath Road, steadily climbing a one-in-six hill. She handled the bike superbly and there was no reason for him to hold her quite so tightly around the waist, but it helped to keep his male ego intact and fostered the illusion that he had some measure of control over her. In reality, it was the other way round, and he was entirely dependent on her but that was something he preferred not to think about too deeply.

The road levelled off and ran arrow-straight across the heath. The fair was up ahead, its side-shows, dodgems, swings and carousel established within a triangle bounded by the A2, General Wolfe Road and Chesterfield Walk. A quarter of a mile from the site, the girl drifted towards the crown of the road, heeled the gear shift into third, then taking advantage of a gap in the oncoming traffic, she turned right into Hare and Billet Road.

The Triumph Acclaim was parked on the right-hand side of the road opposite Hollyhedge House, facing the way they'd come. A number of vehicles had come and gone since he'd put it there early that morning and it was now sandwiched between a Datsun Cherry limousine and an Opel Kadett estate. For a moment, it looked as though it was boxed in but as they rode past, he was relieved to see that he would have enough room to pull straight out from the kerb. Then the girl made another right turn and he instinctively braced himself knowing that they were only minutes away from Pagoda Vale and the man he was going to kill.

An Oxford graduate and former MI5 officer, he was a man who deserved everything that was coming to him. The bastard had started out with every advantage in life and the Establishment had been good to him but instead of repaying them with his loyalty, he had spat in their faces, and offered his services to the KGB.

He had been the catch of the century for the KGB. In fact, he'd been such a big wheel in MI5 that the government had been too scared to prosecute him in case the Yanks decided the Brits had had one Philby too many and that they weren't in the business of supplying Moscow with hard-earned information. So he had been sent home on extended leave, pending re-assignment to some less sensitive branch of the Civil Service and, but for Redmond, he would probably have remained on full pay for the rest of his life without doing a stroke of work to earn it.

Redmond was a bit of a mystery and it wouldn't surprise him if the blond man hadn't borrowed the name. Until Redmond had phoned him up in the middle of the night a week ago, he'd never heard of the man, let alone met him and he'd been tempted to hang up when this perfect stranger had started calling him 'Geordie', but then Redmond had suddenly brought Jago's name into the conversation and he'd rapidly changed his mind. Even so, he wouldn't have come south if Tyler hadn't got in touch soon afterwards to assure him that Redmond was okay. He'd stayed with the jobbing builder back in April when the NSLA had decided to execute the Jew lawyer and knew him well enough to take his word on trust.

He had met Redmond at a houseboat on the Thames near Chiswick Reach the day before yesterday and the blond man had laid it all out, telling him exactly why, when and how he was going to eliminate the mole. Redmond had kept waving a small pocketbook in his face and somehow he'd had the nasty feeling that he was being threatened, but Tyler had been there, grinning like a gargoyle and all palsy-walsy with the blond man, and he'd swallowed his doubts.

Now, forty-eight hours later, he knew Redmond was a man he could trust and respect. The plan was a good one and nothing had been left to chance. Tyler had introduced him to the girl yesterday and she hadn't been told anything more than was strictly necessary. When the job was done, they would split and never see each other again, which was how it should be.

The girl turned into Pagoda Vale and stopped opposite number 26. Telling her to keep the engine ticking over, he dismounted and crossed the pavement. Everything was looking good – a quiet expensive neighbourhood, no kids playing in the street. He unfastened the small canvas haversack he was carrying bandolier-fashion across one shoulder, raised the flap and reached inside, his right hand closing round the specially adapted rivet gun; then he rang the doorbell. A few moments later, he heard footsteps in the hall and a youngish man with dark curly hair and a round face opened the door.

"Hullo, Mr Lawrence," he said cheerfully. "A friend of yours asked me to deliver this."

He took the rivet gun out of the haversack, aimed it at Lawrence and squeezed the trigger. There was a faint hiss as the compressed air was released and a three-inch-long metal dart hit Lawrence in the chest. Modelled on the lines of a humane killer, the arrow head contained a rimfire .22 cartridge which exploded a split second after the shaft had entered the heart.